River Dragon

Tyndale King

Spartan Publishing

Published June 30 2013

ISBN: 978-0-9873841-5-7

Spartan Publishing

www.spartan-publishing.com

Acknowledgements

Thank you to:

Jess for the stories.

Olivia for Colombia.

Farheen, who will understand why.

Gonk, for the tactics.

Barney, for the spidergram.

Lottie, for Freya.

Simon, for the sanctuary of Bestwall.

Adela, especially, for China.

And above all, thank you to family and other beloved animals.

The house stood back, behind a threadbare patch of grass, anonymous amongst its identical neighbours. The paintwork was peeling, the wooden clapboard – a MOD attempt at New England perhaps -- curling away from the brick underneath. The slightly dishevelled man, tall, mid forties, with a shock of dark, curly hair, peered through the window into the dark recesses of the hall and saw no movement. He pressed the bell again and, as the Avon chimes rang out, he rummaged in his music case for the directions. Correct address. But no response.

He turned back towards the bleached street and the car, parked at the kerb. In front of him a few spindly trees offered scant protection from a blazing midday sun, which leached all colour from the long open curve as it wound up towards the barbed enclave of the Marines' camp. About twenty young, shaven-headed and muscular young men ran past in a tight group, temporarily separating him from the car. He paused as they passed, aware of a yawning chasm between him and them. As he slowed, the house door behind him opened.

'Dr Foote?'

'That's me,' he said, relieved.

'I'm sorry. We didn't hear you. He's bad today.'

Young and crumpled, with a lank ponytail, Sandra Boyd must have been pretty once. Now, in sweat pants and a hoodie, she looked washed out and exhausted as she opened the door wider for Foote. He followed her into the front room and placed his music case on the sofa she indicated.

'He'll be down in just a minute. Would you like a cup of tea?'

'That would be lovely. Thank you. Two sugars.'

'I'll let him know you're here.'

She disappeared into the kitchen, leaving Foote to examine his surroundings. He always accepted offers of tea or coffee because it usually gave him a crucial few minutes alone to absorb the atmosphere. His peculiar talents enabled him to read human beings as others might a newspaper page. But their homes, where they felt safest, gave him an insight into their souls, too, which was why he preferred to visit the homes of his patients – he referred to them as clients – at least once during the therapeutic process.

This room was simple enough to read. Wooden Christmas ornaments from Germany – six months after Christmas – on the windowsill. A brass tray, pipe and coffee grinder from the Middle East on the sideboard, a Chinese chest bearing silken tassels and ornate brass discs used as a coffee table. A decent Afghan rug lay under the chest. The rest of the furniture was modern, sleek, and cheap. IKEA had colonised the colonisers, thought Foote.

Only one piece, a family treasure, surely, marred the sea of blond wood. The small upright piano, rosewood and Edwardian with its pierced, brass candle brackets, belonged to a different house from a different time. The lace doily on top of it had undoubtedly the same provenance. Photographs arrayed on the doily showed a beautiful young couple, the young man in Marine's dress uniform, the young woman in a white wedding dress. They were laughing, glowing amid a shower of confetti. Another photograph showed the same couple on the steps of Buckingham Palace, the man again in dress uniform holding up a medal, Foote's hostess wearing a stylish hat with a wide brim and a smile almost as broad. Foote wondered what extraordinary heroism had gone unrecorded, save in the private annals of the Special Forces.

Foote re-centred himself as footsteps came quickly down the stairs. The door swung open onto the piano and a slightly older and heavier version of the young soldier of the photographs came into the room. Crop-haired and dark-eyed, he emanated a physical self-confidence. But he was bone tired. It came off him in waves. Like a sickness of the soul. This boy had no interest in the joys of life any more. Foote stuck out his hand. It was shaken reluctantly.

'Corporal Boyd. Thank you for letting me come.'

'The brass said I must let you.'

His accent was flat, Northern. Preston, thought Foote with a slight shock of recognition. It was the accent of his childhood, the one he had dumped as soon as he had arrived at Oxford.

'Of course, that's why I'm here. But not without you wanting me here.'

'Well, I don't know about that. I'm not sure what I want any more. I've lost my way on everything.'

He looked ready to run, thought Foote. Fight or flight. The most basic survival instincts. Perched on the edge of his seat, balanced on the balls of his feet, either reaction seemed equally possible. Foote hoped it wasn't fight. Though less well known than the SAS, the Special Boat Service had a fearsome reputation.

Sandra Boyd arrived with two mugs of tea, each emblazoned with a commando dagger in a clenched fist, and put them on the Chinese chest in front of them. She was just pulling the door closed behind her when Foote spoke.

'Would you like to join us, Mrs Boyd?'

She flashed an anxious glance at her husband who refused to look her way. She sighed.

'No, you're here for Rick.'

As the door clicked behind her, Foote leaned forward.

'We don't know much about each other, do we, you and me?'

'You're not Forces, are you?' It was a flat statement of fact. Foote was not part of Boyd's world. It was a rejection. Foote had been foisted upon Rick Boyd by his superiors and he was not happy about it. Shrinks were for lightweights.

'Perhaps it's better that I'm not,' said Foote, 'So why don't we start straight in?'

The other man spat it out. 'Simple. I bottled it.'

'Did you?' said Foote gently. 'Tell me about it.'

Boyd was almost disarmed by his neutrality. But not quite. He knew that some of the most effective interrogation techniques were the soft ones. This was soft, but he was hard.

'You must have read the report.'

'I have. But they tell me the bare facts. The what. We're here to find the why. So just take me through what happened and we'll go from there.'

Boyd put his shoulders back, eyes straight ahead, and spoke in a flat, toneless voice.

'Six of us got in a fire fight. My patrol and two other lads. I was in charge. They pinned us down. We had to shoot our way out. I was in front. But then, when I got up there, I couldn't move. Went blank. Just froze. As if I wasn't really there.'

He wasn't really there now, thought Foote as he watched Rick Boyd run through the footage in his mind. It was endlessly interesting to him how traumatic memory could transport a man away from his immediate surroundings and back into the thick of it.

They sat in silence as Boyd watched his inner screen and the minutes ticked past. Then, as though there had been no pause, he spoke again.

'We'd called in air support. They got us out. But I know – the lads knew – that I'd bottled it. I knew they had my back, but I had to tell the CO. I was due a rest, but so were all of us. But when I refused, the CO made it mandatory sick leave. Next time out, they went without me. I failed. That's all there is to it.'

He spat the last words out.

Foote listened as only he knew how. The conversation was over as far as Boyd was concerned, while to Foote, it was merely the introduction. He allowed the silence to linger, and then spoke.

'It's not the first time, is it? Tell me about the first time.'

Boyd looked sharply at Foote, his eyes widened, his fists clenched. Foote tensed for what would come next. Then Boyd crumpled catastrophically. And cried -- great, heaving sobs of ancient grief.

Later, much later, Foote looked at the drained human being before him.

'So now we know the why.'

Boyd had recovered slightly. 'Yeah. And it doesn't make me feel any better. I didn't deal with that fucker when I should have and it fucked me up.'

'You were eight. And you were outgunned.'

'Well, he did for us both – my Mum and me. When she died, I joined up to get away from him, to prove myself. I thought I had. I thought I was rid of him.'

'Bad things lie around like land mines. You never know when you are going to trip over them'.

'Wish the fuck I'd known about that beforehand. It made me a nutter.'

Foote stood up and tapped the photograph of Boyd's medal presentation on the piano.

'Yes. But it's also what made you brave. I'll see you tomorrow.'

The lone cyclist pedalled into view, slowing down as the slight incline demanded more from his labouring heart than it could give. He felt the whisper of the wings of angina hovering over his chest. He patted his top pocket – silly, really – making sure the glycerol trinitrate was there in the tiny phial. That would solve it. Temporarily, anyway. After which, everything would be solved. He stopped and fumbled in his pocket again. The pain was definitely there now and as his trembling hands slipped the tiny pills under his tongue, he impatiently awaited the miracle. Two minutes later, he slowly set off again, wobbling madly, then pedalling faster as the cogs – and his heart - engaged. Tortuously, he crested the hill and clicked the bike into neutral as he coasted down to the lake's edge. Above him, the early morning light touched the great trees, artfully arranged to give the impression of careless nature and setting the autumn foliage aflame.

The new sun danced off the bike's chrome and off the aluminium foil wrapping the bottle in the rear basket. And off the spotting scope, trained carefully upon the cyclist from deep within a magnificent bank of red and green leaves half a mile away. Despite the duct tape covering every metallic surface, the lens gave a flash, an unmistakeable 'tell' to those who could decipher it, but unseen by the man now dismounting his bike and carefully propping it up on its stand.

The glint was picked up from the opposing bank above the fumbling cyclist, where other eyes watched him through the sights of a new, Accuracy International Long Range Rifle.'

'What was that?'

'What?'

'A flash. Up there, in my peripheral vision.'

'Didn't see it, Booksy.'

'It was there. Keep watching. You know what stuff like that in Basra meant.'

'The difference between life and death. I know. But that was the Shatt and this is Surrey, and I reckon His Royal Highness – our dear HRH – has enough hardware round here to keep out the hajjis.'

There was a silence as both men scanned the tree line opposite them, moving their eyes horizontally, top to bottom, pausing for one to three seconds, then moving methodically on, so that no part of the hillside remained unscanned. Cones, doing their thing, the perfect scan. Different at night, where you looked about 10 degrees off and the rods serving the peripheral vision kicked in. Rods and cones. School biology lessons.

For both men, this job was the prize. Back in Blighty, on secondment to SO19, able to go home at night. Although Booksy didn't go home, much. Booksy's wife had walked out with that wanker of a sergeant a year ago. She'd had enough, she said. She certainly got enough, judging from the smirk on the wanker's face when he picked up her stuff. She got enough of Booksy's salary, too. And part of his pension through that blood-sucking leech of a lawyer of hers.

Still, there were compensations. Women loved Booksy. Always had. He'd been to war and survived, he looked the part, and he had enough of an air of menace for them to find him authentically thrilling. Less carnal pleasures made life better too, like a drink in the pub, a drive down the road without fear of suicide bombers or roadside traps, a round of golf with his mates. And as soon as he could get out, he'd work for a security firm and get a nest egg together for his boat. The dream boat, the one that kept him going through the Shatt al Arab and the lousy kit and the worse officers and

13

all the other bloody nutters who fed the wars. Yep. Things were on the up. The only drawback, thought Booksy, was that here you were accountable. People here had human rights even if they fully intended to deprive you of yours. Not like Iraq, where you were effectively immune, whatever you did to the towel-head bastards. At least, until Blackwater cocked it up for everyone.

'Looks all right to me, Booksy. No more flashes.'

'Reckon you're right. A jay's wing. Iridescence, innit.' Booksy was proud of his vocabulary, had to hide it. 'So what's our boy up to, then?'

Both refocused their attention on the man as he carefully pulled on the surgical rubber gloves he had fished out of the pockets of his old tweed coat. Grey haired and clearly tired by his bicycle ride, he looked about 65. But purposeful. He lifted the foil-covered bottle out of the bicycle basket and started to tear off the aluminium in shards. It was a large, plastic drinks bottle, half full of a milky liquid.

'Here we go'

'Subject in sight.' The sergeant depressed the button on the radio clipped to his chest and the slight crackle of static could be heard on the still morning air.

Booksy lifted the LRR up to his eye again and made minute adjustments as his spotter ranged in the binoculars for height and windage and quietly read out digits. Through the sights, he could see the cyclist walking slowly down to the lakeside, trailing shreds of foil as he went, like a jet scattering chaff to decoy incoming stingers, thought Booksy. But this target stood no chance. He bent down stiffly, carefully laid the bottle on the grass and began to lower himself painstakingly onto his knees on the ground.

Booksy – he still did everything by the book – breathed out as he had been taught to do all those years ago, flicked off the safety and began to squeeze the trigger. Then he stopped, as another figure stepped into the cross hairs.

Incredulous, Booksy jammed the sight to his eye as though to feel the evidence of his eyes. It was the Prince, a large wooden trug in one hand, an empty dog lead in the other. On a sodding dawn mushrooming walk, thought Booksy. Today of all days. And he was blocking Booksy's sightline, interposing himself between the bullet and the target.

'No shot, no shot,' hissed the sergeant unnecessarily.

'Fuck, fuck, fuck, ' Booksy growled, breathing in and loosening his finger.

The Prince was talking to the target, the older man leaning to one side on his knees as he propped himself up with one arm at the lakeside. The conversation seemed strangely calm, natural even, when the cyclist suddenly looked up at the hillside across the lake, as though alerted by something no one else could hear. Then he fell straight back. The report came later, though silenced. He was so far away it was like watching a silent film. The way he fell reminded Booksy of a book he often read to the kids. If – and it was a big if – he was allowed to see them. The Little Prince, monarch of a tiny, worn out planet, dies when he is bitten by a yellow snake and falls 'as gently as a tree falls.' Except this time it was the grey haired cyclist who was falling soundlessly and there was a perfectly round hole in his forehead. And he was taking the startled Prince with him. And all hell was breaking loose.

Guy Millington, pale at the best of times, was now positively clammy with fear. He had searched the laboratories and offices with a mounting sense of panic. Finally, he'd called the number the man had texted him that morning. Texted together with a photograph of the six-year-old Millington twins arriving at school that very day. His precious twins, born so late in his life and whom he had given up hope of seeing. He would do anything demanded of him, so long as no-one hurt them.

'He's not here,' he said. He knew his voice was shaking. 'What are we going to do?'

'It's under control,' the man answered. Millington knew, as he put down the phone, that the shame he felt flooding him was well deserved. Laffey had been a colleague for over 20 years and he had just sold him down the river.

Twenty miles away a woman cursed and banged her fist on the desk as she watched events unfold on the screen on the wall. Deputy Chief Inspector Sue Carter's day was turning to ratshit. The headphones she wore were still crackling in her ear and her last words, 'Don't shoot, don't shoot,' hung in the air. The men around her squirmed inwardly and looked dead pan and thought their secret thoughts about the wisdom of women being promoted to high rank in the Metropolitan Police.

The screen showed an unmoving Prince, partially covered by the inert body of the dead cyclist.

'Christ,' said Carter bitterly, talking into her headphones, 'Clean up team, execute contingency plan four. Say again, clean up team, execute contingency four.'

The support officers watched the possible demise of the heir to the throne on the screen in front of them with morbid fascination.

'He's moving ma'am,' said one of the Sergeants, taking pity on her.

It was true. The Prince was scrambling out from under the dead weight of the corpse. The royal spaniel was making it difficult, frantically licking his master's face while he remained on the ground. But he appeared unharmed. Albeit incensed. His increasingly enraged gesticulations as he spoke to someone on his mobile phone, then threw it into the lake, made that clear. The spaniel, a veteran of his masters' tirades, retreated to a safe distance and sat down, panting.

Within seconds, an armed Range Rover screeched to a halt next to him. Three substantial, Kevlar-clad men rolled out of the doors, brandishing MP-7 machine guns and shoulder holsters, while a fourth gunned the engine. Two guards bundled the Prince into the back seat and the third backed towards his open door, swinging his weapon to and fro as he scoured the area in front of him for threats. He climbed in, narrowly missing the spaniel as it leapt for its master's arms, pulled the door to, and the car shot off. The entire operation had taken less than ten seconds.

From his eyrie in the tree line, the sniper watched through the sights of his personalised Walther Wa2000. Crucially, the green perforated cardboard disc over the sight lens prevented reflection, but he knew he had made a mistake with the ranging scope: that flash had been a dead giveaway. He'd been lucky this time, got away with it. Too easy to underestimate the opposition, especially when he had never yet failed. It was time to go. He didn't have long before the occupants of the helicopter now landing on the grass beside the lake decided to investigate where the shot had come from. He moved back into the shadows, pulling off the green gauze and leaf-covered ghillie smock, which broke up his outline so effectively. He'd been invisible, totally assimilated into this natural world for the last 20 hours. He had eaten, drunk and relieved himself right here, burying the evidence under piles of leaf compost in scent-free plastic bags. Even the birds had long since decided this strange interloper was harmless and continued their daily rituals, flying, fighting and feeding around him.

Working fluidly, he dismantled the sniper rifle, unscrewing the various parts and dropping them into a padded, compartmentalised duffle bag. He stripped off the

rest of the ghillie suit, emerging in black jeans and a black
hoodie, which he pulled up over his head. He stuffed the suit
in the bag, slung it over his shoulder and started to descend
stealthily, not running but moving fast, towards the woodland
path below. At a mound of leaves, he began to dig until he
found the handlebar of a dirt scrambler bike. Hauling it up,
he swung his leg over it and clicked it into life. Within
seconds, he was gone. The helicopter arcing overhead never
saw him.

Stuffed unceremoniously in the back seat of the Range
Rover, his bodyguards' unyielding Kevlar digging into his
hips, his spaniel's claws raking his thighs as it leaned into the
bends, HRH Prince Edward, Duke of Cumberland, was in a
foul temper.

'Why the hell wasn't I told?'

The man in the front seat spoke, his neck stiff, his eyes never leaving the road, as if extra vigilance now would compensate for what undoubtedly was the mother of all fuck-ups.

'Sorry Sir. National security.'

'Bloody right it's national security,' the Prince erupted. 'Mine. The heir to the throne. Or had you forgotten? Some damn fool wanders in and gets shot by my bloody lake, so obviously you had some inkling that this was going to happen. Shot, indeed, inches from my bloody side. Bullet parted the hairs on my arm. Yet no one thinks it worth cancelling my morning constitutional.'

A vision of what making such a suggestion would have entailed flashed simultaneously across the minds of all four men. It was a toss up which was more painful – taking on a battalion of assassins barehanded or trying to divert HRH from his plans. And the truth – that although prepared, they had not fired a single shot – was too humiliating. Leave that to the top guys to explain. Sometimes it was good to be a grunt.

Sensing a mute solidarity amongst his protectors, the Prince harrumphed something about their superiors hearing more about it and sat back, enjoying, in a flash of malevolence, the dark red flush creeping up the muscled necks in front of him.

Harold Arthur, Baron Regis of Clutton Champflower, sat back in his deep, leather seat as the limousine door opened. The darkened glass would shield him from onlookers. He had no desire to be spotted by some eagle-eyed shareholder on this, the morning of his triumph. Particularly as the man now climbing into the passenger compartment of the Daimler was not his usual travelling companion. On the seat facing his, Regis could see the Financial Times tantalizingly folded so that he could only read part of the headline. REGIS-BEI and

WORLD B were obvious. He itched to pick it up and enjoy it. But first, he must deal with the essential unpleasantnesses of his life. He indicated the seat diagonally across from him to the new passenger, at the same time leaning forward and tapping on the privacy glass. The car slid away from the kerb while Lord Regis regarded the man in front of him. Though they had met from time to time, it was not a face you would remember easily. Which was undoubtedly the point. Dark, lean, something military in the bearing. But unshaven with anonymous, dark clothing and a scruffy haircut. Clearly, the fees, which were substantial and paid regularly into a Swiss bank account, were not spent on grooming.

Lord Regis prided himself on his grooming. Elegant was the word he favoured; 'dapper' was more used by columnists and rivals because it so neatly encompassed his diminutive stature as well. Regis was short. His height was the only modest thing about him and, like many small men, he had used it as licence to grow a monster ego. As head of a great supranational corporation, his word was law. Even with governments. Especially with governments.

His personality infused the corridors of International Fertilisers Limited and suffused the minds of his subordinates. To a man, they were well educated and well versed in reading his demands before they were articulated, especially Michael Vellin, his aide de camp, who had turned Regis-profiling into an art form.

Regis demanded a certain fastidiousness of dress in his underlings, a highness of mind – the IFL opera society was thriving -- and an age limit. At present, no director or manager was older than 47, a crucial 15 years younger than Regis. Leaving him unassailable. And it would stay that way. He looked inquiringly at the man in black, who spoke.

'It's been contained – barring a minor hiccup.'

'Will that require further initiatives?'

'Only if you want to eliminate our future King as well.'

'Now, that would scotch my wife's social calendar.'

Regis thought of Marcia's unending social whirl of charity balls, auctions and fashion shows, none of which occurred without HRH's endorsement and usually, presence. In fact, Regis had sometimes wondered whether Marcia and HRH had something going on. He thought it unlikely. He made a small and for him, rare, joke.

'Think of the money I'd save.' He tapped the privacy shield again.

'Hope they got the right man, then,' the man said, as he stepped out of the car and walked swiftly southwards on Albert Bridge. Turning his attention immediately to the FT, Regis was borne northwards to his other life.

DCI Sue Carter was ready to quit. Greasy old Briar was here, giving her the hard word, when only last week he was oiling up to her in the bar and suggesting things his wife might not approve of. She sighed. Perhaps if she had succumbed to his dubious charms, he wouldn't have felt the need to make quite such an example of her. Most irritatingly, just as in the bar, he seemed incapable of understanding what she was telling him and kept pushing for more. Surely the man was brain damaged.

'I thought we told our man to stand down.'

'We did. He did.'

Sue Carter felt justified in her shortness. She had said this twenty different ways already.

The Commander raised his voice just enough to allow the officers, studiously avoiding looking interested outside Sue's open door, to hear.

'Then how the hell did a shot miss the Prince by a whisker.'

Sue almost lost the will to live.

'It wasn't our shot.'

'So I'm supposed to believe that SO19's finest, plus a Royal protection squad, were unable to prevent some hit man from getting onto the Prince's private estate and shooting our target seconds before we did. Then having done so, he got away.'

Carter felt light headed from the tension in her neck as she answered. 'That appears to be the case, sir.'

Briar understood, with a twinge of regret, that he'd squeezed this particular situation dry. His arse was well and truly covered and the snooty bitch would be hung out to dry. Maybe if she'd been nicer to him....

'This is not going to be good for your career.'

Sue knew it was juvenile but she couldn't help it. She stuck her tongue out at the slime ball's retreating back. Macintosh, the new boy, caught her in the act and had the good sense to look away.

The Prince straightened his cuffs as he ran up the steps from the Range Rover, closely followed by the spaniel. The royal protection squad took off as quickly as decently possible without spinning the wheels on the gravel, each member longing to lick his wounds in the calm of the bunker behind the Palace. To the equerry, discreetly hovering under the portico, the portents were ominous.

'Who's on duty?' The Prince didn't even look his way.

'Leonie Li, I believe, sir.'

'Good. Find her, now.'

Leonie was awaiting the Prince in his private office. She had already collected together his Mont Blanc fountain pen and the heavy laid vellum watermarked with the Prince's feathers and the legend, 'Ich Dein.'His penchant for written 'howlers' to the great and the good was well known and Leonie fully expected him to exercise his prerogative now. It was this gift for second-guessing the royal wishes that had endeared her to her employer. Her considerable beauty and sharp intelligence had helped, although it wasn't wise to appear too clever around the royal family. Like all members of their caste, they regarded excessive displays of intellect with suspicion. Leonie's First from Christ Church was secondary to her usefulness, and only recently had her fluency in Mandarin and understanding of matters Chinese been noted at all.

She had arrived at the Palace through her tutor at Oxford, a young don at Trinity when the Prince had been studying at Cambridge. Professor and Prince had shared a passion for the Goons and had always kept in touch. Now elevated to Professor of Sino-Russian Relations, the former don had remained of occasional use to the Prince in small ways. When the Prince's private secretary had been searching for a new assistant, the Professor had suggested Leonie. Three years later, she was indispensable.

The Prince swept in and dumped the trug full of mushrooms on a priceless break-fronted cabinet. Leonie cringed inwardly, already hearing the housekeeper's grumblings in her head. The spaniel duly followed and took up residence in his rather smelly basket under the Chippendale desk. The prince was already half way through a complaining monologue, which appeared addressed to no one in particular. Leonie knew better than to interrupt his flow.

'...really is appalling. Can't even walk in one's own grounds without some fool banging away as though I'm a bloody pheasant. I don't care what those infernal politicians say about my interfering: this is going straight to the PM.'

He sat down, scratched furiously at the paper for a few seconds, screwed it into a ball, then threw the pen down. Leonie was already sitting, poised for the dictation.

'To the Right Honourable – the Prince emphasised the title, indicating it was anything but – William Lynton, Prime Minister.'

Leonie looked up expectantly. The Prince was rather good at these letters and this one had real potential as a zinger.

'Prime Minister. Perhaps you know more than I do about who is in charge of this country, but if security exercises are to infringe my morning walks in future, would you kindly have the courtesy to let me know.'

Ten minutes later, Leonie was skipping down the castle steps, jangling the keys to her new Mini. Her shift was over and she was driving back to London for the evening. Along with the mushroom trug, the letter had been handed to a footman with instructions for immediate delivery to Downing Street.

As always, Heathrow Terminal 3 looked more like the third world than the destinations it served, thought Foote as he looked around in vain for a porter to deal with Hester's inordinate pile of luggage. At five in the morning, it was bleak beyond belief. And cold, with the crispness of autumn tingeing the air. Sighing, he found a trolley with the obligatory contrary wheel and dragged it over, wheels protesting, to his wife and daughter. Hester, a handsome woman with leonine hair and a determined expression, started throwing her various boxes and packages onto the trolley, while Freya, their younger clone, nobbled an elusive porter and pressed him into service. Not for the first time, Foote marvelled at his womens' self-sufficiency, their ability to live in a capsule of their own creation. Probably a good thing, considering where they were headed.

The check-in was wide open. No one else wanted to go to Bogota today, it appeared. Considering the cost of the kidnap insurance the University had declined to underwrite, Foote was not surprised.

'I really don't understand why you have to go to Colombia.'

His wife gave him the kind of half indulgent, half impatient glance you accord a senile parent.

'For a man who understands so much, you can be very dense sometimes.'

'I understand that you are going into that part of the map marked by dragons. With our only child. And a sat phone. For three months.'

The only child turned on him.

'Dad, you know this is one of the last places on earth where Mum can study the urbanisation of indigenous tribes in real time.'

'That's because no one else disturbs them. For a reason.'

'Well, I'm not giving up on my first, paid research project,' said Freya.

'Ah, yes, the first job. How could I forget'

'Not the first *ever*. Don't forget, I did the Harrods' sales.'

Hester snorted and leaned over the desk in front of them, piling passports, tickets and excess baggage allowances on the check-in clerk's keypad. She turned back to Foote.

'It's only three months, darling. And you'll be fine. Mrs H will keep you clean and fed at home and Janey's got the office side taped… Anyway, Orlando will sleep on my side of the bed if you're lonely.'

Although a giant and, Foote liked to imagine, extraordinarily intelligent ginger tomcat, Orlando was a bed hog. Foote made a mental resolution to lock him in the kitchen every night.

Hester packed the tickets into her bag, gripped the boarding passes and turned to him.

'Done. We'd better go. We haven't much time before boarding.'

'And I want to do some shopping airside.'

Foote leaned down to kiss his wife. Her returning embrace was fond but brisk: he could see she was already mentally airborne. He turned to his daughter and managed to hang onto her for a little longer than her mother. Then both were walking through security. Freya turned and blew him a kiss. They were gone.

It was with a mixture of longing and relief that he walked back to the car park and searched through his pocket for the £12.00 it cost to park for 40 minutes at London's premier airport.

Two hours after arriving home, Foote awoke from his unsatisfactory nap on the breakfast room sofa with Orlando purring maniacally on his chest. The phone was ringing. Janey, his ever-perky secretary, was on his case.

'Got them off safely?'

'If you could call it that. Last time I looked, the Shining Path pretty much headed up the list of world baddies.'

'I don't think the drug lords will be too interested in indigenous tribes. And anyway, the Shining Path is Peru. You may be thinking of FARC. '

Foote was constantly amazed by Janey's strange bites of knowledge. This one was no doubt furnished by her ex-Para boyfriend, Lance, who was now something in 'security.'

'Let's hope you're right.'

'Was Freya excited?'

'The last time I saw her aglow like that was when she was eight and saw a leopard on safari.'

'She might find panthers in the rainforest. Same thing, without the spots.'

'Is there any rainforest left?'

'Actually, there's quite a lot of it left. I read it in the New Scientist.'

There was a pause while Foote thought longingly about breakfast. Janey broke into his full English reverie.

'It's a different jungle you're exploring today. You're going to meet the lord of the jungle. The Alpha, Alpha male. The Silverback.'

'Yes. The Regis day. Do you think they'll cancel again?'

'He can run but he can't hide. In this brave new world of ours, no one has a choice. Corporate compliance decrees that everyone must have a coach. Even a Silverback.'

'Enter yours truly.'

'Mrs H said to remind you that your good suit is on the door, just back from the cleaners. Shirts are in the wardrobe. They're sending a car for you at 8.45.'

Twenty minutes from now, thought Foote. Damn. The bacon and eggs would have to wait.

At 8.45 sharp a Mercedes pulled up outside Foote's terraced London house. The driver, smartly attired in a dark suit, held the door open for the psychologist as he slid into a

world of climate control and soft leather. Open on the back seat lay a copy of the FT, the banner headline screaming 'Regis-Beijing deal of the century for International Fertiliser.' The Silverback had done it again.

Nancy Hammer was feeling great. Not that she would ever admit to anything less – she was a devout advocate of thinking positively – but today she really was. International Fertilisers was on a roll, her new role as director of corporate compliance and ethics was everything she'd dreamed of, and the Royal visit was promising to be a show worth remembering. Best of all, the old crocodile Regis had finally allowed her to draft in a life coach. Maybe this was how she would get a handle on him.

Deftly, considering the length of her varnished nails, she flicked the FT onto page two. Unnecessary: everything she needed to see was there in 10 point bold on the front page.

And it was a triumph. She looked up at the lean, handsome, hungry-looking man who had just entered the room.

'Good morning Michael. What a coup for the old man.'

Michael Vellin, consigliere to Lord Regis, leaned over Nancy to pick up the newspaper, though she knew he must have first seen it at dawn. She could smell his expensive and exotically ambiguous aftershave. Why did some Englishmen swamp themselves in the stuff? In fact, Nancy felt Vellin was a little too into his grooming, if such a thing were possible. But she appreciated his tidy, clean nails and his white teeth, which she considered almost unheard of among Brits, and the beautiful cut and fabric of his suit.

A lock of hair escaped rakishly from his immaculate coiffure as he dropped the FT on her desk.

'Biggest, baddest deal ever.'

Nancy stared at him. Was this ghetto talk a sly dig at her African-American heritage? Was it racist? Nancy was extremely sensitive to issues of gender, race and age. She was the poster girl for political correctness and proud of it. It made everything so much easier and tidier, cleaner – a favourite Nancy word – if you knew exactly what the rules were. Nothing could get past her. Yet here was Michael Vellin, making her unsure. She decided to ignore him and remained on transmit.

'China. What a challenge. Get the ethics pinned down there, and game over.'

'Exactly what are the ethics of a place where they only allow one child, Nancy? No free speech, state sanctioned death penalties, mass mind control. They want final solutions, not Fertiliser Solutions.'

Nancy felt slightly, indefinably uncomfortable at Vellin's daring to question the new orthodoxy. China was IFL's new best friend. He knew that. Yet here he was, making a joke of it. Sometimes Nancy longed for some of the power the Chinese had to quell dissent. Just until Vellin could see how wrong he was, of course.

She turned away and flicked on the wall-mounted flat screen. A breathless girl was standing outside the Chinese Embassy, surrounded by placard-bearing crowds. Nancy knew what they were chanting. She clicked the control to mute.

'Did you watch the signing ceremony in Beijing?'

'Why would I want to look at – what was it? – those appalling old waxworks. Must say, the heir to the throne has a way with words. Maybe he could write the next press release for us.'

Nancy was irritated. 'Cut it. You're going to have to work with these people. And whatever he said, the Prince is hosting tomorrow's reception, remember?'

'How could I forget? Come on then, Nancy. Show me how. Persuade the great persuader. After all, you managed to get our Lord to see his new coach, Dr. Foote. Who, by the way, is on his way. I hope he's tough enough.'

'His client list is impressive. Eight of the FTSE 100 chiefs. Which is what makes him so desirable. A prize perk. And you know how they all fight for each other's prize perks.'

At that moment, Lord Regis appeared on the TV screen, unscrewing his Mont Blanc pen cap and leaning forward to sign documents laid out in front of him. The camera pulled back from the close up on his patrician features to show an assortment of Chinese dignitaries standing around the table. A single woman stood out. Taller than the average Chinese, beautifully and immaculately dressed, she appeared to be in her late 40's. She was watching Regis intently. As intently as Vellin watched her.

'We owe it all to Ping Li,' he said. 'I reckon she's been working on that relationship longer than anyone knows.'

Ping Li was looking out over Cadogan Gardens from her penthouse terrace. She had lived here for more than 20 years and alien though it was, this was home. Her native land was represented in the elegant room behind her, glorious lacquered chests and exquisite ivories speaking of a time long before a People's Republic. The walls were hung in silk, mounted on batons the Chinese way, and screens ensured no dangerous energy drained through opened doorways. Chi flowed freely here. No entrance and exit lined up. The three bedrooms and bathrooms were arranged carefully at right angles to lines of power and far from the kitchen. A pair of bronze Fu dogs guarded the front door. Ping Li was feng shui-ed to a fault.

The Orientalism sat well with three vast, modern, white sofas arranged around the low, square, lacquered table to look out through the glass wall leading out onto the terrace. As wide as the room, the terrace became part of it when the glass panes folded back to each side. A great, gilded birdcage full of canaries sat to one side by the glass. The other side was balanced by a black baby grand piano, the top covered in photographs arranged in black or silver frames in the English manner. All showed the same young face, as a baby, a toddler, a toothless seven-year-old, a gangly teenager and as an exquisite young woman.

The St Mary's church bells chimed nine and the children below, queuing up for school in their russet corduroy knickerbockers and mustard sweaters, were chattering like birds. The canaries were chattering back, woken from their slumbers by the bright morning light streaming in through the bars. Ping Li folded back the glass doors between their cage and the terrace and watched the little birds fluffing up their feathers in the October sunlight. There was still slight warmth in the sun. She picked up the watering can, filled it from the terrace tap and poured it over the pots. The unseasonable sun was drying out the plants, and though they would be instantly replaced through the expensive maintenance contract with a Chelsea florist, Ping Li could not bear waste. She swung the can to and fro, sprinkling through the rose and listening with half an ear to the Today programme on Radio Four.

A car alarm five storeys below drowned out the newsreader's words, her perfectly modulated English vowels, which Ping Li had tried to emulate every day of her life, shattering into indistinguishable bites by the scream of the siren. The more expensive the car, the louder the alarm. And this was an area full of very smart cars. But a splinter of information had caught her attention. She picked up her mobile, lying by a pack of cigarettes on the wrought iron table in the sun and pressed a key.

'What happened?'

'I can't talk about it now, Mum. But everything's OK.'

'So long as you are.'

'I'm fine. What would anyone want with me?'

Ping Li put down the phone and lit her second cigarette of the day, blowing the smoke down over the graceful treetops below.

The glass tower that contained all the head office functions of International Fertilisers Limited had, from the outside, seen distinctly better days. Architects in the sixties had adopted a functional brutalism that did nothing for the human spirit. Modern hot desking was its apotheosis, Foote thought. How *could* anyone have private thoughts and garner all the energy they needed for a day in an office in a building that drained it away on sight.

Once again, he said a private thank you to the oddest of gods for the oddest of chances that had left him free to pursue his own understandings of the human condition. It might be slow and stumbling, sometimes, but he could refine it on his own terms. No HR controls over Foote. He was the master of his own fate and captain of his soul. And since, over the years, he had discovered that the more certain he was of his own position the less likely he was to be suborned through fear that work might dry up the next day, he quietly armoured himself against whatever onslaught might be coming. Brutal buildings, brutal scars can make.

At a large reception desk in a cavernous space sat a stunningly beautiful girl whose only interest was her nails. A uniformed security man came at Foote from an angle, to intercept him before he could make contact. It looked like a well-practised double act.

'I'm here to see Lord Regis,' said Foote, giving the guard no chance of the initiative. But the guard knew the system better than Foote, and had the initiative well under control.

'We'll let Mr Vellin know you're here, Sir,' he said. Brutal buildings, tight controls. No entry without the proper manipulations. It was a good job he had his own defences well in place.

And then, for the briefest of moments, Foote took himself into the private space that let all his intuitions flow. He called it his limbic lock-in. He deliberately commissioned that central part of his brain that knows everything and registers every minute detail in milliseconds: the place where conscious controls can only interrupt and make intuition stumble; the place where finely-tuned feeling sharpens every perception and makes the richness of the inner world the best guide to understanding.

A sharp observer would have seen only that his shoulders relaxed and that he took a deep breath. But that wasn't the way into his limbic system. Those were simply the outward and visible signs that he had engaged it. Deep in the centre of the brain two almond shaped structures, operating like super sensitive radar, track every thought and every signal coming into the brain. From there, all decisions are made. He hardly understood the pathways himself, just knew that if he trusted them, they worked.

Now he was ready for whatever came next, apparently relaxed but intensely tuned in. It was a state that he had been perfecting since 1997, when the mechanisms of the brain that manage these processes had first been properly described.

'Take the lift to the thirtieth floor,' said the beautiful girl. 'Mr Vellin will meet you there and take you to the thirty-second.'

And so Foote began his ascent to the eyrie from which Lord Regis commanded his vision of the world.

Another double act awaited him first. Like Cerberus, guarding the entrance to Hades, consigliere Vellin had to be circumvented. There wasn't much the ancient world didn't know about the human condition, thought Foote. Even if, in a modern sense, they didn't understand it, the stories they used to describe it showed that they knew an amazing amount about the experience of being human. Though it ran out of steam eventually, of course. Working models have only a limited time-span. Even Newton was eased off his celestial perch in the twentieth century in favour of quantum theories with childish names, like 'string theory.'

Foote's limbic system was in free flow, unbidden and unchecked, as the lift rose through the floors. And as the doors opened, there was Vellin, just like Cerberus, looking in all directions at once as he emerged from a nearby doorway. Grasping Foote's hand and unnecessarily, his elbow too, Vellin steered him away from the adjoining lift – the only one with direct access to the thirty-second floor – and into his office.

'Looks like we made it, this time,' said Vellin.

'Who's the "we"?' thought Foote, knowing that Vellin was alluding to the previous last minute changes of his master's diary arrangements. Despite Foote's extensive training and total absence of ego in therapeutic situations, Vellin was already getting in his way. Foote quelled his irritation and replied blandly, 'The headlines look good this morning.'

'Important to set the agenda, don't you think,'said Vellin, making it instantly clear that he and he alone was responsible for the Regis worship in all the business sections that morning.

'Let's have a couple of minutes before you meet the Lord.'

Foote resigned himself to a little agenda setting, as a surprisingly effete male secretary sitting at a desk by the door was dismissed by Vellin with a curious, underhand flick of his wrist.

Vellins' office was oddly like the smaller inner sanctum to an over-designed gentleman's club or an attempt at a Mayfair gambling casino's anteroom. Inviting his guest on to a substantial leather sofa, Vellin said, in a lower tone and with a conspiratorial edge:

'Regis is an alchemist, really: a magician, organisationally. No one knows how he pulls the rabbits out of the hat the way that he does, and he tells no one how he does it. That's his great strength.'

'Perhaps his great weakness too,' said Foote, then cursed himself quietly for being too quick off the mark. He had broken the conspiratorial atmosphere Vellin was clearly trying to create.

'I'm not sure that's accurate at all,' said Vellin, defensive and stiffening slightly. 'He turns the basest of chemicals into gold.'

He paused to regroup.

'You too have an extraordinary reputation, Dr Foote, but I don't know that he's going to want someone questioning his magic. Still…' he sighed, with an affected world-weary note to his voice, 'everything's got to be transparent these days.'

Reading the message underneath the words, Foote thought it was time to reset Vellin's agenda more along his own terms.

'You do understand the complete confidentiality of all this, don't you?' he said.

Miffed at being read so accurately, Vellin replied dismissively, 'Yes, yes, of course. But we do also have to remember that this is being set up in the Company's interest.'

He was not – quite – cross or crass enough to mention that the company was also paying. But Foote got the message and ignored it.

'That's an interestingly fine line you're drawing,' he said brightly. 'Lord Regis *is* the Company. So if this turns out to be good for him, it's bound to be good for the Company.'

'"Good" is not a word used much around here, Dr Foote,' said Vellin. 'But I'm sure you'll find the right language with him.'

On cue, the camp secretary put his head around the door, saying: 'The good Lord above awaits.'

Ushered through a door on the other side of the office, Foote noted two Victorian evangelical nonconformist wall plaques shining their pious messages. The first said: 'Prepare to meet thy God,'and the second: 'The One above sees all.'Camp humour had an edge to it that he enjoyed.

The thirty-second floor was not Foote's natural home territory. He had heard about it often enough, of course, and felt its ambience in countless movies and TV dramas. It was the way people imagined being in Buckingham Palace until they encountered solid reality. What had struck him on the one occasion he had been to the Palace was the vastness of the space. Cameras never can convey space properly, he thought. The lens needs detail, and so a sense of space eludes the camera's eye. As it fixes on detail, the real impression gets lost.

Far below, the Thames, bright, squandered itself seawards between the limitations of its concrete banks. Sunlight made the Houses of Parliament look flat, as if Canaletto had caught them on a good day but produced only the backcloth for a masque, quickly done for rolling up and storing away. Nothing of Monet and mistiness here. All sharply etched, but *small:* from over thirty stories high. Plenty of time to take it all in too – not like being on the Eye that moves so slowly but finishes too quickly. Looking down on Parliament from the office of the Lord was a perspective sharply edged for Foote from that day onwards.

He focused the lens inward. The first ten seconds are what counts. Everything that's subsequently important between people will have been transmitted in that briefest of preludes to a first meeting. Some people thought it took the first thirty seconds, but Foote had spent a professional lifetime getting it down to what he believed was an irreducible minimum. Ten seconds was his benchmark test nowadays. That's what he kept in permanent memory store and where all his key reflections about anyone he met would later lead him.

For a building that screamed its sub-Corbusier, undecorated, miserable functionality on the outside, the chief executive's office suite deep inside International Fertilisers created a quite different and parallel universe. Huge windows were deeply framed to give a sense of looking out upon the world from a core that contained, cosseted and controlled. That, Foote thought, is the essential difference that plate glass brought into buildings. Where, once upon a time windows were a special and expensive means of looking outwards, plate glass aimed to merge the outer and inner worlds. Boundaries didn't matter any more. A perspective shift was created.

Not here though. This particular Lord had reversed all that. His space defined an absolute perspective on the outside world by making the inside world complexedly refined and the inner frames to the windows, deep.

Foote's peripheral vision took all this in. The brain that gets eighty milliseconds of reaction into a quarter of a second's consciousness can store extraordinary amounts of information. Foote's did, though there was nothing on the outside to show anyone the elegant efficiency of what was going on. Foote didn't go in for show. What he cherished was effect.

There had been a time in his life when Foote thought he was only a chameleon, both socially and professionally; that his only identity came from assuming those of others. But slowly he had realised what a strength this was; if he could both look at the world through others' eyes and have a clarity of his own. From this had come his present sense – not so much of having power but of being able to create the effect in others that he wanted for them. He tried to mitigate any tendency towards pomposity by creating a style with others in which he offered them options of where they might want to get to in their own development. He was of course certain they would pick up what his own best judgments were, and he was not sorry that this was so. For he saw it as his job to help people realise aspects of themselves of which they were hardly aware – aspects which, if some inkling could be created for them, might take them places they could never have imagined.

Foote advanced across the long space between the door and the further quarter of the room, making his way towards the man who embodied IFL. Regis had made IFL and it had made him. Each without the other would die. Symbiosis doesn't get any closer than that.

The impeccably groomed, shirt-sleeved man with greying hair, rose from behind his desk as Foote came closer, removing half-rimmed glasses as he did so. 'Regis,'he said, a briefly outstretched hand making perfunctory contact as he came around the desk. 'You're Foote.'

No 'hello,' thought Foote, just facts.

Turning Foote through a hundred and eighty degrees with the same gesture as ending the handshake, Lord Regis of Clutton Champflower, first and only Baron, life peer, and quondam academic, took Foote to the central group of armchairs. Foote hovered. Lord Regis busied himself with the silver flagon of coffee that had appeared soundlessly behind Foote, whilst he had been advancing to greet Regis.

'White?' he said, pouring it anyway.

'Thank you,' said Foote. It was the first word he had uttered. Somewhere deep inside himself he dug for the energy to get in control of the situation. But, applying the second rule of engagement, he kept quiet.

'Sit, won't you?' said Regis. 'Nancy Hammer has asked me to champion the group ethics and compliance programme.'

Straight in. No small talk. Regis said 'programme' in the American fashion, as if it felt alien to him or it was the only way he could accept it, as some kind of American import that was slightly distasteful to him. Certainly, the new world felt a long way off from the panelled comfort of his office, the low lighting that somehow kept the brightness of the day outside at bay, and the Chinese porcelains that suited the long Chippendale breakfront bookcase so well. Interesting, Foote registered, how the bookcase was pure English, and the porcelain pure Chinese, even if the interior of the bookcases had been fitted with lighting to display contents that were sharper, harder and less demanding than books. And why not choose Chippendale in his Chinese style? But of course that would have meant integration, bringing things together. This way, things were kept quite separate though together, allowing a statement to be made.

'I'd said "yes" before Nancy told me that I had to set an example with my own personal mentor, coach.' Regis said the last two words as though they were foreign to him. 'Apparently you are whatever that is.' He emphasized the 'you' as a challenge. 'What exactly do you do?'

'My job is to look at the world through your eyes and help you make the best sense of it you can,' said Foote.

Regis took his eyes off Foote. He let them wander round his office; not quite caressing, more patrolling.

'Some would say I've made quite a good job of that.'

'But what I'm interested in is what others do not see – and especially in what you *really* think.'

'Oh Mr Foote – sorry, it's Dr Foote isn't it? – if I'd ever let anyone know what I was really thinking I wouldn't have kept all this moving my way all these years.'

His eyes indicated his surroundings.

'But I know there's a shadow side to success,' said Foote.

Was the look that passed briefly across the Lord's face one of irritation at a slick answer, or surprise at something that touched him in an unfamiliar part of his mental system? Foote wasn't sure, but he wanted to know.

'That could be dangerous ground you're on.'

Foote knew it was worth the risk. He was throwing down a gauntlet of sorts. He knew too well that backing off at this point with someone like Regis would mean no hope of getting anywhere in the future. Like fencers in the early part of a bout, the other's probing was to find out about weaknesses as well as strengths and style. Regis had not become the champion he was, and kept his position for as many years as he had, without reading the weaknesses in others very well indeed. Foote could only hope now that the bait was set and Regis' vanity would ensure he felt inviolable.

Regis was used to most men backing off early. He wondered what Foote would do.

'Perhaps,' said Foote. 'An interesting landscape might have surprise views in it and quite unexpected hidden places, some even dangerous; but that's what makes the landscape the way it is.'

Elegant enough, thought Regis. He's not intimidated. He tried a different tack.

'Talking without an agenda isn't a way that I waste my time, Dr Foote. What exactly would we be doing?'

'The agenda is absolutely clear, Lord Regis. It's entirely about you. It's possible that you are not very experienced at talking about you.'

'I would have thought that's rather self-indulgent, especially for a very private man, Dr. Foote. Do we have to talk about me?'

'You *are* the Company, Lord Regis. It has been made in your image – its style, culture, strategy, everything that defines it. So whoever this "you" is, has a very profound effect on everything that "the Company" is.' Foote raised the forefingers of both hands to signify the inverted commas as he spoke them.

Regis noted the affectation and didn't like it. He had been trained in scientific disciplines at a time when it was also an educational requirement that both the written and the spoken word were proper disciplines in themselves, and he rather liked old-fashioned conventions in such matters. Raising forefingers was not, in his book, an elegant means of conveying subtlety in speech. That especially grated on his nerves, like the Australian rising inflection at the end of a sentence.

'Even if what you say is true, Dr Foote, it's not something that we would ever convey in the Annual Report. Company law states that the company is an entity in its own right, not a manifestation of me. Being a very private man I prefer to stay that way, even if Nancy Hammer says I must lead by example through the active support of an executive coach.'

'Naturally,' said Foote, 'And what compliance and ethics need to make clear to everyone in the company is that there is a difference between privacy and secrecy. Privacy may have its proper place, but secrecy is a great danger to a public company. A person usually knows what it is proper to keep private. Anything that's improper to keep private risks becoming secretive. That's when the real troubles arise.'

'Dr Foote, the essence of much of our company demands secrecy. Without it, our rivals would know everything about us. We pay huge amounts of money to make sure things *are* kept secret. Surely you're not telling me you want to lower those barriers for some purposes I don't quite understand?'

Foote gathered himself. The parrying had to be over at this point or it never would be. He had Regis engaged to the extent that, whether he recognised it or not, he was spending time without an agenda. He had started a debate. Was it only going to be a verbal battle, which he could never win because, in the end, Regis held the power to refuse Nancy Hammer's request? Or could he create some means of hooking Regis into a real dialogue that would start opening him up? There would be no referee to define who won and lost. They would both know it, ultimately.

Foote knew for certain that his next words would lock Regis into a working relationship with him that could have real content, or leave it as a relationship with form but no effective substance, in which case he was not interested.

Regis had paused, but went on, because Foote really was better at silences than Regis was.

'If it's my secrets you're after, Dr Foote, you might find me a hard nut to crack.'

'But what if *you* were interested in your secrets that, even *you* do not know, Lord Regis?' said Foote.

He saw immediately that he had a palpable hit. This was an idea that Regis had never, ever entertained. He thought he knew his secrets. The possibility that there might be other matters within him of which he was unaware suddenly fascinated him. For the whole of his life, for as far back as he was aware, he had believed that knowledge was power. What if there were matters of which this oddly tenacious Dr Foote – who didn't work by the rules of winning and losing as he understood them – could make him aware? Might that be something he should risk discovering?

Foote was not going to let the initiative be lost. This was not the time for silence.

'As a matter of fact, Lord Regis, I am probably the only person you will ever know in the business world who is *not* after your secrets. What I am here for is to help you understand them. If that can be done, it makes you more effective. It unlocks energy that is spent and wasted guarding them, freeing it for much more productive use. That's why a Company benefits from a corporate coaching programme. If more of the energies of its people can be put to productive use, then the company has an advantage. It's true of any physical system and human beings are essentially no different from any other physical system. They are sources of energy. Profit comes from how that energy gets used.'

Foote had passed the test. Regis had not surrendered, but something in what Foote had said had made him hungry. So that was what they would be about, these coaching meetings. And he would see if this Dr Foote could help him unlock whatever might be there to be unlocked without actually giving anything back. He wasn't sure it could be done, but he had nothing to lose. He would be doing what Nancy Hammer required of him, so he might at least do it on his own terms and for his own purposes.

'So be it. Let's give this ethics programme a whirl. Get some times in the diary and I'll do my very best to keep them.'

This time, 'programme' came out in the English, not American, form. Regis, Foote noted, had mirrored his own usage of the word. One step forward. That would do for today. There was at least enough of a working deal going to get some diary time.

And then, as he always did, though not always seamlessly, Foote went for the hard lock-in. 'Here's my card, Lord Regis. You have access to me on a twenty-four-seven basis for as long as we are working together. If I am not immediately available I shall always telephone you back as soon as I can.'

Lord Regis stood a little longer holding the open door through which he had just directed Foote, one hand resting on the doorknob, the other holding the card he had been given. He wasn't used to offers of support and it had temporarily jangled his thoughts. He was sure he wouldn't use it. Nevertheless he slipped the card into his wallet.

And then he thought that he would test Foote on that promise, just to see if it held. It was a maxim of his that, unlike Napoleon, who liked lucky generals, Regis liked people who under-promised and over-delivered. It looked as if Foote was over-promising.

Regis was happier now that he had defined a possible weakness. It gave him something around which to settle his understanding of a man who had surprisingly met him with an equality he didn't quite understand. Odd, that little perturbation of his spirit from Foote's visit. Lord Regis was not used to being managed in his own office. He wasn't sure he liked it.

He was already later than he had intended for a curious monthly meeting called 'the Commitment Club' that Nancy

Hammer had started. Damn the woman for getting him into something he didn't entirely understand now that he was there. If Dr Foote wasn't to be put in his place, Nancy Hammer certainly needed crushing into hers. Regis wasn't sure how exactly he would do that, but she needed re-sizing, and definitely downwards. Regis felt quietly pleased with this thought as the outcome of his first meeting with Foote. He could use Foote to hammer Nancy. That would be sport enough for the moment.

Walking to the executive lift, Foote found Vellin again poised to waylay him. At the same instant a door opened and Nancy Hammer, slightly flustered at being late for the Commitment Club, found herself impeded by Foote and Vellin.

'We need to talk about the final details with the Palace,' she said in a rush to Vellin, pleased to be able to say the magic word 'Palace' in front of someone she did not know. Vellin started introductions, but she begged the briefest forgiveness for rushing on. Vellin and Foote moved to the lift where the doors stood open. Reserved for that floor's inhabitants only, it was often on standby.

'It's only the Prince she's obsessing about,' he said. 'Wait until she meets the Queen. That will faze her. Come to think of it, it might faze the Queen.'

' Who was she?' said Foote, the privacy of the lift making it easy to ask.

Vellin laughed, the first entirely natural behaviour he had shown.

'People only ever ask that question once. That's Nancy Hammer, head of Compliance and Ethics. She's the cheerleader for everything that the good Lord hates but must support. It's what the corporate shareholders demand these days. Making money for them isn't enough. It has to be done as if it were being done honestly. Compliance and Ethics is the new way of keeping the Directors out of the courts for doing the things they've always done and will go on doing. Not, of course, that anyone would admit to what I've just said. It wouldn't be ethical to be honest about being unethical.'

Vellin looked rather pleased with himself, thought Foote, as their downward descent ended. As well he might be. He was pulling strings for all he was worth. But that conversation could go no further, either.

'I'll get Nancy sorted out at the end of the day,' said Vellin. 'St James's likes to be in control of the way the Prince appears in public, but actually they're seriously bad at it, and he runs rings around them. How he puts up with most of them I don't know. There's the occasional gem, but HRH scares the shit out of the rest of them and they just say yes to whatever he says until his mother pulls rank.

'Anyway, I shall go and see one of the gems this afternoon and we'll get the IFL announcement under control.

It's really my show, but Nancy must take the credit for the compliance stuff that the new contract has been shaped around – though heaven knows what the Chinese really think about it. My guess is that they can't believe their luck over the way the West wastes its efforts on moral posturing, while they get on with the serious business of polluting the earth, making money and keeping the masses under control. They seem to be pretty good at all three.'

Foote pondered his way back home. His thoughts were not especially well-formed, more a sifting of impressions to see what struck him most of all. Reflecting on immediate events sorted the wheat from the chaff when impressions were what counted. It was funny, too, how often the weaker signals had the greater meaning; as if somewhere on the periphery of consciousness the signals were purer when fainter, like a tantalising fragrance that had great evocative powers.

Foote's ponderings normally did a good job of the sorting out. He had learnt to let them find their own structure. Not much got written down in Foote's private professional world, but the richness of the multi-layered storing of impressions that he was continuously testing and refining let him function at the highest level. Writing things down made them too objective. For that very reason, he had abandoned the writing of scientific papers many years ago. At one time, he had produced them regularly as part of the academic rat-race in which he had learnt the rudiments of his trade. These days, thoughts that had acquired sufficient solidity to be conveyed to others in print only bored him.

He was already putting bits of the jigsaw together. Like all corporate systems that he had ever seen, the fracture lines at IFL stood out much more clearly than the mechanisms that kept it working. But in a world that increasingly looked for heroic chief executives to right the wrongs of the past, where serial failure seemed to be more highly rewarded than success, and where the next selected hero had no greater chances of winning, Lord Regis was a singular example of a man who had created what he surveyed and had stayed to reap the benefits.

That meant that the ghosts would be much more subtly hidden, and the secrets had had time to assume their own identities.

That made Foote's interest only keener. He felt almost elated by what had happened in his first encounter, and was lost for the moment in an early assessment of the way that Regis would be reacting.

Still ruminating, Dr Foote committed himself to the underworld of Westminster tube station, still bright and sterile in its refurbished Jubilee line modernity. Emerging into the Brompton Road at Holland Park, he worked his way across the traffic up the steep rise of Campden Square and to a small road just beyond its southern heights.

An Arts and Crafts church, incongruously large, but popular for local exhibitions, displayed its neighbourly functionality closely attached to the tall, thin house he had inherited from his maternal aunt, a gift that had acquired value far beyond its original owner's wildest dreams. Foote knew, though, that she would have been glad for the only nephew she adored. She had not lived to see him beyond his teenage years, but she had done everything quietly that she could to encourage his promise. As a small boy, he had been conscious only of her presence in the background, his mother's unmarried sister, somehow connected through University College London to the sciences.

Years later, quite coincidentally, he'd gone to the psychology department of that same great institution, at a time when the University of London and its colleges were still part of a residual British Empire based on learning and examination results achieved in distant, hot tin huts for a glory that was still almost Roman.

He put the key into the lock of his glossy, dark green door and entered the quiet house. The new post had been placed on the hall table. Mrs H had gone home, the girls were on the other side of the world and only Orlando was there to greet him.

After lunch, Foote rang Lord Regis's office to get some forward appointments into his diary. His PA – clearly a player – gave him the welcome that makes it clear the caller is not a stranger but not quite within the inner circle.

Farheen knew about inner circles. Indian and of a princely family by birth, she had decided to make her own way in the West on the back of an essentially useless education. By beauty, real brains, fast learning and a becoming softness in the increasingly sterile and unsubtle world of western metro sexuality, she had found herself moving quickly into senior PA roles.

A spell in a Peer's private office had brought her to Lord Regis's notice and, though it cost him a very expensive weekend's yachting party for the peer in question, he had been allowed to invite her away from the cramped but courteous office arrangements of the House of Lords to his own eyrie perched high above them. Farheen had not disappointed. She was exemplary and had learned her boss's foibles fast.

So when Foote asked for six meetings at three weekly intervals, each of two hours duration, she knew how to respond. 'It's not possible, Dr Foote. Lord Regis makes appointments for fifteen minutes maximum. Board meetings are a different matter, of course, and his responsibilities in the House of Lords and to Ministers also have to be fitted in. But his time is very precious and I cannot organise his diary as you request.'

Foote had not expected quite such a firm and negative handling of his request. 'I can't see Lord Regis on any other basis though,' he said, 'if we are to accomplish what I am here for. Look, I'll call you later when you might have had a chance to talk to Lord Regis about it. Would you make clear to him the time commitment that I need?'

Farheen expected to manage the people who wanted access to Lord Regis without difficulty. She generally understood their business and what significance they had for her boss. Neither was true with regard to Dr Foote.

She knew Nancy Hammer and Vellin seemed to have some stake in Dr Foote being there, but she trusted neither of them. Nancy Hammer was all noise and seriously lacked grace as a woman so far as Farheen was concerned. Moreover, Nancy patronised Farheen, which she thought typical of an American woman without any sense of lineage dealing with someone high-born from a third world country.

Vellin she thought of more as a scorpion. She had once watched two garden boys pour a ring of petrol around a scorpion and ignite the circle in a sudden whoosh of fire. As the scorpion became frantic in the flames and eventually sizzled in the heat and the boys had run off laughing, she had learned, aged four, that there were some of god's creatures with whom it was not good to make friends. Vellin was, for her, firmly in that category.

Frustrated by early first attempts to agree a schedule of appointments with Lord Regis' PA, Foote decided to go for a stroll. He knew that he was perfectly capable of holing up in his house for days on end with his books, papers and cat – especially as Hester and Freya were not there to make demands upon his time.

He deeply resented the myriad little jobs for his especial attention that his womenfolk seemed able to conjure out of thin air. They seemed unable to understand the amount of thinking his work entailed, despite Hester's own position as an assistant professor. Foote was entirely capable of staring into space for several hours at a time and longed sometimes for his wife and daughter to go away and leave him in peace.

Early in their marriage, Hester seemed able to juggle her academic duties with the more banal, daily tasks of running a household, while Foote never quite got the knack. After Freya was born, things gradually came to a head. If the house – and the marriage - were to run smoothly, Hester needed another pair of hands. Hence the luxury of Mrs H. Since – thanks to Foote's aunt – there was no mortgage, a housekeeper was affordable. Mrs H had arrived when Freya was three years old and moved into the basement flat under the house. Eighteen years on, she showed no sign of going anywhere else. She was, they all agreed, A Blessing.

Foote wondered whether to light the fire she had laid in his study. No, he would do that when he returned from his walk. Then he would ring the girls on their sat phone as prearranged. The satellite link up was usually at its strongest in the early evening. He picked up his key from his desk, edging the leather fob out from under the now inert figure of a sleeping Orlando and left the house, turning almost immediately left into the church next door.

Inside, the gallery had been given over to the first exhibition of a local artist. Foote went in, still half-musing to himself about Lord Regis and IFL, but really looking to feed his imagination. There, to his surprise but quiet delight, were a series of portraits in pencil and pastel of extraordinary directness and intimacy. If this was a first exhibition, he thought, it's time to have a portrait done before she's better known. He resolved to meet her when he could. The information gave an address in Campden Square itself, on the opposite side to the extraordinary word factory of the Pinters, Nobel husband and noble wife. Foote put the thought of having a portrait done – of Freya? Hester? Even himself? - into a part of his brain that kept treasures in store. Most were treasured so much, they never again saw the light of day. But this, he thought, might be one that did.

Returning home refreshed by the drawings and a swift pint at the Scarsdale Arms, Foote realized that it was still only 5 pm. He would try Lord Regis' redoubtable assistant one more time.

'I'm sorry Dr Foote,'said Farheen as he introduced himself again, 'I still haven't had a chance to speak with Lord Regis. And he's just said he's not to be disturbed.'

'Let's risk it' said Foote. 'It's important I get this sorted out, so that we both know where we are. If he's not on the phone, put me through and I'll deal with the collateral damage.'

Without further ado, Farheen did as she was asked. She couldn't immediately work out whether she liked this quiet man's style or whether he was simply gauche and didn't understand the corporate world. The phone clicked as her boss picked it up.

'Lord Regis,' said Foote, 'My apologies for interrupting you. Farheen did her best to safeguard your time, but there is a matter that's fundamental to how we work together that only you and I can sort out.'

'And that is?' said Lord Regis. No small talk of any kind again, thought Foote.

'We didn't discuss the time that we needed together. If we are going to do what we have to do, we need a couple of hours once every three weeks, at least for the first six months.'

'Heavens above, Foote, I'll be seeing more of you than I see of my wife.'

'Perhaps we'll change that too,' said Foote, somewhat to his own surprise. He immediately understood the subtle enormity of the error he had made. He knew instantly that Regis would trump him because he had entered the verbal game on Regis's terms, so was prepared for the searing shot back.

'I couldn't possibly see her any *less*, Dr Foote. Look, talk to Farheen and set up what we need.'

Putting down the phone, Lord Regis moved from his desk to the armchairs, from where Vellin had been privy to his side of the conversation. Vellin felt a tremor of sympathy for Foote. He knew these challenges intimately, in a way that Foote didn't. It was part of Vellin's relationship with Regis that he responded to such tests and played the game well, though he rarely walked off court without having allowed his master to win. In truth, neither of them really knew whether that was true or not. It was part of the resonating interplay between them that master and servant roles were finely defined and tuned but always kept on a knife-edge of the balance shifting in just the wrong way.

Easing himself into his chair, Lord Regis said: 'Your man Foote thinks he's going to change my marriage.'

'There may be other ways of achieving that,' said Vellin. A look passed between them that was as strong a seductive challenge from Vellin to Regis as one man might send quickly to another. It was not entirely blocked by Regis, who looked upwards from the papers on his knee long enough to let Vellin know that all its implications had been received, read and inwardly digested, then locked away in a part of Regis's soul that not even Vellin had ever quite penetrated. But both knew the atmosphere needed shifting back to the business in hand.

'So you're telling me that Quantum had no idea what Laffey was up to?' asked Regis.

'For us, that's normally their great strength. They let their scientists have direct relationships with companies like IFL, creating all the facilities that are needed without anyone but the scientist and the company knowing what the product really is. Chinese walls between departments, or even between individual scientists, protect secrets. Only the oversight committee is supposed to be in the loop and they convene rarely because the system has always been watertight, worked perfectly, and it's where their reputation has been made.'

'The world was simpler when I started out 30 years ago,' said Regis. 'Nobody inspected anything then. *If* you came from the right stable, they just let you run your hardest on your own terms. We made the world in our own image. But now I feel sometimes that it's moving against us. Too many people prying and too much information swirling around, in ways we can't control.'

'And now Quantum could ruin everything,' said Vellin.

'I never thought I'd hear you sound so paranoid. If your antennae are twitching, we had all better look out.'

Regis laughed. But Vellin's pessimism had also struck a chord within Regis himself. It wasn't something that had surfaced before, but a haze on the horizon had suddenly taken on the substance of a dark cloud. Making light of it would make it go away – for the moment. 'Everyone knows about the Chinese project, IFL's greatest coup so far. My greatest coup so far.' Regis allowed himself a small moment of pride before continuing. 'No one knew about River Dragon, which was – and remains - utterly secret. All Laffey did was synthesise Dragon, as requested, and pass it on to us.'

'So what was he trying to pour into the Prince's lake? And how in hell's name did Laffey turn out to be a rabid animal rights activist on the watch lists?'

'What Laffey was doing may not have been related in any way to River Dragon,' said Regis. 'If he really was into eco-terrorism, he would have been going for effect, an immediate effect, and that's not what the compound does. In fact, I think, as things turned out, there's no risk to River Dragon that I can see. And there's no sample to work with. The stuff was spilled on damp grass and dispersed. And no one was hurt – except, of course, Laffey. And he brought that upon himself.'

He paused, watching Vellin to see if the younger man agreed.

'Odd, though, that the security forces were covering the same ground but from a completely different angle. Is that coincidence or what?'

'They say nothing's coincidence,' said Vellin. 'We'll have to find out what the Police know.'

'We just don't know the rules yet. If everything's strung together – but in unpredictable ways – this world's a stranger place than dear old Newton would have had us believe.'

'One could apply that to the entire Dragon deal. If the Prince hadn't made the remarks he did about waxworks at the Hong Kong handover, there would have been no need to repair relations with China. Ergo, there would have been no generous subsidies for new fertilisers for China. And so Du Pont would have beaten us to it as a result, and there would have been no subsequent request for Dragon.'

'It seemed a small enough contribution to our friends in the East,' said Regis. 'And given in exchange for a great prize. Nor should we discount Ping Li's contribution. She has always had our interests at heart.'

'No, no one could have foreseen how things would work out with her.'

And with that Regis mused quietly for a minute. Ten minutes later, after a quick review, Vellin left.

Millington was growing increasingly desperate. His head was pounding, he felt ready to collapse. The bright white of the pristine laboratory surfaces was searing his eyes. But he had to keep searching. He had gone through half the fridges already, checking and rechecking the numbers on each vial against the master list on the Quantum R&D computers. The task was complicated by the sheer number of protocols: each vial had to be cross referenced and cross checked against several different screens. And he was getting nowhere. What had Laffey been doing? And where the hell was the evidence?

He barked at the assistant who was tentatively poking her head through the door.

'Get me special projects. This is getting me nowhere. I need *everything* Laffey worked on over the past five years. And get personnel to let me have everything we had on him, on and off the record'

At least there was no Laffey wife or girlfriend for the press to get at, thought Millington. That would have been the final nail in the coffin. But whose coffin? Laffey was already dead. And, Millington had to admit, hard to mourn. But the threat to take his twins.... dear God, not them. Millington gripped himself. He had to find the answer.

The assistant's head withdrew and Millington returned feverishly to his task. Time was running out.

Leonie was reversing the Mini out of the royal stable yard, now used for estate offices since the Prince was forced to give up Polo at the age of 55, when she was flagged down. Vellin, ridiculously handsome in dark blue pinstripes, leaned down to the window with a vulpine grin and Leonie felt the familiar flip in her stomach.

'Trust HRH has recovered from this morning? Tell me what happened.'

Leonie knew that Vellin knew she would not do anything of the sort.

'We had an intruder. He was shot. End of story.' As if he would let it go at that.

He didn't. Vellin managed to insinuate even more of himself into the car window frame. So close that she could smell him. Minty breath, Indian Limes and something more animal. She got a grip as she looked up at him. He was a bit too perfect, verging on camp, though she had absolutely no doubt he was interested in women.

'Leonie, Leonie.' His voice was positively seductive. No doubt this was how he managed that most exacting of employers, Baron Regis of Clutton Champflower. 'There must be more to it than that. This is England. People don't get shot in broad daylight with an undercover operation going on.'

'Who said anything about undercover?'

'Might it interest you to know that the dead man worked for International Fertilisers? He'd gone postal.'

'Pity you couldn't have stopped him earlier then.'

Vellin looked thoughtful. Leonie revved her engine.

'I've got to go – it's 3 o'clock and rush hour will start soon.'

'But you're driving back into central London.'

Leonie revved again and Vellin relented..

'You're in a hurry. If you're not going to tell me now, I will have to persuade you over an expensive dinner. How about after the Polo on Saturday?'

'Dinner would be lovely. But my lips are sealed.'

'Let's talk later to check the details for the press conference. Better still, meet you for a drink at the Met Bar. Six o'clock?'

'Fine,' said Leonie, and accelerated out of the yard on her 20-mile journey from Surrey Castle back to town.

It was well past one o'clock, the men were bored and hungry and Chief Inspector Briar was enjoying himself. Not content with the ear bashing he'd given Deputy Commander Sue Carter in her private office, Briar was now conducting the post operational debriefing with all participants present. SC019, a member of the royal protection squad, motley support staff, several Special Forces and the helicopter crew were all there. Plus the Chief Constable, who looked, if it were possible, even less interested than usual. Briar was demonstrating an inhuman relish for the gory details, thought Sue. He was making sure there was absolutely no doubt whose fault it was. Hers. But having been put through the wringer once already that morning, she was feeling no pain. Just loathing.

'Now that you have finished trashing HRH's estate, let's have the facts.'

'We can tell you what we know and we can tell you what we don't know. The unknown unknowns are more difficult.' She wasn't being obtuse on purpose. It was just how it was.

Briar growled. 'Oh, please.'

'Undercover intelligence on the animal rights front indicated that the perpetrator intended to release a waterborne toxin into the lake on the royal estate.'

'Why the Prince?'

'Not sure. We assume anyone prominent would have done, but as an avid and notable supporter of fox hunting, the Prince was an obvious choice. Our fanatic was an ardent hunt saboteur. Many of them are gutted that support for hunting is stronger, if anything, since the ban. Laffey was getting old, he was leaving Quantum and time was running out. Maybe this was his last chance to act.'

'What else do we know about him?'

'He was a loner. Unmarried. No partner, children, close family. A talented scientist and highly qualified researcher who had worked for 40-odd years for Quantum Research and Development. Three months off retirement. Perhaps that's what made him do it: this was his last stand.'

'And who are Quantum?'

'Independent labs which carry out contract work for international bio-agricultural companies. He'd never crossed our radar before and it was only through luck we found him this time.'

'And how was that?'

'Through monitoring of extremist websites.' Lavish new antiterrorism budgets had allowed examination of more than the usual Islamic fundamentalist suspects, and this time it had borne fruit.

The Chief Constable finally spoke, leaning forward and interrupting the inquisition.

'So we found him, tracked him, staked him out -- and then someone else shot him?'

'Yes, sir,'said Carter.

'What a story.'

The Prince's private secretary was almost as grand as the Prince, thought Chief Constable Skinner, as he was ushered into an anteroom at the Palace of Gloucester. Immaculately turned out, with the shiny shoes and manners suggestive of a Guards regiment and Eton, Sir James Finlay seemed only politely interested in the fracas, which had threatened his master's life five hours earlier.

Skinner was about to begin when a side door opened and the Prince himself came in. Skinner leapt to his feet, only to be motioned back into his seat.

'Pretend I'm not here,' said the Prince. 'I just thought I should hear this for myself.'

Easier said than done, thought Skinner. Ears bright red, he launched into his spiel.

'Sir, as you know, new terrorism laws have given us more freedom of action than we had previously. This subject was a 'clean skin' – never crossed our radar before – and potentially all the more dangerous for it. We picked him up through random monitoring of websites and airwaves. Not the Islamic fundamentalist stuff but the civil stuff, which gives any democracy a headache – the fomenters of disorder, anarchists, the complainers and demonstrators and occupiers of Parliament's roof. The subject *was* extreme but only in his violent dislike of hunting and hunters. It was only when background checks showed him to be a senior research scientist, former worker at the government research labs at Porton Down and signatory of the Official Secrets Act, that the alarm bells rang. As a matter of policy, we decided to track him. As back up, we were prepared, if necessary, to take him out. In the event, someone else did it for us.'

'And who was the other gunman?'

'Our intelligence does not indicate that at present, sir,'

'Hah! The old joke about military intelligence,' the Prince snorted. 'You mean you have absolutely no idea.'

'That would be about it, sir. Laffey was a lone operator. No one, apart from us, knew anything about him. His current employers considered him a model employee. Yet someone shot him.'

The Quantum boardroom had hosted many crisis talks in its time. But none like this, thought Millington miserably. His phone, hidden in his pocket, was switched to vibrate in case his tormentor decided to twist the knife already plunged so far into his viscera that he found it hard to breathe. The last emailed picture of the twins, taken as they came out of the school gates, had spurred him onto even greater efforts, but to no avail. It seemed as though Laffey had taken his secret with him.The CEO was tetchy and hungry. There had not been time to arrange the usual M&S sandwich fest and the crisps from the vending machine were not doing it for him. Barely waiting until his subordinates were in the room, he began.

'I've had bloody Michael Vellin on the phone five times already this morning. This is why we have an oversight committee. How the hell was Laffey working on something none of us knew about?'

Jackson, his deputy, tried and failed to muddy the waters.

'We don't actually know that he was. Or that he did it here.'

'The man was our employee. The Police tracked him from here prior to the shooting and he was seen attempting to pour something he had taken from here into the Prince's lake when he was shot. So what the hell was it?'

'He was working on the Chinese International Fertilisers project.'

'You can't tell me he was shot for that,' interjected Porlock, the HR manager. 'If he hadn't got one already, Regis would get a peerage for it.'

The CEO was not to be diverted.

'Whatever Laffey was doing, tonight's headlines will link him back to Quantum. For the first time ever, Joe Public will be made aware of us. We are the most successful, private R&D laboratories in Europe. Successful because no one, except our clients, has any idea of what we do and who we do it for. That's 30 years of secrecy down the drain. And for what?'

'Can't Plod be asked to hold off?'

'Of course not.' The CEO could not make his contempt plainer. 'Just make sure there's nothing for them to find.'

'All the news outlets can broadcast are the facts,' said Jackson. 'We have nothing to hide so let's be clear about them. One of our employees has been shot. He was under surveillance by the Police because he was a fanatical animal rights agitator.'

'Why the hell did we have someone like that on the payroll?'

'Because we didn't know. Because he was one of the best. Because he had useful contacts at Porton Down.'

Taking a breath, Jackson continued. 'There's stuff on Laffey's computer that we haven't got into yet – encrypted – but it seems to link back into the IFL work. We can't tell how. But we've got to have that cracked and cleaned up before the Police get into our records. Just in case.'

At that point the door opened and an unkempt man with a long, greasy ponytail slid into the room. His black T-shirt, proclaiming 'FECK – the Irish Connection' was stretched over an enormous beer belly, which suggested an age far greater than his actual late 20's. Millington looked up sharply.

'Patrick? What is it?'

'Er, you said to find you the minute I got something.' Patrick fixed his gaze somewhere above and to the left of Millington's eyes in habitual avoidance of any human interaction.

'Yes?'

'I think I've found it. The back door. It's just a matter of time now. We're running the algorithms. But we've already got a copy of the compound he was synthesizing.'

He held out a sheet of paper, which was snatched simultaneously by the CEO and Millington. Millington relinquished his hold, only to be handed the paper seconds later by the CEO.

'What the hell is that?'

Millington's eyes raked the paper. His heart sank. 'I have no idea,' he breathed.

Ping Li watched the lionfish extend its delicate striped wings and float with the merest hint of aileron to the furthest reaches of the gigantic fish tank, which adorned the Ambassador's office. Behind his great, lacquered desk hung flags of the People's Republic of China and vast photographs of march-pasts of the party faithful. The usual stolid photograph of Chairman Mao had been relegated to a side wall, evidence of the new wave of collective leadership and the waning of the cult of personality. The Ambassador, scion of a family almost entirely exterminated during the Cultural Revolution, and now, finally, considered safe in the highest echelons, sat on his ornate throne and looked at her. Ping Li was one of China's great assets and treated as such.

'Excellency, there will be an opportunity to speak with the Prince tomorrow,' Ping Li said.

'Good. Perhaps we can persuade him that we are not all waxworks. You will be there in your role as the People's Scientific Attaché?'

Ping Li stood up and inclined her head. 'Of course.'

Marcia Regis examined herself minutely in the dressing room looking glass. Now 58, her true age was satisfactorily disguised by some very expensive and discreet work, most of which involved shoring up the underpinnings of a face starved into gauntness by her punishing diet and exercise regime. Her skin still looked fresh, her lips plump. An excessively critical eye might have spotted a waxy shine – a dead giveaway – but to insist would have been churlish. Her body was perfect, forever 40, and untrammelled by the rigours of childbirth. The midnight blue Herve Leger bandage dress, surely designed for someone half her age or less, covered her curves expensively and seductively. HRH would not be able to take his eyes off her tonight. She paused in her reverie, one chandelier earring half way to her ear, as her husband entered the room. Automatically, she felt annoyed. He was going to say something acid and spoil her mood. He did not disappoint.

'Ah, another fundraiser? More starving children? How much did it cost me this time?' Regis moved behind her and zipped up the final half inch on the Leger.

'*If* you knew how much I improve your image around London, you wouldn't quibble. You should come sometime. And enjoy what you've paid for.' Marcia picked up an atomiser of Joy de Patou and sprayed it into the air in front of her. Then she walked into the cloud of scent. Regis, who had long since ceased to be amazed by such artifice, stepped back a little.

'I'm not very interested in orphans. Nor is IFL.'

Marcia picked up a tiny, jewelled clutch bag and paused by the door.

'Are you out?'

'No. Big day tomorrow.'

'Maria's left some supper in the fridge for you.'

'Will it stretch to two? Vellin's coming round later.'

'Ah, the consigliere. But who's pulling whose strings there?'

Stung, Regis looked hard at this woman he had inexplicably married and wondered what she was thinking. Perhaps it was these occasional flashes of intuition, which masked how very dim she actually was. He made a concerted effort to sound bland.

'I find him useful. He's loyal to me.'

'Don't be too sure. That kind of man is only ever for hire.'

Giving her husband no time to respond, Marcia closed the door behind her. Baron Regis of Clutton Champflower was left to heat up his lasagne alone.

Vellin had stationed himself in a corner with a good view of the door so that he could see Leonie arrive. He heard her before he saw her, the diesel chug of the taxi waiting, the slam of the door and her heels on the foyer marble. The Met Bar was one of his favourite haunts: small, exclusive and sophisticated, in the heart of Knightsbridge.

Leonie paused on the threshold, her eyes searching the early evening crowd and Vellin watched her. She had changed from her safe, Sloaney, royal assistant clothing into something more edgy and black. Her hair was spikier and she looked beautiful and exotic. Vellin waited, excited, for her to spot him. She laughed and came over and Vellin handed her a glass of Dom.

'Mmm. My favourite. Thank you.'

'You look great.'

'I'm on my way out to dinner. With friends. And I'm already late. I have to get there early so I can see my gorgeous godson before he's put to bed. So let's talk arrangements for tomorrow.'

Vellin was smooth. 'I'll arrive at 8.50 with Regis, the Ambassador gets there at 8.55 and you'll pitch up at 8.59 with the Prince. We start as soon as he's in place. The Press will be prepped, and if one of the awkward squad starts, we'll get him later. Now, anything you need to know?'

'I don't think so. Can I give you a lift? I'm heading to Fulham.'

'Sadly I'm off to see the Lord in Mayfair. Vespers. But I'm holding you to our dinner date after the Polo.'

'How could I forget?' Leonie looked at him, half flirting, half serious. There was something about this man, which was unnerving. She was almost glad to get away.

Regis moved the curved arm of a porcelain-centred servant's bell by the side of a low, quietly ornate French marble fireplace. Instead of distant bells clanging, a painting above the fireplace slid noiselessly aside revealing a huge plasma screen. The painting itself was as close a copy of the *Rokeby Venus* as might have annoyed Velasquez himself, with an ornate, trompe l'oeil, gilded frame, which was in fact, completely flat but appeared entirely three-dimensional.

Vellin loved such visual tricks – like the floor-to-ceiling shutters in the library of a great house where he had once stayed, where the substantial, fluted and properly capped pillars between great windows down one whole side of an immense room folded open in concertina fashion, to become shutters that kept thieves out and comforts in.

Here in Lord Regis's drawing room everything was subdued, yet intense at the same time. The panelling was an eggshell, Chinese blue, and the room full of lacquered furniture, none more recent than the late eighteenth century. Ivory carvings and porcelain filled lit glass cases each backed by that special Chinese red that was neither scarlet nor near orange but hovered somewhere between the two. The colour was oddly flat and reflective at the same time, so smoothly was it applied.

Regis too had adopted the disguise of the room. He wore a velvet smoking jacket and slippers of the same material on which the antlers of the crest of his coat of arms – a stag, roaring out his challenge – were embroidered. Softness pervaded all, of which the carpet was the final touch. Woven in the Middle East rather than China, the designs were more geometric than might otherwise have been dictated by a purist; but what had made it irresistible was the depth of the lapis lazuli that had been infused into some of the silks. It was darker than the blue of the panelling and pulled the eye down to its mystery in the quietest yet most insistent of ways. Lord Regis could curb his restless mind simply by looking at that carpet.

Vellin too was in a more relaxed state than he would normally demonstrate at work. He had just left Leonie in the Met Bar, arriving 10 minutes later at the house in Mayfair, which Lord Regis owned. The glass of Dom had relaxed him and the faint hint of future pleasures to come had pleased him. And he always enjoyed this part of the day, the indeterminate part between late afternoon and evening dinner commitments, when he and Lord Regis would often meet. Tonight, they were in Regis' drawing room, easy and at home, and Vellin could almost feel his power sparking out of his fingertips.

The upper floors of the house were little used, though more used now than they had been for years. Lady Regis had a study, bedroom, bathroom and dressing room on the third floor for when she did not wish to be disturbed by her husband's late arrivings. Or, indeed, disturb him with hers – an arrangement that had worked increasingly well for them over the years of their parallel lives. Now, they scarcely met, except to plan diaries and be seen in public together.

Regis and Vellin were just catching the seven-o'-clock news bulletin, heavy cut-glass tumblers in their hands fed by the big square decanters that stood on low tables to each side of their armchairs. They both looked slightly upwards at the plasma screen.

'Police have confirmed,' said the newsreader, 'that the man shot early to-day by counter-terrorist marksmen on the Prince's estate was a 63-year-old research scientist, as yet unnamed, who worked for Quantum Laboratories. Over to our business affairs correspondent, Michaela Green, outside the gates of the estate.'

The cameras zoomed on to a girl who had clearly spent the whole day around the edges of the estate trying to find out what she could. Precious little, was the truth. And while the local pubs welcomed the trade, the local inhabitants were being seriously inconvenienced by the cavalcade of press and television that had descended on the small and sleepy Cotswold town, already weighed down by its own antiquity and the rash of antique shops that tourism in the area had brought.

'Thank-you Hassan,' she said to the newscaster. 'The man shot today on the Prince's estate was reportedly attempting to empty something into the main lake, which connects directly to the local aquifer. The security services, which had been following the man after tip offs, are thought to have taken the decision to shoot, once they discovered his links to an extremist animal rights organization. Although the man remains unnamed, he worked for Quantum Laboratories, a shadowy – and some would say secretive – organisation, which carries out research into agrichemicals on behalf of major, multinational corporations. Clients are known to include de Courcey, Biotechnoz and of course, our own International Fertilisers, which recently announced a ground-breaking major contract with the Chinese Government. The Prince, a long-time admirer of International Fertilisers for their ethical stance, is speaking at a press conference tomorrow following the formal signing of the deal in Beijing last week. This will be the first opportunity for the Prince to be seen in the company of senior Chinese officials since his entries about 'waxworks' in his private diaries, and diplomats on both sides must be hoping that this is an end to the matter. Back to you in the studio, Hassan.'

Lord Regis switched the screen off. They sat in silence, both of them working out how the story was playing. The police had obviously decided to claim the shooting, rather than admit that they were beaten to it by an unknown assailant. Most importantly, the dead man had not been identified as IFL's dedicated researcher and a number of other big players had been smeared by association. IFL stood out only through its association with the Prince, who as the intended victim was therefore the star of the piece. His presence at tomorrow's press conference could not have been better timed. Regis knew that Vellin must have been spinning frantically all afternoon.

'Nicely managed, Michael,' said Regis.

'I have friends in low places,' replied Vellin.

Via a flurry of emails and phone calls, it had not been hard to persuade a cameraman he knew on Southwest Tonight to place some irresistible snippets in front of Michaela that afternoon. Under deadline pressure, she had snapped them up without wondering too hard why. Her reward was a big thumbs up from the desk producers and a bump up to the national news slot they had just watched. The cameraman would wait for a more physical payoff, when he and Vellin next met.

Lord Regis left the comfort of his chair and moved across to Vellin, carrying his own decanter with him. He held out a hand to take Vellin's glass from him. An acute observer would have detected a slight shift from master to servant in the relationship at that moment. Lord Regis filled the glass and handed it slowly back. Their fingers touched around the glass as it was transferred back to Vellin's grasp. Their hands pulled apart, but not abruptly. This was an old, yet still tentative duet, as if the next phrasing were unexplored.

They settled back into their chairs.

'So what did you make of Foote?' said Vellin, wanting to keep the conversation intensely private still but on somewhat safer ground.

'I've never let anyone get as close as he seems to want to get,'said Regis, slightly surprising himself by the intimacy of his reply.

'I'm sure you'll fix the distance, as you always do,' said Vellin, the ambiguities of this interchange escaping neither of them.

'It's what you have to do to *stay* the distance in business these days,' said Regis, shifting the sentient quality of the word and with it, the mood, onto safer ground. 'We don't know where all this corporate ethics stuff will take us, though Nancy thinks she does. But it's not black and white, the way she sees it. We're more subtle than that. An Australian once told me, after he had lived in England for 10 years, that in business an Englishman never told you a lie but he never told you the truth either. I like the room that leaves. It's why the Chinese admire us. Even though their own rules are quite different, they have subtlety too. It's not Nancy's terrain. For example, Nancy wouldn't understand cricket, even though she is so keen on boundaries.'

'And of course she's black and you're white,' said Vellin, admiring the easy flow of Regis's wordplay between meanings, but wanting to provoke a little.

'Regis paused, thinking. 'Maybe it's all the other way round for her. She sees me as black and thinks she's white.'

'Well, corporate ethics is how we won the Prince. It's certainly what tomorrow is all about. The great, public, non-apology couldn't have come at a better time. And Nancy will be in her element.'

Both were silent for a moment. There had been much debate as to whether inviting the Prince to the London signing of the China/IFL deal would be good for the company or not, given the Prince's widely disseminated views about the Chinese. Vellin had wanted the public triumph to be Lord Regis's alone and feared the royal spat might overshadow things. Now he was delighted that they would. Strange, how things worked out. Lord Regis and International Fertilisers could be seen as the peacemakers and a force for good in the world; exactly what was needed to keep questions about the relationship with Quantum low on the list of interesting lines to pursue for snoopy reporters. The public ceremony in the fine rooms of the Royal Academy tomorrow could not, in the event, have been more opportune.

Nancy Hammer could not disguise her excitement at the sight of the Royal Academy as her taxi drew up. She climbed out, paid the driver and flashed her pass at the security guards, already blocking the entrance arches to the Royal Academy at eight in the morning.

The weather was bleak as always in this benighted country, she thought, but nothing was going to put a dampener on this day she had waited for. The long red banners, proclaiming 'Treasures from the forbidden city', hung down the front of the elegant grey building, illuminating its severity. At the bottom of each banner was the IFL logo. As sponsors of this once in a lifetime exhibition, International Fertilisers were everywhere. Many of the exhibits had never left China before – evidence, if any were needed, of the extraordinary influence Lord Regis had over his eastern clients.

Better still, the Prince was positively grateful to International Fertilisers for enabling him to make amends for his waxworks comment. He had agreed to open the exhibition and to attend the Ball later. IFL had made it easy for him by pandering to his pet projects – most of them green – and by trumpeting their credentials. Nonetheless, it was a coup, which no other company among the world's largest multinationals could match.

Nancy walked into the Academy through a side door and made her way to the office she had been lent for the day by the Director. She hung up her coat and jacket, locked her bag in a safe and flicked through her notes on how the reception would unwind. There were three hours to go and so far, she was the only one here. In an hour, she would go and check the seating plans. In the meantime, she found a current Vogue on a nearby desk and flicked through that.

The Prince had made his speech, winning warm applause for his words about Britain's historical ties with China and even warmer appreciation of his joke about 'the problem with bio fertilisers is that they grow far too many plants for one to be able to talk to.' The Chinese Ambassador had graciously replied and the exhibition had been opened. Standing to the side of the dais, where the Prince, his equerry, Lord Regis, the Chinese Ambassador and his aides, including her mother, were seated, Leonie looked around the room. It was predictably full of the great, the good and the decorative, some of whom she was quite sure had no interest whatsoever in Chinese art treasures.

Leonie was enraptured by what she saw. She had visited China only twice in her lifetime with her mother, who had not been keen to show her the country's slumbering heritage. Instead, she had been left for a month with a cousin's family, where she was required to learn the language for six hours a day. It was such a miserable experience that Leonie had not minded when her mother said they would not be able to visit China again. But now, seeing what had been hidden from the world throughout the long, dark years of communism, was a revelation.

She accepted a cup of Chinese tea and breakfast pastry from a waiter and turned to find herself facing Lord Regis.

'I'm not sure how authentic the Ambassador will find the refreshments,' he smiled.

'I don't think he ever eats in public anyway,' Leonie replied. 'I rather like them. They're like sweet dim sum.'

'Ah yes, do you still go with your Mother for dim sum every Sunday?'

How did he know this? Leonie wondered at the things her mother talked about with her friends.

'Sometimes,' she said. 'It's more difficult now, with my job.'

'You must work very hard for the Prince,' said Lord Regis. 'I am sure HRH is an exacting employer. But speaking Mandarin and Cantonese and educated at Oxford, you must match up to the highest standards. He is fortunate to have you.'

'My mother tells me that your Mandarin is more than adequate, Lord Regis. And that your knowledge of Chinese antiquities is unsurpassed.'

'So we've both done our homework,' he replied, amused.

Across the room, the Prince looked up and around. Leonie was by his side in seconds and Regis watched her as she turned in response to her royal questioner and seamlessly translated between him and his guests.

She was so beautiful. Regis found it hard to tear his eyes away from the sleek perfection of her youth, her shining hair, her clear, glowing face, her elegant blue suit an ironic echo of the utility suits once worn by her countrymen in their millions.

Vellin appeared beside him. 'That reptile Campbell wants an interview.'

'Say no.'

'I did. He insists. Says you would want right of reply if you knew what he had.'

'What's he got?'

'Something on Quantum and Laffey but he won't spill the beans until he sees you.'

Regis swore quietly under his breath but followed Vellin out into the hall, where a tall, raw boned hack with stringy brown hair awaited him.'

'Mr Campbell,' said Regis, not extending his hand.

'Your Lordship. Thank you for your time.'

Regis didn't speak. Unperturbed, Campbell continued.

'I have a source who tells me that what Dr Laffey was trying to put in the lake when he was shot was something he was developing in secret for you to sell to the Chinese.'

'There's nothing secret about what we are selling to the Chinese,' said Regis. 'The deal is out in the open, signed here today. They need to intensify their food production in order to feed their booming population. We can help them. Hence the contract – world-beating, I might add, with the potential for the creation of thousands of British jobs and new factories.'

'Do you have any comment on the accusation that you were providing them with water-borne toxins?'

'All our *fertilisers* are water-borne. It's the only way to spread them efficiently, especially in China, where the irrigation methods are basic but effective. But these are fertilisers we are sending them. Why would we want to use toxins?'

'I have information that Laffey put some stuff on the net which suggested he was working on something that could kill millions. My source says Laffey said he was going to prove it.'

'We now know that Dr Laffey, sadly, was not of sound mind. He was obsessed and dangerous, involved with extremists. Who knows what he was planning to do? Whatever, it was is certainly nothing to do with International Fertilisers. As you must know, our aim is to help the world become self-sustaining. Which of course, is why we are so delighted that the Prince is able to be here with us today...'

'But –'

'I think that's enough, Mr Campbell,' said Vellin. 'Now, shall I take you back to the press room or will you be leaving?'

'I'm going,' said Campbell, opening the swing doors to the courtyard at the front of the Royal Academy. Through the arches on Piccadilly came the shouts and chants of protestors blocked by the Police cordon. Regis could hear one in particular, repeated again and again, delivered through a megaphone.

'Don't apologise, Eddie. Ask the waxworks about human rights.'

Nancy's black patent shoes were on the desk, an outrage but she'd earned it. Today was the day of her triumph and petty rules were not going to hold her back. Even her own. She was talking to her mother through the International Fertilisers switchboard – a heinous corporate sin – and was filling her in on the details of the day.

'And then I curtsied and he smiled and after his speech, he spoke to me. *Me,* Mom. A Prince! *The* Prince. Edward the third. I said where I was from and he asked what did I do and he seemed genuinely interested…'

Nancy's voice trailed off as Vellin, who had appeared in front of her, made a line- cutting motion with his hand. Annoyed at being told what to do and annoyed even more at being caught in full flow, she turned her chair a little away from him so that he was no longer in her direct line of sight. She sighed exaggeratedly.

'Gotta go, Mom. Just remember, your daughter fixed relations with China today... Make sure you tell Grandma. Bye... love you too.'

Reluctantly, she removed her feet from the desk and turned to face Vellin.

'Look, I don't want to appear rude, Dr Foote, but for the last half hour I've been telling you about the trivia of my early life. How do you know any of it is of any significance at all?'

'When you've told me what you want to tell me, then I can start asking you about what you're not telling me,' said Foote.

'Like what?' Lord Regis replied. In truth he couldn't decide whether Foote was just irritating him, and whatever was going on was an extraordinary waste of his time; or whether this was the way into that thought with which Foote had originally hooked him – that line about discovering the things about himself he didn't know. And if he was going to do that, was the risk worth taking? Nothing happened without a full risk assessment in Regis' working life. He understood the numbers that went with that kind of thinking. With Foote, there were no numbers. The manner of enquiry and the thinking behind it were strange to him. How could what he had told Foote allow the man to know what he hadn't told him? Well, he had laid down the challenge and would see what he said.

'I've heard nothing about anybody that you've loved,' said Foote.

'Oh, come on, Dr Foote. This is about me and the company.'

'No, Lord Regis, it's about you. You are the company. Read the man, read the company. There isn't a person in the entire organisation worldwide who doesn't want, at some level, to please you. And what would they feel if they knew that they had? They would feel something in that spectrum of sensation that, for want of any better understanding, we call 'being loved'.

'That's very odd,' said Lord Regis, almost musing to himself. He sat on the edge of his chair, staring at Foote, any reflective defensive posture having left him completely. Without any knowledge of what was said or who had said it, Foote knew he had stumbled, not entirely by accident, on to something that touched Lord Regis deeply. That was where he wanted to be.

'And whoever it is you have or haven't loved is part of the whole network of relationships from which you are made the man that you are, and that are buried deep within you.'

'So if I am the person I am, for whatever good or bad reasons, should we not let it lie where it is? I have been using whatever is there for fifty years or so. It doesn't seem to have served me too badly. Is it really necessary to disturb it?'

'But it's not *it*, but *you*, we're talking about. What you are saying is "Is it really necessary to disturb *me?*" To which the answer is the old one about eggs and omelettes. At the moment I'm acting rather like a surveyor coming to do a full structural job on your house. There are nooks and crannies and tests on the way that yield the bits of information that create the whole picture. My job is to look, ask questions and make sense. I could of course do that in part without your involvement. There's enough published about you in the financial and management press to get a superficial view – but that would be rather as if I were a tourist being shown around a great house. What I have come to do with you is to go behind the green baize door and get some understanding of how things really work, not just what is on public display. That's what will let me look at the world through your eyes. It's the inside-outwards view I'm after. When I've got some of that, we shall be in a position to look outwards together, but from an understanding of what filters you use, both to receive from and project into the world around you. Those are the mechanisms by which you make the world your own. That's what I want to get into our working consciousness together.'

Foote didn't often let himself make a speech quite like that. But Lord Regis was swinging between wanting to spar intellectually with him, all defences well in place, and acknowledging that there were depths to which he normally kept the doors quite closed. The brief fascination about organisational authority, being pleased, and something to do with the power of feeling loved, had touched him. Could he really trust Foote where, Regis thought, he would barely trust himself? Foote knew that.

His only chance was to throw some ideas out, like flies to a great trout that had resisted them all before, and see if they caused a flicker of interest. His task here was not to catch and land a fish and make it an unwilling accomplice to his own satisfaction and pleasure – though he had been accused of working that way more than once, and so guarded against it. What Foote wanted was a different kind of compliance here, a kind of which Nancy Hammer could have no conception because it was based on trust rather than mastery or control. And Regis was not a man who had built his life on trust. Utterly the reverse, if the question had ever been asked of him. Which is why he and Vellin understood each other so intuitively. Neither trusted the other but both appreciated that in the other.

A smile played around the distant edges of Lord Regis's thoughts. Perhaps he could do unknowingly with Vellin what

Foote was trying to do more knowingly with him. Perhaps he could learn some ways of thinking from Foote that would let him see further into Vellin's soul. Did he want to do that? He might gain some advantage from this curious situation that half intrigued and half irritated him. For now, Foote had made a convincing enough case, and he could always pull back if he didn't like where things were going or what was happening. He was not really giving over control. But one more challenge was worth it.

'You're not talking about whether I was fed at the breast or not, are you?,'said Regis.

Now he allowed himself an open smile, knowing that of course Foote knew he was being played with to see how he would set matters back on track. If he had been the owner of a great house this would have been the moment when he deflected the structural surveyor's attention from the frayed wiring to a picture that had a great family story attached to it;

or the promise of a future invitation to tea on the private side of the house to which the public ticket gave no admission.

'I doubt you've ever been taken for a sucker, Lord Regis,' responded Foote, smiling in reply to let Lord Regis know they were just playing verbal ping pong and it had no significance at all unless any were suddenly assigned to it.

'Relationships don't last,' said Lord Regis, his hand still on the door that he might open again to see whether or not, depending upon the response that was made, he would let Foote in.

'But you've been married 30 years, Lord Regis.' As he said it, Foote knew he was chancing the door being locked permanently, not opened. It was generally known that Lady Regis lived a life with her husband that had lost any passion many, many years ago. There were rumours of an enduring closeness with the Prince. She and Regis met socially and in preparation for being public, but hardly anywhere else.

'But you'd hardly call that a relationship, Dr Foote. I've almost given up on women.'

A blink memory of Vellin crossed Foote's mind before he continued.

'My experience of complex men, Lord Regis, is that they love in very complicated ways. But they nevertheless have the basic needs we all have which, in the end, are to know that we really have loved and have been loved. Nothing brings significance to life like that. And if we don't have it in a marriage, we might have it with a child. And if not with a child, then there's only desolation.'

Foote didn't know himself, immediately, quite why he had gone for such a bleakly final view, especially when he had just been wondering about how loving men might be part of an undeclared self in Lord Regis. But he trusted his intuition, especially when he said things that he was himself quite surprised to hear himself saying.

And he had struck home. Lord Regis's face looked suddenly tense and drawn and he himself somehow less substantial.

'If we're going to have these ...' and his voice trailed off, as he tried and failed to find exactly the adjective he wanted. Finally, he said, 'Forgive me. I don't mean to insult you. But I need to be absolutely clear about something. I need to know that what I say to you is in absolute confidence and that there are no imaginable circumstances in which anything I say will ever go beyond us. I'm not used to telling anyone what I think, really think, and certainly not in the areas you have been pressing me on.'

'Lord Regis,' said Foote, knowing that the matter was still capable of being entirely closed off if he didn't quite catch the deeper messages Lord Regis was emitting, 'That is my profession and why I am here. Our meetings are about a journey together. If we don't risk trusting each other, we will only go on the tourist trail where anybody can go. All the

140

words published about you go only where others have been before. But we have the option of going into territory that is unexplored. It's entirely yours, of course, but we have the option of doing that together. There was a book some time ago with an enviable title – "If You Meet the Buddha on the Road, Kill Him". Well, to the extent that I'm the guide on this journey into the unknown, to places that neither of us can yet envisage, you can get rid of me whenever you want to.'

Lord Regis smiled again, but this time including Foote. 'No sensible explorer gets rid of his guide before the journey's end. And some guides, like Sherpa Tensing with Hillary, were indispensable. Maybe I'll think of you like that.'

Simply recognising the open door by walking straight through it, Foote said: 'Then tell me about the relationship that did work for you but didn't last.' Flying blind though he was, he knew the elements of what he had said had all been laid non-consciously as clues.

'You're correct that the relationship you mentioned of such importance might be with a child. But it's long and complicated. Let's leave it for next time. But I think we both know where we're going.'

Unusually, Foote found the initiative wrested from him by Regis closing down the conversation. He was quite correct. The 90 minutes were up. But Foote would have preferred to stay. Having created sufficient trust – perhaps not even that, perhaps just intrigue – for that opening of the door, it was bound to be firmly shut again by the time he came back. Next time, Regis would not only have closed the door but closed the shutters to any windows in the room, brought down the blinds and then also drawn the curtains. And going into a room for the second time never held quite the surprise and discovery of the first. In addition, the person had a chance, having once opened the door and then closed it, to rearrange their internal furniture for public display at the second time of opening. Foote felt a slight sadness at what had happened, though some quiet satisfaction that his intuition had led him where it always did – to the heart of the matter – though he never knew in advance how the territory would appear.

Regis did not bring the blinds down quite as quickly as Foote had imagined he might. Despite the press of the day, Farheen was instructed to keep the next half hour free. It surprised her. Timings in the diary were never changed without her having an immediate sense of what the more important person or matter was that had arisen. This time, all she knew was that Dr Foote had left and Lord Regis was alone.

Had he seen it, Foote would have called the time that followed reflective. The trendy management consultants who had never entirely cracked the way of peddling their wares around big business would have been murmuring things to do with mindfulness. Lord Regis simply sat still in his chair, closed his eyes, eased his legs out to full stretch and let the pictures of his mind screen themselves into his visual recall.

He sat that way for a whole half hour, not so much rearranging the furniture of the room within his mind that he now knew he would let Foote enter, but inspecting himself in a way that he hadn't for years. Perhaps, not ever. Having inspected it in surprising detail, and quite enjoying the sense of being his own surveyor, he knew how he would take Foote around it. That felt safer.

Time to think had engaged corners of his deeper consciousness that were usually not visited at all; and by being not visited they could feel unknown and even, sometimes, unknowable. Foote had provoked him into illuminating these dark recesses and he no longer felt he would be surprised by what he saw. Foote would not catch him out again in the way he had, when he had suddenly mentioned loving a child. Perhaps Foote had done all he needed to do, actually. But, dammit, Foote was only here in the first place because of the Hammer woman, and he couldn't cancel Foote because she would wonder why. No,

Foote had earned his right to be taken into the room again, but it would be a conducted tour rather than somehow poking about together, at risk of being startled.

So the parallel processing of a fine mind, highly tuned to a wide variety of complex tasks in hand, settled themselves into familiar grooves again. The perturbation Foote had provoked had been sorted, filed, made ready for future reference in the 'do not disturb again' folder, and Regis was ready for the day ahead.

Foote tried never to drive in London. Although he had lived in the metropolis for almost 30 years, it rattled him for a number of reasons that added up to an overall sense that he and the State were fundamentally in a state of tension. Were there to be some extraordinary time when his loyalty to his country might be tested, he could feel that he might not be on the side of what passed for law and order.

This surprised him, when he thought about it, but his logic was clear. Through a quarter of a century of political correctness, he had lost any kind of a relationship of trust with the State he lived in. It in turn had lost the sense that people lived freely under the law by enacting such a spate of laws that no-one could live freely at all. The sense of being free-born had almost gone.

For some people, one response was to leave the country altogether. It surprised him that, in the UK, there was net outflow of people. Despite hysterical tabloid headlines, it was a fact that more took up permanent residence abroad than came to live here. Of course that didn't count the unknown numbers of illegal immigrants; nor the great waves of migrant workers from within the new accession countries of the old Eastern bloc, whose EU status now let them come at will to make restaurants in London better places in which to eat, or to show the building trades what decent workmanship was about. All that would tip the net outflow balance if it were properly accounted for. But it wasn't. A government that couldn't even count properly hardly deserved one's trust, Foote thought; and a government that then used such figures selectively in its own interest, deserved it even less. It wasn't safe to trust those who didn't offer trust to the people who placed them in power. That left him feeling very uneasy, as if he nursed a grievance that might one day kick off into active, burning action.

Climbing into the car had let this internal rant loose in Foote's half-conscious awareness. He had promised his wife he would take several boxes of books that had been stacked in the hall at Campden Square to an old colleague of hers now living in scholarly bachelor retirement near Shepherd's Bush. As happened too often these days, the University library had cleared its shelves of tomes that hadn't been borrowed for a good many years. Books that could and would never be replaced – whatever future scholars might need – were sold for a few pence each first, to any academic staff who might want them and next, to antiquarian booksellers who, in truth, had little sense of where their value might lie these days too.

The ex-colleague in question was fascinated by the beauties of Roman water supply systems – not simply the great aqueducts that curved their ways with impossible millimetric precision across remarkable distances and impossible terrain, but the much larger mileages of underground systems of which hardly anyone knew anything. These conduits snaked, exquisitely arched and hidden in damp, earthy darkness right across the ancient Empire that they had served. In addition, there were leather-bound books of the British Empire's waterworks, mostly from India, with exquisitely drawn and detailed copper-etched maps of siphons, sumps and pumping marvels from India's northern territories to New Delhi's Imperial developments and the efforts to get Bombay connected to a clean water system. All of these would be lovingly stacked by the aged man Foote had promised them to; and as he had a telephone call with Hester promised for this evening, it would be a small jewel in his crown to have done as he had promised.

Foote often felt that he was in some kind of useful servant relationship with Hester. The car was part of that. The need to take their daughter's remarkable amount of kit to and from university each term, together with Hester's intermittent demands for carting her anthropological expedition equipment to Heathrow, or wherever it was she was departing from, had resulting in Hester insisting that they buy a four-wheel vehicle with substantial space in the back.

Foote had been absolutely firm that they couldn't have a Mitsubishi Shogun monster parked in Campden Square; and unusually for him, had been brutally insistent that he simply wouldn't drive such a vehicle around London. As Hester didn't drive at all, her belief that the biggest workhorse that could be found would meet her requirements very well didn't take any account of the difficulties of parking such a beast in a residential setting. They had settled, after a lot of argument, on a Mitsubishi station wagon. Its diesel clattered into life and Foote edged his way around the Square and down towards Kensington, all imagination temporarily suspended as he managed his way into another life-denying, London traffic excursion.

The streets around the back of Shepherd Bush are not exactly mean. To imagine them so would be wreak grave injustice upon the hyperbole of the estate agent's jargon that made Victorian workers' cottages desirable and expensive dwellings for the middle classes. They nevertheless lacked any sense of joy, whilst parking on both sides ruined whatever sense of proportion or vista any of the streets might ever have had. Foote always noticed a complete absence of trees too, in this part of London which, he thought, might not have been such a difficult bit of urban improvement to have arranged.

At that moment the car engine died. Quite inexplicably and utterly without warning, his accelerator gave him no power and he coasted to a halt. There were no parking spaces into which he might have slid and so he found himself stuck in the middle of the road, twenty yards away from the house he wanted. It was next to the alleyway and blank graffiti-ed wall that marked the end of the cul-de-sac where he had hoped to double park briefly whilst off-loading the boxes in the back.

Foote sat in bafflement. He had no knowledge of the workings of a car engine. His only response was to turn the dead engine off then turn it back into life. The only sound was an engine turning over and over without a spark of response. It neither coughed or juddered, nor gave any evidence that a whirring starter motor might have any effect other than to make an extraordinarily ineffective noise. He tried again. The same. And again, the same. Baffled, he sat there looking forward helplessly as a gang of youths, white and black and hooded, swung round the alleyway on to the road ahead of him. He could see at a distance that their postures started fixing on him, as they pointed to his car and nudged each other their mouths opening in what looked like raucous comment on his predicament.

Foote's heart started pounding. For some curious reason he was alone in his car with feral youths bearing down on him, laughing and jeering. Sweating, he banged a fist on the central locking button, cocooning himself, trapped inside a car that he loathed and about to become the target of he knew not what.

Seven youths, shouting and jeering, started banging their fists on the car, thumping the windows, kicking the wheels, standing on the bumper, pulling the windscreen wipers up and letting them flick back on to the screen whilst he sat there. In fear he pressed staccato blasts on the horn, and then realised he was only egging them on and no-one would come to his help. Why should they? Only a police car would do anything. He fumbled for his mobile, only to find he had left it at home on the hall table. He hadn't imagined anything like this. There was no means of help. And meanwhile the youths kept up a mounting drum roll of banging all over his car in a way that they had all caught a rhythm and were going to batter him with it inside.

Uselessly, he tried to start the car. In his tension he pressed the accelerator hard on to the floor. With an extraordinary surge of power the engine burst into roaring life, a huge black cloud of diesel smoke billowing out and swallowing in it the youths who had been bashing the back door. Knowing nothing of where they were, and seeing very little through his side mirrors but enough to keep a straight line, throwing the one on the front bumper flat on his back to shouts of hate and eyes that had turned from casual violence to pack rage, Foote hurtled backwards until he could swing the car back into the road from which, only a few minutes before, he had found his way into this hellish trap. Knowing nothing of what damage he might have done to any of them, he careered his way to the main road and gathered himself enough to stop at the turning, gather some semblance of control, and join the sort of orderly jam that usually made him rail at London driving. This time, he felt suddenly relieved and secure that he had become anonymous and safe. On automatic pilot he returned to Campden Square, where he sat in the car and smelt his anxious, sweaty self dissolving into tears.

Deeply wounded images now came edging their way into Foote's troubled state. The young Andrew Foote, lying in a school playground, aged eight, bruised and bleeding, hearing the laughter of the boy they all feared, whilst he punched him in the face to show the anxious, curious, admiring, fearful crowd how people got knocked out. The particular bully hadn't had the force of punch to do it, only enough to make a nose gush blood and to make little Foote – 'Footie' they called him – double up, winded with a blow to his solar plexus. None of the crowd could have known that at home his father called him a sissy and tried to get him to land punches on the held-up palm of his big, raw hand to toughen him up, whilst his mother ineffectually kept telling him not to worry the boy. There would be no comfort there for his wounded body or, even less, his battered pride.

Now, again, he was going home to an empty house. Foote knew that he had married Hester because she had the capacity to take control of him. 'Bully him' would be too strong, though it had echoes of how things had been two or three years after they had married, and Hester was adamant that he should be just as much involved in Freya's care as she was. Then she had gone back to her university job and Foote had had to fit his own life around her professional timetable. He loved Freya, but sometimes wished the way they had brought her up together could have felt more like a gift that he gave than the duty that Hester ordained. But there it was. Could he ever really have told Hester what an awful experience he had just been through, even if she had been there? Would she just have been scornful that he hadn't delivered the books? And how to deal with them now? And so he felt himself slowly merging back into a present that only made sense when understood from the past.

Easing himself out of the car into the quiet of Campden Hill Square and back through his own front door, Foote dropped the experiences of Shepherd's Bush into the cauldron in which simmered everything that happened to him; and from which he could retrieve original constituents as if they were entirely fresh, yet where they also contributed to the complex brewing process that let him enter other people's worlds.

Foote had been back in his home after his ill fated expedition to Shepherd's Bush for less than an hour when Farheen had called. 'Lord Regis,' she said, 'has an unexpected space in his diary tomorrow. He has an hour-and-a-half free at eight thirty. If you were available, he thought it might be an opportunity for you both to continue your discussions over coffee and bagels.'

Foote gasped inwardly with surprise. 'A palpable hit,' he thought to himself with delight. Nothing would stop him being available. Without so much as a glance at his diary, he said immediately: 'Of course. I shall reorganise my diary. Let Lord Regis know, if you would, that I look forward to being with him.' As Farheen assured him she would and ended the call, he sat in his chair and mused.

If Foote was surprised, Farheen was amazed. She knew her boss's patterns well enough to know that the diary time she had just given away was sacred and never, except under huge pressure from others, blocked for anything at all. Indeed, Lord Regis religiously had three occasions during the week built into his diary, which he called 'sacred time' – space and time for reflecting. It was what made him seem so decisive in meetings. He had worked things out for himself in advance, played scenarios from all angles, and in the process consulted no one but himself.

Whatever data he needed for his own private musings was readily to hand summoned easily in advance. Two young, recent MBA graduates were kept permanently busy getting data into the shape where he could most easily digest it. The sense he made of it was always his own work, though, never the sum of others' opinions. That was what had always made him so formidable in business.

But now Lord Regis had broken his own rule here, and Farheen had not seen that happen before. Dr Foote must have something important to say, she thought; and she looked at him with added interest when he arrived the next morning at the appointed time.

Following instructions, Farheen showed him straight into Lord Regis's office without prior announcement. That was odd too. Only Ministers of State were normally treated in such a fashion; but that was done, as Farheen understood, simply to flatter and create a potentially reciprocal sense of ease of access between them and Lord Regis. This was quite different. Lord Regis somehow *wanted* Dr Foote there – something she had never seen before. That he might be needy was new to her understanding of him.

Before Foote had eased himself into his usual chair, Lord Regis was straight into discussion. He held a state of alert tenseness around him – not born of anxiety, but the tension of someone firing on all cylinders and bringing all their faculties to focus upon the task in hand.

'There was... there is, rather, a woman in my life. From much earlier in my life. And I have a child by her. The child... she does not know I am her father. I love her mother still, more than I care to admit and more than I think she does me. She's significant in other aspects of my life too. As I am for her. But the girl... our daughter... I barely know. What I do know of her makes me intensely proud. But there is no way of showing her I love her.'

'So what are you thinking, and what is in your thoughts?' said Foote.

It was a deceptively simple question. It made no assumptions but allowed him to keep a very steady, involved gaze entirely upon Lord Regis; and at the same time created the most natural assumption that they were there together only to explore his thinking. Later Foote would shift that to feelings, too, but in such a way that Lord Regis would hardly notice that the focus of enquiry had shifted. Foote's only job now was to listen with every particle of his being, absorbing in his deepest level of understanding what he was being told. From there, he would make sense of it in a way that he could slip back into Lord Regis's working consciousness, so that it became his own.

This was Foote's especial skill. It was something that he had discovered intuitively and worked on over many years.

Then, at a professional seminar once, as he listened to an American woman talking about thinking and feeling and ways of accessing the deeper mechanisms of the human mind, what he had always known, but had not systematised in his thinking, suddenly became clear.

She made him almost gasp with delight at the self-deprecating but incisive elegance with which she talked about her own discoveries over three decades of listening to people. With sixty people present, he felt as if she spoke only to him. He had determined then to learn a great deal more from her, and had. And even knowing other people must feel much the same about her, he was nevertheless certain that her life's work had purpose only in focusing his own. It was not something he could tell her, of course; just live it out over the time that he got to know her professionally and go on treasuring it and feeling made completely whole by her.

Richly furnished from this source, his gaze rested on Lord Regis. It opened up channels of information that even Lord

Regis was surprised to hear himself conveying and yet, at the same time, felt completely safe in doing so. Gone were his earlier uncertainties. Curiously, he was no longer conscious of having to remind himself of his decision to let Foote know things that he had told no-one ever before. The flow of his own speaking felt completely right: right in a way that required no questioning of it.

Lord Regis had entered a very special state of dependency without knowing it at all. Indeed, he would have hated the word being applied to him. Even to Foote, who knew exactly what was happening, it seemed much too limited a word for the complete naturalness of the experience. But within the limitations of the word there was great depth. For the experience that Lord Regis had entered came from that most remarkable part of the brain whose job was to engage at the deepest level of attachment with another human being. Most human beings experience it consciously when they fall in love. They have, if they have been fortunate, known it non-consciously as an infant enveloped by the adoring gaze and burbling of a mother – whose whole existence is wrapped up in the joy of the baby who has been tuned into her body rhythms in the first nine months of its development, and from whom it will continue to receive life itself.

Dawn streaked across the Thames as Vellin eased his way through IFL's outer glass shield, the lobby, the good-mornings from the security men and into the temporary helpless comfort of the lift. Today Lord Regis was off to China. Early morning meetings at the beginnings of those trips were sacrosanct. If Vellin ever allowed himself the extra enjoyment of feeling conspiratorial that pervaded almost every action in his life, to a greater or lesser degree, it was on these occasions.

As he swung his way through the outer office door, Farheen looked up and smiled in greeting as he strode straight for Lord Regis's closed door, hand outstretched to walk straight in. He always did, for these meetings anyway. The usual tray of coffee would be there and Lord Regis would be carefully packing the small attaché-case he carried on the flight, filled with the papers that only he held secure. If there were an expensively executive equivalent of a Government minister's red box, this case was it. Farheen knew its contents and Vellin believed he did, though sometimes he was not entirely sure he knew them all.

'Not even you, Michael,' said Farheen, as his hand was almost on the doorknob. 'This morning, there are to be no disturbances.'

'I'm not a disturbance,' he said, pausing and turning to her and leaning forwards slightly as he walked towards her desk, ready to start the piercing friendly encounter that usually got him his own way with anyone subordinate. He had long practiced the art of making himself non-resistible.

Irresistibility was for other occasions, when the pay-off was much more private.

'This morning you certainly would be.' Farheen was remarkably impervious to Vellin's charms. She saw them for what they were, offered to herself and others on an entirely self-interested basis. It was part of her instinctive and highly tuned distrust of Michael Vellin. A long line of Indian princely forbears left her with an almost in-born capacity to tell who a flatterer might be, as against a true friend. There had been plenty of violent deaths among her ancestors whilst that bit of social genetic evolution had been sharpened into a survival skill that still worked very well in the London jungle. Lacking insight, Vellin had no sense of how clearly she saw the scorpion within him.

'Ah,' he said, computing quickly the cause of his being kept away from the inner sanctum, 'It's the first of the confessionals, is it? How much longer? I thought he was flying to Beijing this morning.'

'We have a block on ninety minutes. And the flight's been moved to tomorrow.'

With a slight shock, Vellin realized that somehow, he had been left out of the loop. His Lord's movements were his business, almost more than any other's and he would normally have been the first to know of any changes. He looked suspiciously at Farheen to see if she had done this on purpose or was enjoying his displacement, but there was nothing to see.

'So he *is* taking it seriously,' said Vellin. Farheen, wanting information too, let herself relax enough to make Vellin experience the slight softness that would make him think he had won her over. Without missing a beat, she said, 'Whatever *it* is. Tell me, Michael, what it's about, this meeting with Dr Foote.'

Farheen didn't see many people coming into the inner office of Lord Regis whom she felt that she herself would want to know. Many would be interesting to know. Plenty were powerful and famous and almost all of them men, whose business from charity to investment to strategic politicking to international affairs at the highest corporate and governmental levels took them through Lord Regis's door. But it was rare that Farheen found herself interested in any of these people because she sensed that they were fundamentally good. To her surprise Dr Foote had appeared so; the way he had gone about meeting Lord Regis on his own terms had a directness that appealed to her.

'As part of the new corporate ethics regime, Farheen, Dr Foote is our Lord's coach and mentor. Even the most senior people have to have someone to whom they can bare their souls. In this brave, new, Nancy Hammer world of compliance, transparency is everything. Even our own good Lord must be seen to be *complying.*' He stressed the last word with a cynical shift in his tone that made it sound the least likely act that Lord Regis would ever perform and that he, Vellin, and Farheen were complicit in that shared knowledge. But Farheen was proof against his conspiratorial tendencies.

'Complying with *what*, exactly?'

'Good question, Farheen. Call me when he's out.'

Vellin left, unaccustomed to being out of place and time with at least an unexpected hour on his hands and no place in the private world that Dr Foote and his boss were testing for themselves. In need of comfort, he left the building and took a taxi to Maiden Lane.

Rules, the oldest restaurant in London, with the best English food in the world, had been owned by only six families in over two centuries of catering to the whims of the demimonde behind Covent Garden. It had recently started a breakfast club for members only. Even eating there by himself, Vellin could see and be seen and feel wrapped in its cosseting attention. The fact that more and more of the waiters were Polish actually added to its charm. They had an ease about being of service, whilst keeping a proper distance, that English waiters lacked and Vellin found intensely reassuring. Fried eggs, black pudding and the best back bacon, from a Tamworth Old Spot reared and sacrificed especially for his breakfast, were what he wanted just now. He would return in time for Foote's departure. Indeed, being there for Foote's departure might add some spice to the morning.

The world was re-ordered in familiar ways and he settled into a less fractious frame of mind. In the same way that a boa constrictor that has just swallowed an animal whole will lie contentedly for three weeks, while its digestive tract performs a minor miracle, so Vellin sat at his immaculately white-linened table in Rules, temporarily content.

Harry Regis pushed a sunflower seed through the bars towards the gaping beak and watched as the little bird expertly shelled the husk and dropped it. The sun setting over the square below tinged all the trees with gold and lit up the ice in his glass. He moved back towards the white sofas and sprawled out, relaxed. He *was* relaxed. And here, in Ping Li's house more than anywhere. He was at the top of his game, his legacy was not in doubt and now, perhaps, with this man Foote, he could get to the bottom of the small things niggling away at his subconscious.

'Dinner, Harry?'

Ping Li came out of the kitchen holding two plates, which she put on the table. They sat, picking up the ebony chopsticks and ate naturally together, like man and wife. Regis found himself positively enjoying it – an unusual sensation for a man with so jaded a palate. The thrill of being able to command a table a London's most exclusive restaurants had long since worn off.

'It's a long time since you cooked for me,' said Regis.

'It's a long time since you and I have been in public together.'

It was true. It must have been 20 years or more. Yet Regis looked at her and found her timeless. She would be forever fixed somewhere between 40 and 60. He knew she would remain that way until she died – her skin unlined, her figure that of a young woman. How Marcia, that triumph of artifice, would envy her. But Marcia still wanted to be desirable, sexy, youthful. Ping Li had probably never dreamed of such a thing. Yet Regis remembered being intoxicated by her, his brilliant student, his passionate lover. Her external façade of serenity only fanned the flames when they were together. And they had shared so much.

'I didn't like being there, you and I with Leonie, Harry' said Ping Li, 'I felt we were tempting the fates.'

'It was inevitable. She works for the Prince.'

'But if anyone ever finds out she's your daughter…'

'No one knows. No one will ever know. She is our – extremely beautiful, it must be said – secret.'

Regis felt a wave of something rare and unfamiliar wash over him. Mild regret? Uncertainty? Was it the final acceptance that Leonie would be his only child? Today, for the first time in his life, he had felt a powerful desire to show her off, to smother her with gifts and affection, to lay claim to her. Even at the height of his courtship with Marcia, ensnared by her sexual and social power, he had not felt this desire to possess, to own. He knew enough to know that these feelings were universal to all fathers, and that his had just been left to stultify in a dark cupboard under the stairs of his consciousness. Perhaps that's why they were so undeniable now they were allowed into the light of day. He had felt almost overwhelmed, as he had gazed into Leonie's bright, beautiful face that afternoon. He had last seen her as an awkward teen, when he made his chauffeur park outside her London day school at four o'clock just so that he could watch her.

Without even trying to understand his own motives, he had looked for an Anglo Chinese face. There were several, but Leonie's was unmistakeable. Already, her mother's determined expression was there and the brace and pigtails couldn't hide the beauty she would one day become. That one glimpse had sustained him for ten more years. But now, he realised with astonishment, he needed more.

Marcia had never wanted children and Regis had never felt it necessary to force the issue. If he wanted a child, he knew she was there with Ping Li. But then Ping Li had cut him off after his marriage. Regis had been surprised and as close as he ever got to hurt. But Ping Li had been adamantine. And he had lost his lover and his daughter.

Flushed with warmth and food and companionship, he asked, 'Did you ever wonder how it would have been if things had been... different?'

'They could never have been different. My family would never have allowed it.'

'Ah yes. The perils of being high born in a communist country.'

'At least I got out because of who I was. And then, when I had a daughter, I could keep her. Anyway, you felt you needed a more... suitable... wife when you left academia.'

He felt the sting. Be careful what you wish for. He had chosen Marcia, it was true, when he was rising rapidly through the ranks and he needed a star by his side. Already the daughter of an Earl, Marcia had impeccable contacts – as a young child she had shared baths with the Prince, for God's sake – and a faultless gift for spotting new talent, which was what had originally brought the brilliant and still young Harry Regis to her attention. At 29, freshly escaped from his junior donhood at Cambridge into the siren arms of a big chemical company, he had been standing lost at the country house weekend where Marcia's father, the Earl, had hosted the newest intake. Unerringly, Marcia had homed in on

Regis. Dazzled and charmed, he had seen doors open, which he had never even known were closed.

Years later, before their mutual contempt had hardened, she would tell him that he was her greatest creation. It was partly true. Through the years her contacts had formed the cadre around Regis, which had ensured that once at the pinnacle, he stayed there. Relentless years of dinner parties, charity balls and art galleries had paralleled Regis's equally relentless rise to the very top. Certainly, Marcia had a sure touch. When Regis first donned his ermine at 51, Marcia knew the form and guided him through it. But it was all so sterile. And now he needed more.

'Our daughter is so lovely, he said wistfully, 'a kind of physical representation of what might have been.'

What was wrong with him tonight? He felt slightly unhinged by all this delving into his psyche that had been going on. He, who had been whole, was no longer intact. A chink in his armour was widening, the wool of his self unravelling like a knitted sleeve. He felt panicky. Not such a great idea. Certainly not his idea. Damn that PC bitch Hammer.

Ping Li spotted it immediately.

'What is wrong with you tonight, Harry? If we had lived together the romance would have gone and the nitty gritty would have worn us down. This way, we can still be friends.'

Regis laughed it off, though he felt a pressure on his chest he could not explain.

'Always so cool-headed. So, my darling, what concerns you tonight?'

Ping Li switched immediately into official mode. 'The Ambassador must be sure that Quantum won't leak.'

'As my best research assistant ever, you are more than qualified to assure the Ambassador that no one will be able to work back from Laffey's plastic bottle to River Dragon – or anything else.'

'But Quantum staffed Laffey on projects for International Fertilisers. They have his files. If they work out what he was really doing for you and what the implications are… China doesn't need any more international scrutiny of how we manage our population problems.'

'I would have thought that the western world would be delighted if Chinese men died out.'

'The truth is not as simple as that, as you well know.'

'The truth is that your kinsmen asked for this substance in the first place.'

Ping Li broke away. 'We could talk about this forever. I need your assurance that this will not leak from Quantum.'

'You know I don't control Quantum. And they do have his computer. Even though they don't understand what's on it. Or how to get at it.'

'It would be best if they did not get the opportunity.'

'It's already in hand.'

Patrick Stiles – Paddy to his few friends – lived alone in the upstairs annex in his grandmother's house. Which was fortunate because no flatmate or lover would have been able to endure the squalor of his kitchen, where rotting slices of pizza lay limply on the draining board, mixed up with used, takeaway Styrofoam coffee cups, donuts and half eaten *doner* kebabs. His grandmother had ceased to remonstrate and Paddy's parents had long since 'sodded off', as Paddy put it, to their place on the Costa del Sol. From there, they sent him occasional cheques and snapshots of them looking orange and crispy in their place in the sun. Both cheques and snapshots were an affront to Paddy – the first because his mother could have banked the money for him if she could only learn the basics of online banking, and the second because she flatly refused to buy a digital camera and therefore could not email the pictures.

Despite his mother's pleas – and probably as revenge - he refused to heave his bulk onto a cheap flight to Malaga. Part of the reason was his obsession with air accident data. Although none of the airlines which flew millions daily to the sun had ever had an accident, one was well overdue in Paddy's estimation. The turnarounds were too short, the fuel was too skimped and he knew, from a documentary he had seen, that the airline staff handing out drinks and crisps had had as little training in evacuation as the airline could legally get away with. A conspiracy theorist to his marrow, he was convinced that he was the next statistic.

In addition, going to Spain was too much effort – and meant spending too much time away from the mainframe – though Patrick could always have taken a laptop with him.

The annexe contained two rooms – a bedroom and a kitchen/living room. A rudimentary shower room was crammed in under the stairs. While both rooms were unremittingly squalid, there was one shining exception. The desk, which stretched across one end of the entire bedroom and where Paddy conducted his cyber life, was pristine, dust and grease free. An open bookcase divided the room behind his big, rolling desk chair and from there on, towards the bed, anything went. Clothes were strewn across the floor, more food and takeaway containers littered every surface and a stale smell pervaded every atom of air.

Paddy didn't care. He sat at his great console reading the entrails of computer code and divining answers from the ether. He was crooning to his machine.

'Come on, baby. Give it up. I can feel it, we're so close. No one knows we're together. We can do what we like. I want to discover your innermost secrets.'

Briefly, the banner headline 'Quantum R&D' flashed up on the screen in front of him and as Paddy hit a few more backstrokes, various sub-catalogues opened and closed. The expensive firewall posed little problem, especially as Paddy had interned with the company who installed it. The back doors were there, as they always were.

'Let's just see what's here... ah, that's it,' he breathed as a new screen opened. 'Let's just make sure they don't know I'm here, my lovely, visiting in the black of night. Softly, softly, catchee monkey.'

The television screen on the wall above and to the right showed a reporter doing an earnest stand-up to camera in front of the Royal Academy. Imperial red banners bearing a dragon motif furled down behind her and her breathless delivery gave no indication that the reception had been ten hours ago.

'It appears that the Prince may have redeemed himself in the eyes of the Chinese hierarchy. Certainly, there appeared to be a distinct thawing of relations between the People's Republic and the heir to the throne. This joint venture between International Fertilisers and China – a pet project of the Prince's for the company's renowned ethical stance – should cement cooperation further…'

Paddy wasn't hearing anything. He was in, and muttering to himself as he pulled up what he was hunting for.

'Now what's naughty Dr Laffey been up to… and why's he hiding it?' He tapped a few more keys. 'You beauty. Time to open up.'

Suddenly, it all went wrong. As Paddy watched in disbelief and then despair, the lines of data he was examining began to disappear, one by one. Frantically, he tapped keys, banging his hand down in frustration on the keyboard as the lines he was reading vanished into thin air. Deleted by someone else who had breached the firewall.

'What the fuck? You cockteasing bitch. I've done everything for you. I'll show you. Fuck, fuck, FUCK.'

The whole point of the building was its anonymity and its proximity to the grid, for it slurped power out of all ratio to its size. This was a computer server house, in the outskirts of Twickenham, and it held the key to no less than a third of the computers in the United Kingdom. More than that, with the advent of Oracle and Cloud, it was the pathway to stored data which, although considered safe once it arrived at its destination, was considered fair pickings on the way there and back. But for the man standing in front of a bank of servers, nothing was sacrosanct. As the machines' lights flashed and the giant air coolers hummed and clicked around him, he was focused on a screen of data that he was manipulating via a small palm-held device connected to the server by wires. As he tapped in code, lines and lines of computer date were being deleted from the screen.

'Somehow Laffey's files have been erased. There were no copies – company policy. Nothing leaves the Quantum building, ever.'

Vellin and his Lord were standing by the panoramic window of his office, ostensibly looking at the Thames below them but in fact being conspiratorial. They stood closer than normal conversation needed. Whether the precipitous nature of the view made it feel safer despite the barrier of the glass or whether, as was Vellin's preference, his boss was kept within the smaller bounds of personal space than social intercourse might normally require, was hard to define.

'Nancy will love that,' said Regis. 'It's only a matter of time before she has her thought police scanning our innermost thoughts for dissent. Sometime I think all this corporate governance is just a screen for her control freakery. Bloody woman.'

Since the Enron scandal, part of the corporate game was to be seen to be whiter than white. The trouble was that the people who had been invading large organisations, creating the compliance and ethics fear game, couldn't distinguish between what was being properly left to grow in the dark – like a seedling in a cupboard – and what was secretive. And between the two, privacy had become a dirty word. It could be justified as being 'commercially confidential' to the outside world; but on the inside world nothing was left to germinate untended by the Nancy Hammers of this world in case what had been planted was an illegal substance. The Nancy prism, the way she saw the world, would mean all attics being abolished by law in all houses because some people grew cannabis plants in them.

Was someone of Foote's persuasion being let loose on Nancy? Regis suddenly wondered. They ought to be. What a rotten experience that would be, trying to prise open anything in whatever might pass for Nancy Hammer's soul. He envisaged it as a Salvador Dali post-apocalyptic wasteland of broken machinery and body parts.

Regis suddenly found himself not a little surprised at the vitriol he felt about Nancy Hammer. He didn't like such feelings when they could not be used to some purpose, and he could see none they would immediately serve. Nancy Hammer was a fact of his corporate life, the way things were, and he would have to suffer her for now.

Regis allowed his mind to settle itself back into its smooth running state. Vellin, in any event, was someone he could be direct with about secrets.

'Well, just wait until she hears from Quantum. She's expecting a big fat file on what Laffey was doing for us and she ain't gonna get it. Still, nor will the police. So now they only have the samples they dug up to work on.'

The matter was of huge importance to them both – Vellin because he had to deliver, Regis because it had to remain completely closed. Further investigation seemed pointless at present. As things stood, the public story that Laffey was a crank doing something that had nothing to do with anyone or anything, except his own fanaticism, seemed to be holding up and getting stronger. That would do for the moment.

'OK. It seems to be sticking. Let me know whatever you find out. At least I am prepared for the fury of a woman thwarted.' They smirked, very slightly, together, Vellin's registering a microsecond after Regis's lips twitched. Whatever neurons mirrored one person's emotional state within another, Vellin's were highly polished reflective mechanisms that kept him perfectly in sync with his master.

Nancy Hammer's capacity for incandescence was never far below the surface. Normally the simmering kept everyone around her on their toes and she rarely allowed it to boil over. On this occasion, she surprised even herself by the force with which her rage poured over the hapless Millington and

Porlock, who remained standing whilst Nancy sat tensely behind her desk, addressing them as if they were fourth formers brought before a furious head.

'How the hell do you expect anyone here to keep anything under control if you can't even tell me what the man was doing for us,' she raged.

The Quantum men had already had ten minutes of it, being incapable of giving Nancy any answer that would satisfy her. It had started cold and steely. It was getting hot and increasingly out of control. They hadn't really known who Nancy was when she had demanded they come to see her. The corporate systems at IFL only forced Quantum's attention through endless pieces of paper demanding signatures for almost everything which, in the long-standing relationship that they had enjoyed through Lord Regis, they had taken as routine.

Last night, in hasty preparation for this meeting, they had called up the varied manifests, supply relationship contracts, confidentiality and exclusivity agreements that bore Quantum's signature below IFL headings, and were aghast at what they had seen. The early morning meeting they had had with their lawyer hadn't made them feel any easier. The secrecy they had imposed as part of their own special place in the market they served had been massively suborned by Nancy's increasingly detailed documentation since she had been at Corporate.

What for Quantum was a routine signature in an on-going relationship was for Nancy the noose she was deciding not whether, but when, to pull. Porlock and Millington sensed that, but neither could put it into words. They had never been in such a position before. Hitherto, they had called the shots because Quantum always delivered on its own terms. Not this time, though.

Nancy was in full spate, firm on the moral high ground that she always took. She had adopted that as a source of power in a dirty trick she had pulled to become head of the sorority in her senior year at the mid-Western university she could barely afford to attend. Her main rival had a reputation with the boys. Nancy had been told the night before the last major election speeches – 'presentations' as they were called – that her rival was unexpectedly pregnant. At the time there was not much social support for a pregnant senior year student. It terrified the boys, and parents saw only the investment they had made being wrecked at a late stage. It was a lonely place to be for the girl who had been too free with her favours – loved a lot for the fun, let go fast when it became too horribly real. Lola, the girl in question, knew her parents would do whatever they could to get her the abortion she would need if she got the sorority post. She wasn't sure she could count on them otherwise. Her dad was pretty strident about losers. She had a lot riding on the vote. She didn't know that Nancy knew.

Nancy had not had the same success with boys. It wasn't that she wasn't good looking, in a hard, athletic kind of way. It was that the hardness was un-tempered by any of the softness that, she had observed, seemed so attractive to men and for which she despised both them and the girls who had it. But she couldn't bitch about that in public, she knew. It was a sure vote loser.

And then she wasn't totally sure about the pregnancy story. One of the boys from Lola's camp had spilled the beans – a Lola reject no doubt. He had been more persistent than most boys in his own interest in Nancy. He knew he stood no chance with Lola but, if Nancy were to win, he stood every chance of being her beau whilst she was sorority head. And so he had told her what he had heard.

So the final campaign presentations came; Lola first, Nancy second. In all the hype, balloons, trumpeting and banners of crowds of late adolescents starting their final year at university, quiet only came when the contestants took to the platform. Lola played it well, got lots of laughs and left the microphone to loud cheers. There was no doubt she was popular. Nancy began with the deepest feeling in the pit of her stomach that she had lost before she had started. But her speech was stronger than she knew. She was bright and she had actually formulated policies that met some student concerns very well indeed. In the popularity stakes she was not the winner, but in the likelihood of getting things done she came up stronger. It would have been a very close vote and she might have got it.

But, in the anxiety of trying to win, Nancy couldn't work all that out. It would have taken a sophisticated political analyst to see the trends, which Nancy wasn't and never would be. The next two minutes taught her that she did pain well and it stuck permanently.

It was customary for each candidate to end their speech with kind remarks about the opponent – making preparation for being a gracious loser. Nancy did just that, and then heard herself saying – almost as if she was not the person who decided what she might say next, but with a voice rising to the excitement of the occasion and her own tension: 'But there's one thing I do want to say in closing this campaign: Does the sorority really need someone who is managing a pregnancy as well?'

Lola, sitting on the platform where Nancy still stood, flooded instantly into tears. Her world collapsed as she rushed off stage. The ensuing silence was so stunning that everyone present could recall it for years afterwards. Normally at this juncture the vote would have been by hand, each campaign manager shouting the name of their candidate and asking for hands raised in support. In a close-run contest where the hands were too confusingly numerous, everyone present would have filed out of the hall and been counted and then re-assembled to hear what the tellers reported. And so the evening would end in cheering and shouting. An election would have been played out with all the Razzmatazz that they would see for the rest of their lives at every congressional, gubernatorial and presidential election campaign throughout America.

Not this one, though. Lola's campaign manager said, quietly into the microphone: 'I guess that's that, then.'

And Nancy got the first power job she had ever had. From then on, honing skills with the additional force of law within her, she lacked any quality of mercy.

Millington and Porlock could have known none of this. Theirs was not the world of the human mind. Their world liked microscopes, computers and the hum of laboratory machines doing their endless titrations of exemplary fluids. They were disciplined, secretive men for whom passions were deeply hidden and turned mostly into money. Power came from knowledge that no-one else had and it was kept that way.

In contrast, student Nancy had gone public with private information – and won. She was braver than they were. Since then, her life's work had been to keep human mess at bay and under control. And here were two men who had the power to fuck everything up and looked as if they had done so, leaving her with nothing to hang on to. How she despised them.

'Let me make it clear again,' said Nancy, 'so there is absolutely no misunderstanding between us. We operate on clear expectations and clear guidelines, and it's part of your contractual relationship with us that you, as our supplier, do the same. The contractual penalties for not doing that are equally clear. So where do you suggest we go from here?'

'We would of course give you everything we have, Miss Hammer. The problem is, it's all gone.' Porlock had to take the corporate lead. Millington had always wondered why the senior management got paid so much. Now he had an inkling -- they were the first to get shot.

'For heavens sake. We spend millions of pounds with you. We trust you. You do the most sensitive stuff for us. Surely someone's got a copy!'

Millington thought Porlock needed a bit of support, not really understanding, scientist that he was, that truth can land you in a lot of trouble too.

'There was no need. We pride ourselves on being a paper-free organisation. It was on our intranet, absolutely secure, firewalled, everything. We have no idea how anyone got anywhere near it.'

Porlock groaned inwardly. He knew enough to know that the only way of managing this kind of situation was to keep shtum.

Millington waded deeper in.

'In any event, whatever we've lost was completely encrypted. Our best man was unable to break it before we lost it.'

'So,' said Nancy, moving like a chess player who is about to take an opponent's queen and knows the other hasn't seen his mistake just yet, 'you don't think it's possible that whoever was able to breach your impregnable firewall might also have been able to crack the code?'

Porlock couldn't bear Millington having another go. He tried his best to close it down. 'It's irrelevant. They didn't *steal* it, they *wiped* it. The whole file. Every last digit. It no longer exists. So, though we don't have it, they don't either.'

'And what,'said Nancy, going for checkmate, 'is the actual evidence of that? How can you stand there and tell me that someone hasn't got something when the only certain fact is that you don't have it? What's to have stopped them taking a copy of the encrypted file, then wiping your system clean, and then working for as long as they need to until they've cracked it? You really are in trouble.'

And Porlock knew that he was. The fact of the matter was that someone had breached every security procedure they had, left no traces except a glaring hole, and disappeared. Just like a sleeper agent, lying dormant until needed, the flaw in their own systems had surprised them from within.

Somewhere, deep inside himself, he retained a vestige of hope that bastard Laffey had built in a failsafe, which destroyed his work after a period of inactivity. But he knew it was too much to hope for.

At that moment all the fight went out of him. Bluster he might, but it wouldn't get him anywhere. For a while, he simmered beneath Nancy Hammer's lashing then, to retrieve something of the position, he said:

'Well, whatever was going on in Dr Laffey's private life was not authorised by Quantum. IFL's work, though, was high on the secret list. Only Laffey knew what Lord Regis's purposes were and whether there is any connection. I don't know if you are aware of how far Lord Regis wants that exposed at this juncture. Perhaps you could let us know.'

Nancy recognised she had just made another enemy. Briefly it crossed her mind that this was the way it always seemed to be, and a smidgeon of self-pity flitted across her consciousness. No one understood her. As Millington and

Porlock left, more on their own terms than Nancy had intended, she knew that if she decided to take on Lord Regis, her career would be ruined forever. She might be the smartest ethics and compliance officer the executive world had ever seen, but she would be unemployable.

She closed her eyes and sighed very deeply and very slowly. Nancy Hammer took things very seriously indeed and sometimes it was a heavy load. A migraine was definitely coming.

Paddy hadn't felt this bad since he was knocked off his number one spot in the world wide Korean 'MMORPG, or massively multiplayer online role-playing game,', *Banshee*. Until then, he had remained at the very top for two weeks – no mean feat when the two million players known to be playing online worldwide at any given moment were considered. Of course, they were all Asian. Paddy was the only Westerner he knew who could match the guys he met online. And from their names, none of them were born further west than Sri Lanka.

Frantically, he docked his laptop into the mainframe and rummaged in the front pocket of his padded backpack. He pulled out a disc, carefully enclosed in a smooth, titanium cover, and shoved it into the slot in the computer. A few taps later and he visibly relaxed. The lines of code he had seen disappearing into the ether minutes ago were still there on the backup copy he had downloaded as soon as Millington had brought him Laffey's computer.

'Still got you, my beauty, ' he said. 'They can't keep us apart.'

The police forensic labs at Hendon processed more than 20,000 samples of gunshot residue, blood, bodily fluids and myriad other substances every week. But neither scientist felt much inspired by the clump of turf sitting on the workbench.

'Where did you say this came from,' the senior scientific officer asked.

'Believe it or not, the Prince's estate,' said the other. 'Dug up by our lads from the Regiment.'

'I'd have liked to see that,' said the first man, who had developed a jaded view of the Special Forces ever since his brother had beaten the clock and now made multiples of his salary running a private security firm in Paris. 'Our lads, digging up shit.'

'At least it will be organic' said his junior.

There was a short pause as the first scrapings were added to a test tube with an universal indicator, which showed immediately that the contents were anything but natural and benign.

'It's some kind of acetaldehyde agglomerating alderesterase. That's all I can work out. Sadly, that covers most of the chemical world.'

'Yep. But what's it doing there?'

'Apparently the perp was emptying it into the aquifer via the lake. But he was stopped. And it poured onto this bit of grass.'

'Well, it's all buggered up. We'll never be able to tease out the elements, even with spectrum analysis. Mud, grass and animal waste – it even smells like shit.'

They both looked at the piece of earth with disgust.

'Not exactly sodding CSI, is it?'

Leonie loved polo. This was fortunate, because the Prince enjoyed nothing more. In four years of royal service, she had stood on the edges of more practice pitches than she cared to remember, often functioning as an ad hoc 'stick chick' when none other was available. Palm Beach, Santa Barbara, Argentina, New Zealand, Cirencester, private estates, vast Estancias, it didn't matter. Polo players were all the same. And so were their girls.

She had the uniform down pat. Little silk dress, cashmere cardigan and flat sandals. Shoes always flat, for divotting. The glamour girls at the Guards polo club had never quite cottoned on, giving themselves away in their sky high Gina's and Louboutin's, which sank up to their expensive spines and snapped when they were asked to get out there and stamp down the chopped up turf.

Today was the International Fertiliser's Queen's Cup, attended by her Majesty herself, together with her son and heir and various other members of the Family. The Royal Enclosure, where the guests of honour, accompanied by a select group of invitees, ate lunch and watched the polo from a private stand, was separated from the rest of society by several white picket fences, assiduously guarded by flunkies who would have made a pit bull blanch. Comfortable in the knowledge that the Prince would be busy with the players, Leonie stood on the perfect green, rolled that morning, and watched the spectacle.

Pennants fluttered all around the pitch – the size of eight football fields. At the far side the teams, both stick and balling as they warmed up the horses, looked shrunken in the distance. The England players, much taller and broader than their Argentine opponents, were playing to the crowd, enjoying the adulation.

The Prince's middle son, George, was playing at number 2. His 7 handicap was a source of great pride to his father and of great anxiety to the rest of the Family. Still, as George never wearied of pointing out, if he had been allowed anywhere near the front line in the Army, he would never have needed to prove himself on the polo field. He was cantering slowly past his grandmother's tent, helmet in his hand as he waved at the legions of fans who had turned out to see the golden princeling.

The Argies were playing amongst themselves, warming up their horses with sharp sprints and turns as they chased the practice balls. Unlike the four, seven goal players fielded by the Brits, the Argentinians were a team of assassins, completely unbalanced. Their godlike Adolpho Cambiaso, handicapped at 10, was balanced by a talented four goaler at number one. The other two were both seven goalers, thus bringing the total handicap up to the required 28. In fact, Argentina was easily able to field a 40-goal team, but the problem with being the best in the world was that there was no other single country able to match them. Only the great Argentine Open, the 'Abierto', held at Buenos Aires' Campo de Palermo every December, ignored the handicaps and welcomed all comers. Otherwise, total goals were strictly matched for competitions.

The players were moving back towards the stands, ready

for the throw in, when Leonie felt Vellin's light touch on her

back.

'Miss me?' he said.

'You're only just in time,' said Leonie reprovingly, not

taking her eyes off the players.

'I'd never have thought you'd be a polo fanatic.'

'It's strangely gripping after the first 1,000 matches.'

'I forget, this is work for you.'

'Not today, it isn't. I'm off all weekend. So let's have a

drink in your magnificent marquee.'

Leonie took Vellin's arm and looked up at him. He was

wearing a bone white linen suit, a striped shirt and a panama.

It set him off perfectly. Instead of looking effete, he looked

as dark and red blooded as the Argentinean players. His

physical presence was overwhelming. Leonie had seen him

many times in sleek consigliere mode, bespoke suits and

discreet cufflinks, his considerable focus tuned in only to

Lord Regis, but today he was most definitely concentrating on her. It was thrilling.

At the bar, Vellin handed a glass of champagne to Leonie and raised his.

'To being off duty.'

'Leonie needs to know that Michael's never off duty.' Nancy's high, forced, American tones broke rudely into their mutual absorption. 'One way or another, he's got an agenda.'

'Not today, Nancy. I can't believe there is anything in the Code of Conduct which could possibly govern a glass of champagne with the prince's assistant,' smiled Vellin.

'You sure of that, Michael? If this is a company event – and as the International Fertilisers' Queen's Cup, I believe it is – it's covered.'

Vellin grabbed a bottle of champagne from the bar and grabbed Leonie with his free hand.

'Come on Leonie. Time to give those Argies some bargie. They've beaten us for the last 19 years.'

Giggling, Leonie allowed herself to be dragged away from the tiresome American with the painted talons. Unable to decode the broadest of hints, Nancy followed them, staggering slightly as her heels sank into the grass. Her ridiculous pink suit and hat were more suited to Ascot but then, Americans always did overdress, thought Leonie.

Nancy caught up with them both at the white picket fence and barged into their conversation again.

'Leonie, you know the rules. Can you explain them to me?'

Her voice took on a wheedling quality which made her, thought Vellin, even more nauseating than usual. Why had her mother had not suffocated her at birth?

'Gotta keep to the line, Nancy' he said, 'I'd have thought you would appreciate that.'

Nancy ignored him, looking straight at Leonie.

'He's right, actually,' said Leonie in as mollifying a tone as she could muster. 'Once a player has the ball, it's forbidden for other players to cross his line. You can get beside him and hook the ball out or ride him off but you can't cross his forward path. It's obvious, really. You can't have two tons of horseflesh colliding at full gallop.'

'Health and safety,' added Vellin, 'You would understand that, wouldn't you, Nancy?'

'I'd still like to read the rules,' said Nancy. 'How do I get them?'

'Just go over to the umpires – they're wearing the zebra striped vests – and ask for Mr Hurlingham.'

Vellin wasted no more time. He dragged Leonie off towards the stands, the girl giggling hysterically. Nancy watched them as they left, knowing she was being mocked but unsure of what to do. She didn't approve of the Prince's assistant behaving like that. Fraternisation between colleagues was strictly frowned upon at IFL, with co-workers being asked to leave if they were foolish enough to fall in love. Perhaps she could work up something to cover Vellin and Leonie. After all, Leonie was a key asset and as such, invaluable to the firm. And Vellin needed his wings clipped. She collared a passing waitress.

'Where can I find Mr Hurlingham? I need a copy of the rules.'

'I'll just go and ask,' said the waitress. She never returned.

Hours later, the sun was a great golden ball behind them as the car roared in over the Westway. London's usually sclerotic streets were unclogged, gilded motes of dust hung in the air and the Audi TT made the most of the road, speed cameras permitting. The roof was down and Leonie was leaning back in her seat and admiring the view – mainly that of the man beside her. She had never seen Vellin so vividly. He lit two cigarettes and passed her one. Leonie didn't smoke but it felt sinful and so did she. Their eyes met as she took the cigarette.

'Eat first?' said Vellin. Leonie could have asked but she didn't bother. She knew what would come next, as certainly as night would follow the shimmering day they had just spent together.

There was a time of the day that Foote treasured more than any other. On an old sofa, lying propped with cushions and his cat settled comfortably on his abdomen, he would open whatever reading matter was most engaging him at the present time. Then, reading slowly and thoughtfully with an occasional sip of his favourite island whisky, he let its wisdom pass slowly into his own accumulated understanding of the arcane ways of human beings.

This evening was such an occasion – a Saturday contentedly bereft of his family, doing whatever they were doing in South America, though come to think of it, he had had no word from them for a few days. He would try them later but for now, he had unalloyed time doing what he did best. If he was feeling just a little bit pompous and ever so slightly pleased with himself, he knew he was transforming the knowledge, under conditions he couldn't specify, into insights that astounded the highest in the land. 'Astounded' might be too strong a word. It must be the whisky. 'Intrigued' might be more accurate. Yes, that would do.

Such thoughts intruded pleasantly into his consciousness whilst he turned a page or stretched out a hand to stroke Orlando or sipped the alcohol that contained its own special bit of a mountain stream transmuted into a kind of alchemist's elixir. Real gold, he could say.

The phone shattered his calm.

A minor affectation of his was to have an old candlestick telephone standing on a nearby table, its earpiece hanging down in its cradle. Though elsewhere in the house a modern digital system satisfied the requirements of his wife and daughter for instant access, here in his study a carefully reengineered instrument from the early 'twenties rang out with the kind of tone now heard only in black-and-white movies.

It required two hands to manage it properly – one to hold the main part of the instrument, one to hold the small, fluted earpiece horizontally to the ear. He stretched out to try and get at the ear-piece one-handed, couldn't reach it, and lifted himself enough for the cat to walk disdainfully off his stomach and, with erect tail showing huge disapproval, disappear to wherever the stirrings of its nocturnal instincts took it. Getting up, he found that the ringing had stopped but that immediately the doorbell buzzed its own insistent demands. And then there was the sound of someone shouting hello, and Janey walking in.

'What on earth are you doing on a Saturday evening with that bundle of papers under your arm,' said Foote. 'You must have something better to do than see me.'

Janey smiled quietly – a look upon her that Foote cherished.

'I was just passing so I thought I'd drop this off for you. I called from just outside to see if you were in. But there wasn't an answer so I let myself in and then saw these back lights were on.' She had with her the first draft of an academic paper that Foote was working on. He had recently largely abandoned typing on his computer for the benefits of voice-recognition software; and Janey produced the finished document.

'Well, how about a drink? Have you got time?'

'Thank you but no. Lance is waiting outside. What I really wanted to hear about though, was how things went with Lord Regis.'

He had acquired the habit, over the years, of talking to Janey about what he was doing. He justified it on the basis of saying that if she was better informed, she could do her job better. But the truth was also that she asked very intelligent questions and sometimes said things that gave him real pause for thought. It wasn't that she had ever been a psychologist or wanted to be; but she had a remarkable capacity to see people for who and what they were, and her insights sometimes made Foote aware of how he could over-analyse things and miss the essence of a person. He thought about psychopathology, whilst Janey used her street-sculpted intuitive self to predict what might happen next.

'I know I shall enjoy it but I'm not sure about him. For him it's chess. For me it's watching how a chess master makes moves while being one ahead of him all the time. So far, I think we both know that. Doubtless we shall surprise each other. That's it, so far.'

Janey knew she would get the detail from the notes that Foote would dictate. But she liked to have a sense that he knew that she knew he was much involved in something. It made them a team in their own quiet way, from which they both drew a great deal of strength.

Janey had left a big corporate environment for a less-demanding life with a boss that she could trust and who was doing work of which she approved. A spell as secretary to a very highly-regarded paediatrician in Harley Street had taken her into the privileged world of medical confidentiality. She much preferred it to the competitive secrecy of the commercial world. But she also missed the pressure and excitement of the commercial world.

Working for Foote gave her the confidential world whilst not being entirely divorced from the mysteries of the commercial. And she liked his dependency on her. Lance, who was waiting for her outside, had simple views about men and women. He had not survived in security without being pretty macho on the way, keeping his intuitive side fixed only on the job and not on his relationship with her. She liked that in him, and valued what he did. But the reflective side of Foote held her fascination.

''Bye, then,' she said, 'unless you want to join Lance and me for a tandoori.'

Foote was touched. She knew he was alone on a Saturday night and this was her plan to see he was alright. That knowledge was much better than a tandoori, and he declined as Janey knew he would; but the warmth stayed with them both. Foote had been looking forward to making an omelette. Some mushrooms and grated cheese with it was as far as he would commit himself to any culinary art form; but he had his book and would settle down to that again soon. Then the phone call.

Leonie couldn't remember what they had eaten in the riverside brasserie downstairs. In truth, she had been ready to drag Vellin upstairs the minute they arrived in the parking lot beneath his warehouse apartment. Instead, he steered her out to a table overlooking the water and ordered more champagne. Up river, last of the sun sank into the west. And while she reached burning point, he had gone a little cooler, like the air. He watched her speculatively as if trying to gauge the level of her passion. He had fed her with his fingers, while she ate like an automaton. After what felt like aeons, she was standing in his hall, tearing off her clothes and his. Leonie had never felt such wild lust. As her knees gave way, he picked her up and carried her to his bed.

Foote found the satellite phone Hester had left him and set it up with its little umbrella on his desk. Hester, knowing that he was officially a technophobe, had run him through the procedures several times but still he felt a little unsure. He should have asked Lance. Somewhere in the man's past history of derring do, there must have been more than a few satellite phones. Security meant black ops and abseiling and guns and being 'exfil'd' from hazardous situations. He thought of calling Janey back. But it was 10.30 pm and he didn't like to interrupt their post tandoori bliss. Especially as Lance was a lot bigger than him.

Instead, he switched the machine on and watched the coloured lights run along the side. Was it ready when they all turned green? Or didn't it matter and were a few red ones acceptable? He felt like the apes when they encountered the vast black monolith at the beginning of *2001: A Space Odyssey* and spent their time patting it uncomprehendingly. He had drunk a few more Taliskers than strictly necessary and was fumbling, he knew. But he was seized with a sudden desperate need to talk to his girls. He missed them.

He pressed the pre programmed number and hoped for the best. Miraculously, after some clicks and buzzings, he heard Freya's voice, startlingly clear, in whatever jungle swamp she was standing.

'Dad?'

'It's your father.'

'I know,' she said affectionately, as he realised that of course, his name would be displayed to her – as hers was to him – on the screen.

'How are you both?'

'Great. We've started interviewing the tribe and we're getting good results. Mum's really excited. She wants to do a book. And maybe bring a film crew back here. You wouldn't believe it. It's just what she hypothesised. They're so –'

There was a distant satellite beep and her voice disappeared as miraculously as it had come. Foote stood for a while, looking at the phone which was now not showing any lights at all, sighed and plugged it into its charger.

At least, he consoled himself as he drifted off to sleep in bed some 15 minutes later, his only daughter had sounded happy and excited.

From the depths of Vellin's king size bed, Leonie could track his movements by sound. He was rummaging in the fridge and the coffee machine was hissing. She lay back in the crumpled linen sheets and looked through the doorway into the main room. It was minimalist in the extreme. The acreage of plate glass, oak floor boards and white pillars visible through the open doorway was unrelieved by any furniture, save one vast, red sofa. There were no curtains, rugs, tables or chairs – just two stools by the breakfast bar, which separated the kitchen area from the rest of the huge space.

The only enclosed room was the bedroom, one wall of glass hiding wardrobes and reflecting the great river outside. Naked, Leonie padded over to the mirrors and started tentatively pressing on the edges, trying to find the hidden spring, which opened the door to the concealed bathroom.

'Mmmm,' said Vellin appreciatively as he walked into the bedroom with a tray, 'I knew there was a reason for all this glass.'

Leonie glared at his reflection, 'Where is the loo door? It was there last night and now it's gone.'

Vellin placed the tray on the Zanzibar trunk at the foot of his bed and walked up behind her. He leaned gently into her as she regarded their joint reflection in the mirror. He was too beautiful, thought Leonie. His dark sleekness was even more pronounced in this bright, white environment, as though he had chosen it especially to set himself off. Leonie could smell his warmth and feel the rough linen of his dressing gown. She was ready to turn back into his arms when he pressed the top left corner of the mirrored panel. There was a click as it swung open. Leonie walked through the door, shutting it firmly in his face.

His disembodied voice came through the crack.

'See how compliant I am.'

'Nancy would be proud.'

When Leonie opened the door again she found Vellin lying across the bed, a bowl of granola, yoghurt and blueberries in his hand and a wide smile across his face.

'Breakfast?'

'This isn't what real men eat.'

'I do. The great thing about this particular breakfast is it won't go cold if you don't eat it immediately.'

'I underestimated you.'

'Never do that.'

Denham airfield did very well for Lord Regis and his ilk. Ever since Tiger Moths had flown the summer skies above the western edge of London's creeping conurbation, the aerodrome had supported weekend pilots whilst those who trained them amassed the hours they needed for their commercial licences. But quietly, over the years, it had acquired the really profitable side of its existence in being a base for executive jets. Corporate indulgence in two powerful jet engines and a sleek body bought not just the convenience of a plane always being available: what counted was not having to go through endless hours in waiting areas that, however expensively panelled and exclusive they might be, could as easily be the anterooms to hell.

Lord Regis had just stepped out, and as Farheen came round from her side of the car to join him, he looked exasperatedly around.

'Why the hell don't we know where Vellin is? I expected him here before I left. Get hold of him as soon as you can and tell him I don't know what the code is. I need to see him face to face. He knew that.'

The both knew Vellin's mobile was off. Farheen had spent the forty-five minute journey from central London trying him incessantly and leaving messages that he should ring. It was unlike Vellin not to be at his master's immediate call. They both knew that and were puzzled in their own ways. For Regis it just went to profound irritation.

And it wasn't only irritation that Lord Regis felt. Airports, even small ones, are not conducive to a sense of intimacy. They are, in their nature, transient places. Without his consigliere, Lord Regis felt oddly anxious. He had a sense, very unusual for him, that the world around him was not entirely under control. It had echoes of the time he had first been told of the only child he had ever created. He knew instantly that his world would never be the same, but it was not possible to define how that would be. And so it was now. He felt perturbations he did not like at all; and Vellin was not there to give him the comfort of familiar conspiracy.

Farheen knew only that for a creature like Vellin to disobey his master, he must have other, much more compelling needs of his own.

The insistent ringing of the phone finally roused Leonie from her post breakfast, post everything torpor. She was cocooned around Vellin's sleeping form, his mussed hair and nakedness giving him a vulnerability she had never seen when he was awake. He was completely out cold now. She drummed her fingers on his hip and whispered in his ear. 'Michael, wake up.' She slid her hand further around. An iron grasp encircled her wrist.

'You're insatiable.'

'No. The phone. It's been ringing for ages. It stops then starts again.'

Not showing any great urgency, Vellin wandered across the floor and out into the main room. He pressed the speaker button on the phone as he reloaded the coffee machine. Farheen's immaculate English filled the room.

'Lord Regis just flew out to China. He's not pleased that you weren't there.'

'His flight was at two this afternoon.'

'He brought it forward. He was anxious to get there quickly. We tried your mobile all night but it was on voicemail.'

'I see.'

'I am to give you a message, which is: tell Vellin I don't have the codes.'

'How very cryptic. Thank you.'

'You're welcome.'

Farheen rang off. Vellin continued frothing milk and shaking cocoa powder over the mugs but his mind was elsewhere. He was frustrated with himself. He had missed a trick. He had lost control, however momentarily. He never, ever did that. Time to get this girl out of his bed and get back to work. He set the tray down on the bed, neatly evading Leonie's entangling arms. He felt a fleeting pang of regret. But only fleeting. He had other interests and she would not impede those.

'Duty calls.'

'I thought it was your weekend off.'

'His Lordship has decreed otherwise.'

Nancy was anxious to leave and the damn driver was nowhere in sight. She had settled into the back seat of the Mercedes and spread her briefcase out over the next seat. Her case was standing by the boot ready to be loaded in. Her BA flight to Beijing was due to depart in two hours and she wanted some shopping time in the terminal. She had discovered that some of the labels she favoured would keep a few, hard-to-source items exclusively for their airside boutiques. They would then hold them for her return or even bike them to the office, once she was back. It made Nancy feel special and she was longing for her fix.

She got out of the car and looked around. A tell tale puff of smoke was issuing from behind a wall. Nancy smartly exited the car, slammed the door and marched over.

'I have been waiting for ten minutes.'

The driver, an old-timer named Eric, was sitting on an upturned waste bin enjoying his cigarette.

'Mr Vellin asked me to wait.'

'Why? I'll miss my flight. It's the only scheduled British Airways today. And I'm *not* taking China Airlines if I do.'

Eric seemed disinclined to stub out his cigarette but took a last, lingering puff and dropped it onto the asphalt where he crushed out the stub with his shiny black lace up. He could not have done it more *slowly*, thought Nancy in a rage. Quite apart from smoking on company property, which was forbidden, he was failing absolutely to show her the respect she considered her due. Worse, he seemed to have protected status at International Fertilisers. An old soldier, Regis' favourite driver, imperturbable and loyal and reputed to share the odd pint with his Lord and master on the way home. But loyal only to Regis, she thought savagely. If she were in charge, this old guy would be out of here on skids.

She turned back to the car, so incensed that she was considering driving it herself. And there was Vellin. Immaculate, smooth and smiling. At least he knew how to present himself. Part of the course at any decent American business school. And his teeth were good. Why didn't the Brits get it? Especially those scientists at Quantum. Some of them seemed to be culturing their lab samples on their teeth. Disgusting.

Vellin handed her a manila envelope.

'His Lordship needs these. Urgently.'

'I'll see he gets them. I was hoping to hitch a ride with him but he took off three hours early without letting anyone know.'

'Great men are driven by different tides.'

'That jet is for the use of all senior executives.'

'Perhaps you'll remind his Lordship.'

Nancy got into the car, slammed the door and pointedly kept the window up. She tapped on Eric's glass screen with the manila envelope and was swept away.

Foote was woken by the strange beeping of the satellite telephone. Good. It was obviously recharged and the girls were getting back to him. He pulled on a dressing gown as he scrambled down the stairs to his study. He pressed the on button and put the phone to his ear.

'Hester? Freya?'

There was no reply.

'Hello, hello? Hester, is that you?'

'Andrew, listen to me.'

He knew immediately that Hester was terrified. The hairs stood up on the back of his neck in sympathy, even though his wife was 10,000 miles away.

'They're beating down the fencing now. Somehow, we've stumbled into something rotten… they're bad men….'

'Freya? Freya?' he almost sobbed.

'With me. I've got her. But I'm so scared, Andrew. They're shooting our people – Maria, Luis... ' Her voice was quavery, Hester the indomitable. He could actually hear automatic gunfire.

'Tell me where you are. Who shall I ca-'

Abruptly, the phone bleeped and went dead. Sick with dread, he looked at the handset as if it could give him some answers. He was utterly impotent. The two most precious beings in his life were in danger and he could do nothing. He sat down with leaden legs. He needed to think, think hard.

Nancy was feeling good. Before boarding the flight, she had bought a jacket at Chanel, a cunningly constructed day dress at Lanvin and some shoes from Louboutin. They would be sent to her home after she returned, the assistants had promised. After being preboarded and cosseted, she had eaten a light supper, changed into her pyjamas and pashmina and slathered her skin with her special in-flight hydrating gel. She had inspected the contents of the British Airways vanity bag – not as good as Emirates or Singapore but pretty good all the same – and packed it away for overnight visits. She snuggled down into the duvet and put her eye shade on. She lay back for a few seconds on her bed, and breathed deeply.

Abruptly, she then sat up and pulled the mask up onto her forehead. She reached down into the well between her bed and the window and pulled out her briefcase. From this, she extracted Vellin's envelope. It sat in her hands for a few minutes while she thought. She fumbled for the spotlight switch. Then she opened it.

The contents were not illuminating. A list of names and codes covered one side of the single sheet. Nothing rang any bells. Turning it over, Nancy confirmed that the back was blank. It was meant nothing to her. Yet Regis had wanted it urgently and had not entrusted it to email or fax. And he had wanted it for this meeting with the Chinese. Therefore it was company business and therefore Nancy was entitled to look at it – as she was with any official documentation produced by International Fertilisers. Indeed, to deny her sight of such a document would be a prima facie case of non compliance.

Thus confirmed in her decision, she slid the paper back into the envelope, re -stuck the seal and put it back in her case. She then rang the stewardess, asked for water, took a sleeping pill and lay back down.

The Forbidden City held the same relation to Lord Regis's hotel window as did the Houses of Parliament to his office's view upon the outer world. In consequence he could look down upon them both. He stood there, contemplating the outside world whilst really lost in thought; rehearsing in his own way the format of the meeting that was coming up.

At one level it was just a formality. He knew that the Chinese knew that he knew that neither of them could back off at this stage. Truth to tell, neither of them wanted to. The Chinese needed what he could deliver. And he was the only one who could deliver it. But it was a devil's compact. He took all the risk and the Chinese could deny everything – not only because they had control of every bit of the apparatus of the State, but because in practice they could deny they had ever given him leave to do what they had asked. The rewards, of course, were huge. But the science fascinated him too. Try as he might, he had never been able to find any reason that they would hang him out to dry; any more than he would betray them. On that basis, it felt like proper business - - even if he should have known, had he thought about it, that it was simply wrong.

A knock on the door interrupted his musings. To his consternation, it was Nancy who responded to his invitation to enter.

Without a pause Regis said cheerfully enough -- and in genuine surprise, 'Nancy! I didn't know your schedule was bringing you to China this week.'

'Perhaps Farheen forgot to mention it to you. I was hoping to ride in the *company* G5.'

He noticed the emphasis and continued smoothly.

'How extraordinary. Farheen never forgets anything.'

They both knew this was true, and that therefore Lord Regis had actively avoided having Nancy as a travelling companion. Or at least, Farheen had divined his allergy to Nancy and looked after his interests as she always did. Nancy immediately went through half a dozen permutations in her mind as to what compliancy failure she could indict Farheen on. But in the same instant she understood that in doing so she would only expose Farheen's victory on her boss's behalf, so she   tucked the matter away for future revenge.

Indeed, if corporate HR was now generally known as Hate and Revenge, Compliance and Ethics was fast overtaking it as the part of the corporate system that people least trusted and most feared. Like the newspeak in Brave New World, the words had been tortured out of all resemblance to their original meaning. Not that Nancy cared. She wasn't, as she so often said to people, there to be liked. She was there to be right and have them be the same. And she believed profoundly that in the end she would be, if not loved, at least respected.

Lord Regis did not consider either a likely option for Nancy. He intuitively understood the nature of her tyranny and the insecurities upon which it was based. She was for him a necessary evil in his corporate life, but not one with which he especially wished to consort. And especially not right now.

'I heard things were moving fairly fast over here and so I thought I ought to get up to speed first hand,' said Nancy. 'Anyhow, I thought it would give me a chance to see how the compliance people here are bedding down. I'll just piggyback on your schedule if that's OK.'

Regis heard no question in that final statement. It was an assertion of what she intended, not a polite request to intrude. He was aghast. There wasn't anything he either could or would want to accomplish on this visit with Nancy at his elbow.

'Most of it is only technical stuff, Nancy. It wouldn't really interest you. It's just us boffins together.'

'The great thing about my job is that I don't know what would really interest me until I see whether it does or not.'

Regis groaned inwardly. He had just heard the great *carte blanche* excuse for people like Nancy to exist at all in corporate life. Their only business was to be inside other people's. The utter unproductivity of it made him want to scream. He gathered his thoughts as to how to deal with her, then decided to pull rank.

'I don't know how to say this, Nancy, in a way that you'll find entirely acceptable, but there are times when you are going to have to trust that some people must be trusted. As Chief Executive, worldwide, I'm one of them.'

'Then this is a crunch-time discussion. And I'm glad I'm here. Because unless I have open access, at my own discretion, to anything that is happening within the company, I am unable to satisfy the compliance authorities.'

'Even if it compromises the company's most valuable contract? The Chinese don't like unexpected new people being inserted into situations, especially very delicate ones, for purposes that they don't entirely understand or sympathize with. Don't we have to take account of cultural sensitivities too? Isn't that what multiculturalism and diversity are all about?'

'The world we're in requires a corporate conscience. My job is to be that, and to build that capacity. If it's a learning experience for the Chinese, then maybe it should be. And you can't be serious that it would compromise the contract. That's all been announced hasn't it? If not, I think I need to know.'

Lord Regis was saved from an immediate lie by a knock at the door. It was room service. He could have embraced the waiter.

'Thank God, breakfast,' he said, and set about pouring some coffee and constructing a smoked salmon and soft cheese bagel – happily available in Beijing – which, he had discovered, seemed to get him through almost any morning's work. Nancy, meanwhile, remained ready to resume the battle knowing she had the upper hand. Lord Regis chewed reflectively, and then rejoined the debate. He had seen a way out but it required a little calming down of Nancy. Getting her on to policy issues was one way of engaging the male side of her brain and getting her to bat on his wicket – a metaphor, he thought, she would hardly appreciate; let alone the yorker he was planning.

'Nancy. I thought we were managing ethics and compliance through mentoring arrangements for all the senior people throughout the company. I don't want a system based on fear. I want one that is embedded in people through their understanding what ethical behaviour really is, so that they are compliant as a matter of good practice, not through force. Forced compliance has no long-term value to us. Isn't that what we agreed? And if it is, then there have to be some areas where people are free to make their own judgments, even if they are made in private. The company has to take that risk because it's not conceivable that you can be everywhere all of the time, nor can all of your people.'

'"Private" is just another word for "secret".' And what I have to police is secrecy. Because that's where things go wrong. Think Enron. Think Anderson, think... '

Lord Regis knew he had her on the defensive now. She knew as well as he did that Enron and Anderson were the disasters that were never far from corporate minds. Investigations by the CESC and others had unleashed all this compliance stuff upon companies now spending small fortunes on the likes of Nancy. He cut her off.

'Okay Nancy. Let's put our cards on the table. I'm going into some extremely private meetings which are concerned with the long-term strategic developments of International Fertilisers' relations with the Chinese government, and hence essential to our commercial future in China. There isn't time to background you in the whole history of that and its implications, even *if* I were clear about them all myself. Added to that, you're a woman, you're American, you're black, and you're in China.'

'You could be sued for every word of that.'

'In the States, maybe. But China is one of the most racist and misogynistic countries on earth. And you're insisting on walking into meetings at the highest levels of Chinese political and commercial sensitivity. Tell me, how do your seminars on cultural sensitivity deal with that? And do you think you are going to benefit the company or do it damage?'

'That's not my call. I'm here to do my job.'

'But it *is* your call, Nancy, because as the most senior person in your function and a member of the Board, where you carry responsibility for the Company, not just your function, you have to decide what is best for the Company. You can't wriggle out of your responsibilities for the Board position you occupy. It's my judgment you will do damage to the company if you insist on coming into the meetings to-day. But it's your call. At this level, judgement counts. You think about it. I shall be at the Ministry of Culture one hour from now. The car will be here in forty-five minutes.'

'I know,' said Nancy, suddenly smug. 'I'll see you there.'

'That's not the way it works, Nancy. If the Chinese see us arrive separately they will know we are not operating as a team. If you come, you come with me. Cancel your car. Be at my car if you're coming.'

'Okay, you're the boss,' said Nancy. 'See you there.'

Nancy left, risking the slight smile that was on the edge of the corporate seduction she thought she had pulled off. She had shown him she wasn't afraid, and she couldn't believe she could do anything to break the deal or harm the company's interests. The thought that her unexpected presence alone would damage her boss's standing in ways that were too subtle for even him to understand was beyond her. The Chinese fascination with saving face was something of which she had no comprehension at all.

Regis had the phone in his hand already as she left, and started dialling a number he knew by heart. No matter that it was very early morning in London. He had less than half-an-hour to get the googly in flight.

Vellin shuffled through the papers on his desk then stared through the window. Regis was safely out of the way for a few days and with him, Nancy. Nancy the nemesis. Nancy the nightmare. If he needed anything to confirm his ambivalence about the opposite sex, she was the crystallisation of it. And she hated him as much as he hated her. He knew that. Despite the fact that he despised her, he recognised her unerring ability to see things he was able to hide from others. Even if she was too obtuse to put it into words, she recognised the unconscious roots of Vellin's hold over Regis for what they were. If he could read himself accurately, the truth was that fear was mixed with his hatred.

Although Vellin would never have made his predilictions clear to his boss, the tension between them lead to rare moments. Like the other night at Regis' flat. Still, Vellin felt confident of his ability to keep things on the tightrope. He had no wish to compromise his power by changing the dynamics of their relationship. But in one small corner of his soul, Vellin was glad to have some power over his master. Like a remora fish, servicing a great shark, he sometimes tired of the scraps of flesh trailing from his master's maw and longed for prey of his own.

In his own orbit, Vellin saw himself as a predator, a successful one, living alone and choosing how and with whom he spent his nights. His other self raved at night in Islington canal-side warehouses where buff, hard, young men would make it clear what they were seeking and take him home. Or if too urgent, they would find a hidden corner and ravish each other. On the darkest nights, he would cruise alone, glittering and narcissistic, on a north London heath, searching for instant gratification and the mouths of strangers. Holding such power over strangers was exciting, visceral and to some extent, compensated for the powerlessness he sometimes felt as Lord Regis' creature.

Despite himself, his mind wandered back to the night he had spent with Leonie. There was something different there, if he could allow himself to examine it. He had enjoyed many female lovers but love never entered the picture. As Leonie was beautiful – undoubtedly -- and useful in her role as assistant to the Prince, what more could he ask for? As the son of an antiques dealer with a special knowledge of Arts and Crafts, he enjoyed his little William Morris joke. If there was an infinitesimal sense that Leonie could be more than beautiful and useful, he wasn't attending.

Vellin always expected that Lord Regis might contact him wherever and whenever he needed him. He prided himself on always being available. But being woken by the dedicated mobile at three in the morning, made him struggle into consciousness. He could imagine Regis in his hotel room, standing, flicking through his private notebook, getting geared up for the day ahead. That was what usually happened – an early morning call from Regis half a world away, ensuring that Vellin would provide whatever it was he needed by the end of his working day.

The immediate tone of this call had an unusual urgency in it.

'Michael, wake up fast and listen,' said the distant voice, a conspiratorial edge apparent. 'Nancy Hammer has turned up here in full cry. She's insisting on being at the key meetings. I cannot possibly do what I need to do with her in tow. Get her back to England. I don't care how. There's only forty-five minutes before she wrecks the first meeting and if that one goes down, the rest will follow.'

'It's the middle of the night here,' said Vellin, 'Nancy won't believe anything she gets from me at this time of day.'

Still annoyed by Vellin's absence at Denham, Regis applied the thumbscrews.

'Michael, I can't spend time on the detail with you. All I know is that if she's waiting in my car in forty minutes from now, you won't have done your job. Just do whatever has to be done.'

Hester was sitting in her tent, tapping the day's work into her laptop. The battery was running down; the generators were off for the night, so when the power died, she would have to sleep. But she wanted to get the day's impressions down before then.

The upper Guaviare river was alive with sound, even at this hour. The tree frogs, monkeys and cicadas competed for airtime in a discordant symphony. The cicadas always won, a permanent refrain from sunset until just before dawn. Their song rose and fell in waves, ebbing and flowing, sometimes quiet, sometimes almost deafening. It was a wonderful sound; one she had first heard on a childhood trip to the Everglades with her parents.

Hester's mother, Florida born and bred, had wanted to show her only daughter the vast wetlands, which covered the southern tip of Florida. Hester's father, a Professor of Zoology, had been happy to investigate the manatees, alligators and crocodiles as they travelled slowly on a houseboat through the waterways among the mangrove swamps. A deck on the houseboat roof provided a birds' eye view of endless, matted green jungle. A barbecue hung out over the back, where her mother grilled steak every night, while her father puffed on his pipe to keep away the mosquitoes.

That was where Hester first fell in love with the cicadas' song. Her most precious souvenir on returning home to London from Florida was a cassette tape of the nightly chorus. She had played it every night at bedtime until the tape finally stretched and snapped.

Forty years later, the sound still lulled her to sleep. She yawned and rubbed her eyes and shut down the laptop. She eyed the sat phone. Was it too late to call Andrew? She felt a rush of affection for him, for the life they shared. She imagined him sitting with Orlando on his lap in the study, the little fire – a real one, despite all the strictures about smoke in London – burning in the grate.

Then she thought again. No, it would be five in the morning in London. He would be asleep in bed. Would he mind? She wanted so much to speak to him.

Deciding, she picked up the small aluminium briefcase and carried it outside to her folding camp table. She took out the handset, extended the aerial and holding the phone face up to the sky, waited for the satellite to line up. The iridium sign flashed up immediately. The satellite was available and somewhere overhead. The service was so much better than when she had been a young research student, like Freya, thirty years earlier. Then it could take up to half an hour for the signal. Everything was so much better now. The kit was lighter. The fabrics were breathable. The wellies – essential for wading through the Amazon basin – were now lightweight, with neoprene linings and strong soles. And best of all, she could enter her findings directly into her laptop and download them back at the university at home.

Keeping the phone face up, she tapped in her home telephone number. Then she heard the gunfire. A burst, silence , then another burst. Then screams.

Maria, Luis's young wife, who made the morning arrepas and hot chocolate, ran towards the tent, tears streaming down her face.

'E muerta,' she sobbed, collapsing.

'Who's dead?' gasped Hester, bending down over the girl. As she tried to haul Maria up again, a red stain spread across the girl's shirt.

'Maria? Oh, God......Maria?'

She laid Maria back down on the ground, fumbling clumsily for a pulse while trying to pull her scarf off her throat so that she could clamp it to Maria's chest in a frantic attempt to stem the bleeding. She struggled with the dead weight of the girl, then a voice from behind her pulled her up.

'Mama?'

It was Freya's baby name for Hester, only used when she was hurt or frightened and not used at all for at least five years. She was standing in the open doorway to the tent, sleepy and confused.

Hester held out her arms and Freya ran into them. There was a sound, recognisable but distant and tinny. Hester tried to calm her breathing and listened.

'Hello? Hello? Hester, is that you?'

She picked up the satellite handset just as several men, dressed in green jungle camouflage and carrying AK47s, burst into the clearing a hundred yards away.

'Andrew, listen to me.'

She didn't pause for his response.

'They're coming now. Somehow, we've stumbled into something rotten… bad men.…'

'Freya? Freya?' he almost sobbed.

'With me. I've got her. But I'm so scared, Andrew. They're shooting our people – Maria, Luis...

The lead guerrilla had reached her. He gestured with the gun, slung on webbing across his chest. With weary understanding, she handed the phone to him. And he crushed it underfoot.

Nancy Hammer was standing in front of her dressing table, both checking and admiring the manufacture of her appearance. She felt triumphant and as ready as ever for the unknown meetings ahead. She had decided, unusually for her, that silence would be a good ploy. There would be a lot to take in and her antennae needed to be highly tuned. Conversations in translation always made things more difficult, and she already knew she didn't have a good ear for the Chinese singsong cadence in their speech. There were none of the soft, drawn vowels she could naturally accommodate from wherever they came in America. It was actually physically tiring listening to Chinese in translation. The slightly reedy voices didn't help. So silence might give her the best chance of making sense of what she was about to hear, knowing already that she was a long way behind what all the other participants knew.

The telephone ring surprised her; Vellin's voice even more so. But she found herself shifting from surprise to more than a little delight as she listened.

'Of course,' she said. 'Sure will. I guess he can cope on this occasion.'

Lord Regis came across the hotel lobby to see Nancy standing by the car that was drawn up immediately outside. She looked at him with barely suppressed excitement, as if she had been awaiting him with some anticipation.

'Lord Regis. I've just received a call from Michael, who says there has been a call from the St James' Palace. The Prince would like me to speak at a lunch he's holding. Apparently, he especially wanted me to be there after the Royal Academy session we had. Michael says he's especially concerned about corporate ethics and wants someone who can talk about that side of things from a practical point of view. I think it would be good for the company if I showed willing.'

'If you're sure, Nancy,' said Regis, wondering how the hell Vellin had pulled that one off.

'I will need to take the company plane back to make it in time,' said Nancy.

Regis smiled a little inner smile to himself. So Nancy did have her soft spots. She knew as well as he did that there were strict policy guidelines about what the corporate jet might be used for. Getting from China to London to fulfil a wholly frivolous lunch engagement at St James's Palace did not fit the guidelines, however much Nancy might dress it up. What was good for Nancy was the only test being applied this time. She needed his approval for the use of the jet, and in giving it, even he would be going out on a limb. In these days of shareholder power and freedom of information, being questioned why a corporate jet went back and forth to China, at what cost and who was on board and what was the urgency and to what purpose, could make a nasty headline if the AGM results were not quite what the analysts expected.

On the other hand, she would be gone and she would owe him. Regis paused a beat to show her that her request was out of order.

'Do what you think is best, Nancy,' he said.

He couldn't after all appear too enthusiastic about her impending departure. But they both knew he had said 'yes' without saying it, and that it had put her in his debt, which altered the balance of ruthlessness with which Nancy had always previously maintained her independence.

'Then I'll get on with things immediately,' she said.

'And I'll let our hosts know so there are no airport problems,' said Regis. He left her, slid into the limo and breathed a sigh of infinite relief.

And then she leant into the car and handed him a letter. 'Michael asked me to let you have this,' she said. And as he took it, Regis knew that she had already read the contents, sealed though it appeared to be. But there was nothing he could do. She was gone in the same movement as she had leant into the car.

Then he began to think how his hosts would be elegantly relieved by Nancy's sudden absence. It would puzzle them slightly when he told them that it was at the Prince's request. Their understanding of the way corporate power and the palace managed their relationships was not well developed. This incident would not shed any light on that but simply add to their uncertainty of where the Prince's influence reached into the English system. 'Influence' without the clear authority to back it was not familiar to the Chinese view of the world. Tiananmen Square would not have happened if it had been.

Democracy develops subtlety and deviousness, thought Lord Regis. Despotism likes dark corners. China was stuck between both at this stage of its development. In trying to find how a political philosophy might emerge in the absence of communism and the rise of a free market economy after 4,000 years of Confucianism, China knew only that the future lay in managing the internet.

'Netizens' were where the future lay. Citizens had sufficed for the previous two hundred years of development in the western world but wouldn't do for the future of China. Citizens always wanted rights. China was only recently prepared to permit RAM.

It wasn't surprising they couldn't understand the unseen aspects of a British constitutional settlement that was never entirely settled anyway, evolving as it did through the personalities of the royal household and the variously elected members of what was still called Her Majesty's Government. Could any other nation, Regis wondered, as his mind slipped into freewheeling, find itself with a prime minister who had no formal mandate from the people for his power?

Lord Regis brought himself back to the present. His thoughts had been a pleasant diversion, spared from Nancy. But now he had to prepare for his hosts.

His mind was settling into the patterns of what he planned to say when the mobile phone he always kept in his suit pocket vibrated against his heart. He put down his papers, pulled it our and pressed the green button.

'Regis.'

It was Dr Foote. Before Regis could suggest calling him back at a more opportune moment, the psychologist had burst into a long, garbled account of something to do with his wife and daughter and Orinoco tribesmen. It was obvious he could not - should not - be interrupted. The man was in extreme distress and despite the awkwardness of the moment he had chosen to ring, Regis focused intently for about a minute. When Foote paused to breathe, he spoke.

'Where are they?'

'Colombia.'

'Who has them?'

'I don't know. They were living with the Guayabero Indians, a tribe facing extinction, on the Upper Guaviare River. Then they were attacked. Hester shouted something about armed men. I could hear the shooting. Then the phone cut off. I didn't know what to do. I still don't. I can only think you might.'

'I may know someone who could help. Sit tight and he will call you. In the meantime, ring the Foreign Office and ask them to contact our consulate in Bogota. They may have some information.'

Privately, Regis had not the slightest conviction that the British Embassy in Colombia could help at all, but Dr Foote needed something to do to fill his tormented mind.

He pressed the red button, searched through his phone address book and found another number, stored under the single letter 'S.' He pressed it, spoke succinctly when his call was answered and gave Dr Foote's home number.

'Do anything you have to do,' he said, 'All my resources are at your disposal.'

He sat back in the limousine and thought about the man into whose suddenly human hands he had committed his secrets. As the ultimate power player, Regis could see certain advantages in the situation, although he regretted Foote's pain. However, it would not hurt to change the balance of power in their relationship somewhat. He had been uneasy at the one way transfer of information. He had felt uncomfortable baring his soul, even though, for some reason he could not explain, he trusted Dr Foote completely. Here, he could reclaim some of the initiative. Regis understood minutest shifts of power on levels others could barely comprehend.

Also, selfishly, the thought of losing Foote to a domestic disaster bothered him more than any discomfort he had felt initially in exposing his inner thoughts. After the first few meetings, he found himself positively craving the chance to examine things he had never before held up to the light. Now that the dam wall had been breached, he was unwilling to hold back the flood. He wanted to see where the swirling waters would carry him. But to do so, he needed his guide.

Seb put down his phone, his mind already scrolling through contacts and fixes and long ago adventures in foetid jungle arenas. He was glad it was Bogota; he already had some mates up to not much good nearby, and he hadn't seen them for a few years. Especially Shimon, a one-time Mossad negotiator and full time badass. They were based in Caracas now. They would all be up for a foray into the unknown, especially as they would get danger money.

And he knew a bit about Colombia. The Revolutionary Armed Forces of Colombia, or FARC, were the usual enemy – of the state and of the people – and he was sure they had taken Professor Foote and her daughter. 'Los sequestreros' were a fruitful growth industry for FARC.

Their main income came from growing and trafficking narcotics – mainly cocaine – and they used local Indians as mules. This lady professor's subjects were probably running one of their factories. Her lost tribe would be acquiring mobile phones, laptops and sharp trainers as quickly as they possibly could, and co-operation with the FARC guerrillas was the fastest, if most lethal, way to get there.

He also knew that FARC tended to treat its hostages well so long as they had a perceived value. They would calculate that an English lady professor and her daughter would definitely be worth something – even if it turned out to be much less than they had imagined.

He cast his mind back to other hostage stories he remembered. The best known was Ingrid Betancourt, the French-Colombian politician who had been returned, unscathed, after six and a half years. Not a single bullet was fired, though only Colombian President Uribe knew what had been given in exchange for her life. She had, reportedly, been decently, if not well, cared for.

Then there were countless other stories of the children of rich Colombian families being kidnapped for ransom. One in particular had stayed in his mind. The child was given a birthday party, complete with balloons and a cake, by the guerrillas who held her. She was given a catalogue from Fallabella, the fanciest department store in Bogota, from which to choose her presents. Only 13, the child chose survival over playthings, picking a swimsuit, new boots, socks and waterproofs from Colombia's Harrods. She, like many others, was freed quietly after payment.

The area where the professor and her daughter had last been seen was bang in the middle of the demilitarized zone. Cleared by government forces, it was supposedly free of guerrilla activity, However, Seb knew well that it was nonetheless home to airstrips and processing plants, all of which moved frequently under the cover of the jungle canopy.

He had a twinge of nostalgia. This would be more fun than Baghdad and definitely more entertaining than Kabul. He was going to enjoy it.

When he had first agreed to work for Regis on a retainer, he had not imagined that this peer of the realm and master of the universe would have much need for his unique services. He had been wrong. There had been constant assignments, almost on a rolling basis. If the papers ever got hold of a fraction of it, Regis would be up the river without a paddle. Or up the Orinoco, in this case.

He took out a new, yellow, American legal pad – a habit picked up from working in Iraq and Afghanistan with US special forces - and started sketching out what he would need for the exfil.

'So Miss Hammer is not staying, Lord Regis?'

'How do you know that so soon?' thought Regis to himself. Less than 30 minutes' drive through an increasingly snarled-up Beijing was barely time enough for the Chinese internal information system to have discovered Nancy's plans. But they had. Which, of course, meant their telephones were tapped. That meant that they knew of Vellin's call to Nancy and so had been aware of everything sooner than he had himself.

Perhaps, more significantly, they had heard Foote's call to him, and his to his man in black. It amused him to call his pet mercenary this; some reference to a long ago film he could not imagine how he had seen. He could only imagine the Chinese would have found both calls bewildering. However, it bothered him that they should know anything about his private life and he reminded himself to get a few, significant numbers, including his own, changed as soon as he returned to England.

'Is it possible that the flight planning arrangements for her urgent return to London could be expedited?' he asked.

'Everything will be in order, Lord Regis. It is not a matter that need detain us.'

Walking down the interminable corridor of a Chinese ministry building, the official went on:

'We had two rooms set up for your meetings today, Lord Regis. Here on your left,' he said, pointing through the half-open door of a room where Regis could see one side of a long board table with officials seated and waiting attentively, 'are my colleagues attending the meeting that would have taken place had Miss Hammer been with you. They know nothing of our project of course, but have been deeply involved with the long-term contractual relationships between International Fertiliser and my country.

'It would have been a meeting to review the very early stages of how the contractual arrangements we have agreed appear to be working, and what we need to do to make sure that they go on in a favourable manner for us both. A great deal of documentation has been prepared for this meeting. I think Miss Hammer would have found it a model of its kind. We would not have wished for her to be disappointed in any way, or to have left feeling any kind of disquiet. While we Chinese do not comprehend your western corporate fascination with the matters that so engage Miss Hammer, we do understand the rules within which you have to function.'

Standing in the corridor outside the half-open room, Regis was quietly staggered. Within 30 hours – once again suggesting they were aware of Nancy's movements long before he was – they had pulled together everything to create a completely plausible meeting for Nancy's benefit.

It was a measure of the importance of the real meeting, the one of which Nancy would never have known. And a measure of the regard in which they held Regis himself. It would have been easy enough to cancel the other meeting and leave him feeling, in a very Chinese manner, a serious loss of face.

'So let us attend the meeting for which we so value your presence here in Beijing,' said the official.

Although they had never met before, this man seemed absolutely conversant with everything that connected Regis to the most senior – and hidden - parts of the Chinese hierarchy. His grasp of matters both Chinese and western impressed Regis but did not particularly surprise him. This was the Chinese way of doing things. This man, still only in his early thirties, could only be a rising star with a powerful protector.

His career path thus far would have been entirely pre-ordained by whoever talent- spotted him and plucked him from the Communist Party School. In his mid twenties, he would have been sent to an arduous, far-flung posting, to prove himself. There, as master of a faltering factory or as governor of some uneasy province, he would have been expected to prove himself, following a strict party line, increasing productivity and ticking all the boxes, all the way.

His protector – and there would have to have been one, Regis knew – would have been occupied with infighting to keep his protégé on the rise. It was not unknown for powerful patrons to attempt to destroy the reputations of their rivals' placemen in order to enhance their own. The ultimate prize was so great that almost any action was justified. Even if the protectors wished to remain in the shadows, having their man as one of the top 10 or 15 in a country of one billion people meant access to unimaginable power and influence.

Regis knew that the highest ranking members of the Party were tightly connected to each other and to their own, individual dynasties through dense, internecine webs, which owed their first loyalty only to each other. Each family controlled a fortune through a vast network of subsidiaries, many spread out across the globe. It was through the head of one of these subsidiaries, which had first approached Regis, that the original IFL deal had been struck. It was only after years of close work that the question of anything more had been raised, and then so obliquely that it was almost indefinable.

The deals with IFL had been signed by a high ranking member of the Politburo, though whether a second rank or more senior member it was impossible to tell. Regis still had no idea of the identity of the member, but he knew they would need to have a solid power base. In a Politburo of seven members, the plot to test the substances provided by IFL in the autonomous regions would need the support of more than one member, Regis knew. Yet, executed as it was by those further down, it was infinitely deniable.

At this level, there were few clues. He could have been one of the last of the Mao era generals, establishment Communists still dedicated to keeping China's military might, or one of the new, younger technocrats, who had attended the Tsinghua communist party university and focused upon economic growth and accommodation with the West. Either could have represented the new China; the old militarism hand in glove with soft power.

In the same way, the young man before him represented the ultimate discipline of the East combined with a disarming understanding of the West, thought Regis. It was impressive, as was the inky blackness of the man's hair – a small vanity Regis had spotted in every official of note he had ever encountered in China. He thought idly of the fortune he could have made simply by introducing black hair dye to this country – no need then for vast chemical contracts. It was the classic advice given to aspirant entrepreneurs – sell millions of something cheap, rather than just a few of something expensive. Grecian 2000 was a dead cert here: like their Western cousins, the Chinese had their own obsessions with youth.

This man was probably connected to the Ministry for Internal Affairs, thought Regis. That meant border control matters, amongst which Tibet was a paramount concern. Certainly, it had featured prominently in the careers of the last and the new President of China. Internal affairs was probably not the only Ministry involved, but certainly the one with which he mostly dealt. It was also where responsibility lay for China's population control policies and their implementation.

As a long disputed Chinese territory, the mountainous Autonomous Region – known in China as Xizang Zizhigu and to the rest of the world as Tibet – was a convenient test-bed under their control.

The physical appearance of a boardroom in China differs only marginally from a boardroom anywhere else in the world. Furniture and design apart, boardrooms are for meeting on the basis of power.

The only exception to this universal truth is to be found in the creative industries of the west coast of America. There, power is subsumed in the creative processes and boardrooms feel more like a coffee shop, or adult playpen, than places of serious business. It was not a fashion that Lord Regis imagined would catch on soon in China.

In the centre of one side of the long table, his back to the shaded windows, was an older man, his jet black hair at variance with a face which betrayed the passage of at least half a century. This was a senior party member responsible

275

for the portfolio which included IFL, Regis assumed. Though maybe only a cats paw for another, even more powerful individual, he seemed to make happen whatever he wished to happen, from any part of the Government machinery he needed.

Lord Regis had often envied the nature of central control that he witnessed in China. The senior people spent a great deal of time resolving strategy but almost none about fighting for their own territory once strategy was agreed. Responsibility was equally shared, of course, just as it was in the command of great armies. Why England had disabled its industrialists and was now systematically disabling its generals too, despite desperately needing them, was a paradox Lord Regis pondered often.

In China he was entirely relieved of having to worry about where authority lay. They were right, he thought, to resist the West's demands that they become democratic as well as developing a free market economy. Democracy slowed development up. Look how many years it had taken to get the channel tunnel rail link up and running. China couldn't afford that kind of snail's pace. But America feared the speed with which China could develop her industrial might. Only implementing a democracy might slow that down to a manageable pace. No wonder America was adamant about the Chinese becoming democratic. As with everything between nations, in the end, underlying philosophies gave way to considerations of power.

Next to the party member sat a man Regis knew. Hu Quinglin had been head of a US-based Chinese subsidiary when they first met at a conference on agri-solutions to world hunger. Always on the look out for new worlds to conquer, Regis had carefully fostered their budding friendship, flattering Hu with useful introductions, dinner with the Dean of Harvard, high table with a fellow of All Souls. Only later did he fully realise that Hu had been there all along with the express purpose of enlisting Regis and IFL's help. A

277

revolutionary fertiliser and then, ultimately, the Dragon project, had been the result.

To Hu's right was a general in full uniform. His build was powerful, and Regis could detect the squat musculature of the northern indigenous tribes in his physique. He knew him to be the military commander of everything that included the allegedly autonomous region of Tibet. His absolute responsibility was for law and order. Though technically he reported to the Central Council member responsible for Tibetan affairs, his actions were autonomously determined. Anything affecting Tibet strategically was his concern too. And professionally, population control matters interested him very greatly. Though in not averse to loss of life in any circumstances, he preferred it not be done unnecessarily. Efficiencies of action were of considerable logistical interest to him. Indeed, it was not only the remoteness and relative inaccessibility of Tibet but its well-mapped water systems that, in the case under discussion, especially intrigued him.

China knew exactly what every rising stream in Tibet contributed to each major water system. In this particular matter, absolutely nothing was to happen that involved the Tibetan headwaters of the great Mekong river, which flowed through the inestimable delta lands where southern Vietnam and Laos nestled in its folds. All control would be lost if the trials were to be leaked.

Their interest lay to the northern and eastern faces of the Tibetan mountain ranges. West and South might be of interest later, when the strategic values of this first experimental trial had been properly understood.

To the general's right were two men who were unmistakeably boffins. Thick spectacles and pens sticking from their top pockets were an international uniform. The power of the pen was still much valued by the Chinese, despite their facility with everything electronic. Education to the highest international levels was still regarded as a national resource to treasure, revere and continue developing.

These scientists had existed entirely within the communist system and understood its capacity to transform science into public policy very well indeed. They would be jointly responsible for what was about to be presented.

Thank God Nancy wasn't here. Lord Regis knew very well that the alternative meeting to which they would have been taken would have been conducted in Chinese. What the interpreter said would have been totally rehearsed and would have borne no relation to anything that was actually being said. It would have been a charade entirely for Nancy's benefit.

Here, the common language was to be English, not only as a very high level courtesy to him but because, with the exception of the general and the senior party member, everyone else present had done their doctorates in the USA. The general had learnt his English the hard way, in China. The origin of the other's was obscure, but its fluency was remarkable.

He made his greetings. The size of the table forbade a handshake, but the acknowledgements of each with a slight formal bow settled the meeting into its format. On the one side of the table, the Chinese. On the other, Lord Regis, an esteemed supplier but not a colleague.

The older man whom Regis had not met before now rose. He introduced himself, starting the meeting as he did so in impeccable English but with a distinctly French accent to it: 'Lord Regis, this Committee of the Central Council is delighted to welcome you. You and your company, International Fertiliser, are honoured friends of China and major contributors to the present success of our agricultural developments and our capacity to feed the people of China. This meeting does not concern that, however. We have come together today to hear from our esteemed scientific colleagues what the results are of the first trial of your new compound. This trial has been conducted in Tibet, in one region that shall be nameless. Its results will, I think, interest us all.'

Regis noted that he had given no name and had used the formal style of introduction on behalf of the Central Council. It flashed through his mind that this was as smooth a spook as any Regis had met. Again, he marvelled slightly at the effectiveness with which the Chinese state managed itself.

The younger official who had originally escorted him now walked down the length of the table and, pressing a button, made a screen coverering the end of the room slide down. A picture appeared on it, projected from somewhere that Regis could not see.

The picture that covered the screen was of a mountain village. The official sat to one side of the screen, just in case the technology required any further intervention.

The senior boffin – three pens rather than two in his top pocket – pressed a button on a small wooden block in front of him and the screen showed a satellite view of mountain ranges. Down the centre of the photograph, wonderfully sharp in its images whilst covering, Regis guessed, some one hundred and fifty miles north to south, were the sharp-edged peaks of a continuous mountain range. To either side of this main range were secondary north-south ranges separated by a long valley on either side of the main high ridge. Each of the two valleys had a river flowing along its floor, broken by tributaries coming off the mountains on both sides. Each had clear evidence of vegetation below the snow lines.

'This is the site of our study,' said the man. 'You will see that the tributaries flow east and west from the central range to create the river in the two valleys flowing south. Each of these rivers is also fed by the waters coming off the smaller ranges to the west and east of the main ridge. This is the map of the water system.'

With that he pressed the button again, and every single water course was picked out in blue. Thin lines staggered down from the valleys, joining an increasingly large blue confluence that thickened as it went south in each of the valley floors. There was a remarkable symmetry on both sides of the central range.

'You will see the similarity of river networks to either side of the range,' he continued. 'I will not trouble you with the details, but the volume of water flowing through the two systems is essentially identical. This area was chosen because not only were these characteristics desirable but also because over the centuries, human habitation has developed very similarly in both valleys in relation to the natural geography.

'This has happened although the two valleys are effectively cut off from each other. There is no trade of any kind between them. There are only two passes across the central range, climbing to more than three thousand metres. There is no commercial activity that would warrant such a journey. In consequence there are no casual relationships between merchants and local women.'

Here he pressed the button again and every village was shown in orange. The naturally balanced ecology of their development was in itself fascinating. Lord Regis could suddenly see why human geography – a subject he had always slightly despised as a pseudo-science - might have its attractions after all.

'The experimental design was to introduce the new compound – the chromatothanatogen -- into the tributary rivers here, here and,' button press, 'here.' On the eastern side of the central range and in its northern half, about twenty little rivers went a deeper blue on the screen and the villages that depended upon those water sources went a deeper orange.

'Simultaneously we introduced the original fertiliser, from which our chromatothanatogen is synthesized, in the equivalent water courses on the western side.' There the rivers went light purple and the villages deep purple.

'That was 18 months ago. We know of course, the incidence and pattern of births in the region over the past 50 years. It is important to state that there has been no effect from our previous one-child policy in the Xizang Zizhiqu, as there was no implementation of it in the autonomous region.

'There were two questions that we wished especially to test. First, did the new compound have the effect we seek? The animal studies were especially encouraging. However, there is no experimental control of our subjects here, as we have had in the laboratory studies, because the conditions are completely natural. The only variable we have introduced is that the compound on the east side is synthesised from the compound on the west side.

'The second question we wanted to answer is what happens to the compound further down the water system. Does it dilute or stay effective? Both these rivers run into lakes, both of which have hydro-electric dams at the downstream outlets. In those lakes we have freshwater fish specific to those lakes and we will study them over time as well as the populations around the lake shores.

'As with all new compounds there is always some difficulty in working out what would the correct level of water-borne dilution. These are not, after all, still water systems but fast flowing rivers.

'We found that the villagers do have a form of collecting water by enlarging a pool where their villages and the riverbank coincide. Water is drawn from this pool for all domestic purposes. The men might from time to time drink from mountain streams away from their villages if they are herding animals. But they are rarely away from their villages overnight and the main evening cooking of the day will be done from water that has been drawn from the pool and then boiled. As a result, we can assume that they are generally exposed to the compound in their daily drinking water.

'You will understand that the numbers we have had to work on are not huge. In the 20 villages on the eastern side there are 542 family dwellings scattered over some 75 kilometres north to south, in which there are one 130 women of child-bearing age. Fertility rates are not high in this population, each woman producing on average three children over a twenty-five-year child-bearing span. Male to female live birth proportions are almost exactly 50:50. There are no observable seasonal fluctuations in birth rates. For the purposes of our study, we have been interested only in live births occurring in the second nine months of the study and in still-births and spontaneous abortions occurring throughout the whole period – that is to say, live births where the conception will have occurred after the introduction of the compound 18 months ago or failures to produce a live child at any stage after the introduction of the compound. I must add that the population is generally very hardy and healthy and live births are the rule. Still births and deformities are the exception.

'So in the nine month period in which we are especially interested, we would have expected there to have been about 12 live births, of which six would be male and six female in this population. Of course, over such small numbers and short runs of time the general trends and averages might not have been at all observable. Indeed, this is one of the scientific problems in the global warming debate.

'I will not go into great detail about the population on the western side where we were testing to see if the original fertiliser produced any specific birth-related effects by itself. Suffice to say that we expected a very similar number of births to the norm.'

Lord Regis found himself becoming unexpectedly tense. A great deal hung on this outcome. He leaned forward, watching the boffin's outstretched finger reaching for the button that would produce the results slide.

And there it was. Intense concentration from every pair of eyes around the table. A simple bar chart with purple and orange histograms. The legend said that female births were cross-hatched; male births were solid colour. The numbers of births were up the left hand axis, zero to twenty. The bottom axis simply alternated; male, female, male, female. The purple male bar measured 6, the purple female 4. The orange male bar measured 1. The orange female, 10.

No-one spoke. Everyone knew the numbers were very small, probably too small to be statistically significant. But it looked tremendous. Could it really be so simple? The incidence of male children controlled by a single application of a waterborne chemical? The results of the first ever chromatothanatogen trial never ever to be published – and forever unknown to anyone except those in the system where secrecy was absolute.

Even to Lord Regis's scientific mind, the data looked as impressive as he could possibly have hoped. But how would the Chinese evaluate it?

'We believe,' said the boffin, 'that this first set of data is considerably clearer than we might have expected. As good scientists, we would have anticipated no difference between these two populations. The huge difference between them is quite clear. We have, as you might expect, calculated the extent to which this might have happened by chance. The probabilities are extremely low: this could have happened by chance less than one time in a thousand. We have in fact checked all the data for the last 25 years from these two populations, and there is no record of such a strong deviation in births for males and females in any nine-month period. The same is true of all possible consecutive nine- month periods on a rolling basis in the whole of that time. Are there any questions gentlemen?'

The silence around the table was absolute. Lord Regis felt the tension beginning to drain out of him. Until now everything to do with the project had been hypothesis and possibility. Here was data of an extraordinary kind. Laffey, the mad bastard, had got it right. He felt euphoric. But he had to play the detached science game nevertheless.

'Might I start,' he said, 'by offering my thanks for such a rigorous piece of work and congratulations on the elegance of the presentation and findings. I have come to expect nothing else from the disciplines that you practise so well here in China, but it is nevertheless a special pleasure to see them so well demonstrated. Thank you.'

As he spoke, Lord Regis bowed slightly to the most senior person present who sat impassively in reply. No other acknowledgement or response would have been appropriate; as it was, it was perfect.

It was time to show his own expertise.

'I have two brief questions – though it may of course be too early to tell. Has anything been determined yet about population or other effects in the dam waters? And is there anything to be known yet about the persistence of the compound in the village water drawing points?' The question of breakdown was of special interest to Lord Regis. He had been part of the student research group that first found the field evidence for the way DDT persisted in soil and water systems long after its apparently useful application life. He had come to realise that such considerations deserved attention very early on in product development; a lot more money could be made if no later claims arose because of products being rushed too soon to markets. Bhopal and dioxins haunted every commercial chemist's mind.

'For the first,' said the senior scientist, 'I can tell you that we have had a parallel study of fish going on in the dam waters. We set this up right at the beginning of the project. It appears to have other interests as its main focus, so that none of those working on it know anything of our other interests. As part of the work they are doing, they are required to strip all trapped fish of their roes and send the stripped material to one of our laboratories for analysis.

'We have observed two things in the developing data -- though before I continue, I should say that none of these effects have been observed on the fertiliser-only side. The first observation is that in the dam to which the compound flows, the incidence of male as against female fish caught has declined sharply among immature fish. In mature fish, the substance of the male roe looks pale and inert compared with the normal healthy deep pink of healthy male roe. We shall continue this study to see what happens to spontaneous recovery rates, if and when they occur, now that we have halted the experimental introduction of the compounds to the headwaters. We do not yet have any clear understanding of the toxicology of the pale roes. But we are working on that in order to understand more accurately what the precise effects of the chromatothanatogen are in the fish population. We have also observed a shift in the male-female balance of water snails. Although not extensively researched in the past, we are starting demographic studies under the auspices of a conservation programme so that we have baseline data for any future work in the same water system. The World Wildlife Fund is delighted to be supporting that work. We fortunately can manage the detail of it.

'On the question of human reproduction around the dam, there is nothing definitive we can say at this stage. There are mostly male migrant workers around there. What we are doing is tracking whatever live births they generate over the next two years at least. Unfortunately we may not know all the girls with whom they have casually cohabited; nor the other men with whom the girls have had liaisons. Also our anti-Aids programmes among migrant workers mean that their fertilisation rates are unlikely to be the same as the mountain valley populations. But this is always the trouble with naturalistic field research. By no means is everything under control. Nevertheless, we shall learn some things that over the years ahead will make us gradually wiser if, as seems to be the case, we do have chromatothanatogen that can be used.'

Lord Regis admired both the depth of thinking and the fluency with which the ideas were presented. Nor could he prevent an envious thought about how wonderful it must be to be able to do what one wanted without being surrounded by red tape. How curious to feel so free in a communist country, he thought, when we have been taught in the West to think that it is we who have freedom.

'Again thank you,' he responded, 'And on the question of the persistence of the compound in the village water supplies?'

'We have observed that within one week of stopping the use of the compound, there is absolutely no trace of it detectable in water drawn from the village pools nearest to the points at which the compound is introduced to the water. Downstream and nearest the dam, it takes a month for the pools to clear. We don't know at this stage whether the substance degenerates in water, and if the speed of degeneration is related to concentration; or whether it is simply a kind of flushing effect – as typically happens when a substance that should not be there gets flushed through by clean water, which is what usually happens. '

At last the General spoke. 'I think, gentlemen, that the scientific service has done as we requested. It has conducted its work under naturalistic conditions and has today provided us with information that demonstrates that the compound Lord Regis has synthesised for us has the capability to manage male fertility within water-borne systems. I shall now recommend to the Central Council that policy is developed on the basis of the capability we now have. I think that is all. Thank you and good day.'

As the people at the table rose to leave, Lord Regis found a restraining hand on his own arm and a slight pull to keep him in the room. The older man beckoned him to walk with him towards a window from where Beijing lay scattered before them.

'We were pleased to hear about the success of the press conference last week, Lord Regis.'

'I am glad the members were satisfied,'said Lord Regis,

'We are most satisfied, on many fronts. The fertiliser, River Dragon. Everything has been excellent – except, of course, for the potentially disastrous case of Dr Laffey. I understand he chose to test the special compound in the most public way possible.'

'He did, but we contained the situation. '

'Yes, we know he is dead' said the man, 'and that your police are pretending they executed him, at least until they discover who actually pulled the trigger. Unfortunately, your police are testing some of his compound at their research facility. We are concerned that it might be traced back to the work IFL was doing for us.'

'There is no possibility of that. The substance was spilled onto grass. My information is that the sample the police have is entirely corrupted. In addition, your research confirms that its precursor breaks down after a period in the environment.'

'We certainly hope so. While minor anomalies in the birth rate in our autonomous regions can easily be explained away, the effects of the androtoxin – Dragon's Breath – will be more drastic and will need different handling. And while we are better able than your country to contain information, even the remotest regions of China are infected by the internet. We have tried to contain its pernicious effects, with some success, but information always leaks out. Which is why we will experiment on the most remote peoples and we will ensure that their communication networks are degraded before we start. Meanwhile, we have been working on an explanation – the breach of a mine wall in a cadmium mine. As you know, while we need this precious substance for all our electronics, it is poisonous to man. A sudden, catastrophic run off into the aquifers might explain away any mass poisonings.'

These were the inner – and most secret - workings of the Chinese system, thought Regis. The one child policy had encouraged families to keep their male children and abort the females. For years, the international news headlines had trumpeted the plight of unwanted Chinese girl babies. But now the policy had shown the wisdom of the old adage, be careful what you wish for. Yes, the population was full of strong young men, able to work for the new China. But there were no longer enough young woman for them to meet and mate with.

The imbalance in population demographics had become a matter of great, long-term strategic importance to China. Twenty five million men between the ages of 22 and 35 had absolutely no prospect of finding a Chinese wife. Chinese male labour could not be exported at any great rate, though a surprising amount had been managed in Africa. Unofficial figures signalled that the number of men without brides would increase exponentially over the next 20 years as China set out to redress the balance of her one-child policies. But social problems were not easy to resolve when they took two generations to do so and ordinary human desires were blocked. It could cause a great deal of unrest.

Instead of growing into a vibrant mixed society, China was becoming predominantly male, with large groups of potentially troublesome young men, sad and lacking sexual partners, with nothing except work to divert their energies. Like rogue male elephants, thought Regis. Recent research in Africa had shown that the policy of extinguishing older elephants in order to deal with overpopulation had resulted in large groups of rudderless, adolescent males roaming destructively through the bush. African wildlife experts now preferred to cull entire families, in order to leave the hierarchies intact.

The androtoxin was a last, desperate attempt to halt the testosterone-fuelled desert that China was in danger of becoming. It could never be used in mainstream China, but in the autonomous regions or indeed, parts of the new colonies, it could. Certainly in Africa – China's newest and most assiduously courted colony -- where women often worked harder than the men, it would be invaluable, thought Regis.

'Tell me,' said the Council Member, changing the subject, 'is it not the case that in four weeks' time you will be announcing your half-year results? I hope they will be as the analysts predict.'

The slight interrogative raising of the voice at the end of that last observation left Lord Regis uneasy. Could the Chinese possibly have something up their sleeves, he wondered. A bid for IFL was not entirely out of the question. He had often been warned it could happen. His own view was that this was exactly the wrong time for China to be buying up companies in the UK. It was not an easy place to do business and, unlike manufacturing generally, IFL could not easily be transferred elsewhere in the world.

International chemicals, like pharmaceuticals, were essentially a knowledge industry with many dead ends lurking among the breakthroughs and money-spinners. This needed great depth of scientific endeavour. He wasn't sure China had that yet or, if a whole company of western scientists was bought by China, whether China could manage such a crew.

But he wouldn't want to be the one to convey that message to a Council Member on the first occasion the topic was raised. It would be held against him forever. Yet if he went along with what he thought was being hinted at, he would have crossed a line. The vilification he would get in his own boardroom and the financial press was something he would not wish to experience.

Yet hadn't he crossed a line already? The fertiliser was of course acceptable, but the chromatothanatogen compound?

The great River Dragon, named for the most powerful sign in the Chinese zodiac. And worse, the androtoxin, Dragon's Breath? Both developed only to prevent life or to end it? This was playing God – a vanity to which the greatest scientists were prey and from which Regis was certainly not innoculated. He had already crossed a line. But China would be grateful.

'It would be good to surprise them by making it other than they expected,' he heard himself saying, not sure where such a Delphic reply had come from amidst his mental turmoil.

'Can we help in any way, Lord Regis?' This was an opening that would not come often.

'A forward payment on the new contract would make a difference and please our shareholders,' Regis replied

'We had been thinking something similar, Lord Regis. Would 40 percent be suitable?'

Regis was stunned. What an extraordinary testament it would be to his powers of persuasion to go back with such a gift to his accounts. There would be an immediate rise in the IFL share-price. Once again, he would be voted best company leader of the year in those international journals, where such matters counted. He had recently begun to covet being made a Knight of the Garter, and wondered fleetingly if this would help. Had any industrialists had ever been given such a personal honour by a grateful sovereign?

'That would be more than generous. I am much indebted at such forward thinking on the part of the Peoples' Republic of China.'

They both knew that such an act could only be noted in the most polite and impersonal terms. Equally, both knew that it bound Lord Regis to this Council Member forever. At this level of government, triads did not have the faintest fingernail hold. But the social obligations by which the triads cemented their existence were entirely understood at all levels in the system.

'But it is we, Lord Regis, who are indebted to you. You bear the most risk and we value immensely what you are doing for China. You have helped us find a solution that will offer us the chance to change the shape of China's future quietly and without impinging on public awareness while it happens. There will need to be other solutions too; but there again, you have shown your willingness and ability to help. That is an accomplishment for which we would wish to show some personal gratitude to a very good friend of China.'

It was a promise, and Regis stored it in a separate compartment of his mind, to be taken out and examined at a future date. Who knew what the future would hold?

'Please keep us informed, Lord Regis,' added the Council Member. 'If you hear any more about the Dr Laffey situation. We would not like your intrusive press to start digging.'

'We have, as you know, a press over whom we have very little – indeed no –direct control,' replied Regis, 'But they lose interest very rapidly. As you know, they are considered a pillar of our democracy.'

'America wants to control everything and call it democracy. We do the same and are called totalitarian. Human rights are only tools of mind control, not rights of any kind at all. So it's fashionable in the world to have these human rights at the moment, but they will destroy the world. Islam understands that very well, and it is not as tolerant a religion and system of thought as Confucianism is. It's a curious world, Lord Regis, for often nothing is as it seems.'

He rose to go. Within a couple of days of Regis' return, there would be a discreet visitor from the Chinese Embassy. After some formalities, he would be told how and where and when a very large additional sum of money would be transferred to his company's accounts against the value of the contract he had signed last week. It would be called an advance payment and it could be lost over the next five years.

A payment for his real services to China could never appear in the books. Garter Knights were not known in China. But battle honours blazoned on the IFL balance sheet would do very well for the time being.

On his way back to his hotel. Regis experienced the familiar feeling of bathos – the anticlimax he always experienced when he had stepped up to the mark – and won. His last thought as he sank into a bath was that Nancy would have to be dealt with one way or another. His perception of her had changed. She had become an unnecessary evil.

The doorbell rang and Foote opened it wearily. A man stood on the doorstep, moderate height, lean, fit-looking but otherwise nondescript. He put out his hand.

'Doctor Foote?'

'Yes.'

'I'm Seb. '

Foote stepped back and indicated the interior of his house. He shut the door behind his visitor then squeezed past him, showing the way into the study. Mrs H had lit a fire and the remains of some toast and tea littered the desk. The man moved straight to the satellite phone on the desk and started pressing buttons and testing connections.

' Was this how you were communicating?'

'Yes,' said Foote miserably.

'Tell me exactly what happened, where they were to the best of your knowledge, and how much time has passed since you alerted Lord Regis.'

Foote looked at his watch. Already, he felt as though a lifetime had passed although in the real world, it was just three hours. But even in three hours, Hester and Freya could have been killed, or worse.

He had always been aware of the dangers inherent in the expedition. The insurance brokers had made that clear. Colombia had long been riven by a drugs war and the

Colombian Government's decision to send in special forces under the new 'Democratic Security' policy had only made the situation worse. Criminal armed groups had forcibly displaced the remaining 700 or so Guayabero Indians eastwards, from their traditional territory in the Middle Orinoco onto reservations. From there, violence between government forces and the gangs forced them on again until one of the last nomadic tribes in the Colombian Amazonic Region was in danger of extinction.

Hester, an acknowledged expert on tropical forest Amerindians, was the obvious -- the only – choice for the final, definitive study of their diaspora and absorption into Neo Colombian society. She had won a field research grant from the Royal Anthropological Society for three months' study with the Guayabero and academic papers to be published upon her return.

As a budding anthropologist, fresh from Oxford with a first, Freya had been invited to accompany her on a research studentship. Freya had been intensely proud to have earned her place on the trip in the face of stiff competition. It would be noteworthy. Like most of Hester's schemes, the expedition had been well – immaculately even – thought out, and it had not once occurred to Foote to try to stop her.

Now he regretted his complacency. He loved his wife and he adored his only child. The thought that he might not see them again was unthinkable. Yet the presence of this man in his study was proof that the situation was so far beyond his control that he would have to entrust their lives to others.

Seb broke into his thoughts.

'I have a map here,' he said, spreading out a large folded sheet over the debris on the desk. 'Show me where their camp was.'

It was a large-scale map of the Orinoco basin. Following the tributary westwards from the Atlantic coast, Foote traced the mighty river with his finger up into the wildest and furthest reaches of the basin where the wide blue line became

311

a thread. His finger stopped at a tiny dot on the map, marked Barranca.

'There,' he said.

Leonie rolled over and watched Vellin's naked back, his waist wrapped in a white towel, as he made the coffee. This was becoming a habit, a delicious one.

They had met for tea in a Chelsea patisserie to discuss a lunch the Prince was hosting. It was the thinnest of pretexts, but Vellin had seemed as keen to grasp it as Leonie had been to create it. The café chairs and umbrellas were corralled into a roped off area. From her seat, Leonie could see a small child and a dog amusing themselves by rushing into vertical jets of water, which appeared at intervals out of the paving stones. The child's delighted gurgles and the dog's constant startle reaction, despite the predictability of the fountains, made a charming picture, and people were stopping to watch and laugh. Leonie was waiting for her appointment, the last of the day, at the celebrated and costly hairdresser in the building above the café. She looked down at the menu and wondered about chocolate tiffin.

'You look very beautiful today.'

Leonie looked at Vellin, dark against the sun and her head swam with what they had done together.

'I'm waiting for my hair appointment.'

'Your hair is perfect.'

'It needs tidying up.'

'How long do you have to wait?'

'Another half hour.'

'Plus the length of the appointment. Too long to wait. Come home with me. Now.'

Even as she was getting up, Leonie heard herself say feebly. 'I have to work tomorrow.'

'That's tomorrow. We have time.'

As the taxi left the kerb, they had fallen on each other like starving hounds.

Back in his crisp white sheets, miraculously changed since the night before, Leonie lay in Vellin's arms and floated. Now it was lunchtime, her day off was almost over, and she was due back on duty at 4 pm.

Vellin perched on the side of the bed and looked at her.

'Could you do something for me?'

Leonie thought that she would do anything for this man, she was so deeply in lust.

'That depends on what you can do for me.'

He grabbed her head and pulled it to his chest. 'You know what I can do for you.'

The very thought made her weak. She had had lovers before. Callow boys at University, one married man, nothing lasting. This was different. This was a grown up man, capable of turning her into a passionate woman. She closed her eyes and reran the film of the night just past. Her hands coiled around his waist.

He was talking, insistently. Leonie came out of a haze of desire to hear him say something about how much it would mean to him.

'What?' she said lazily.

'Nancy. The lunch we discussed yesterday. You need the right participants. I need a favour. Whatever it takes, get her on the list. She worships your Prince, would die for him. He won't mind another sycophant hanging on his every word.'

Leonie played for time while her mind scrambled. 'I'll have to think about it.'

'No time. She's on her way back from China.'

'Not for *this* lunch, surely....'

His silence spoke volumes. Leonie sat up, the sheets falling away as cold outrage overwhelmed her.

'You *didn't.*'

'It was essential, Leonie. Regis called in the middle of the night. He *had* to get rid of her. It was the obvious, the elegant solution.'

'It was not your solution to offer. Nor mine. The Prince is most particular about his invitations and believe me, this is one he will not be issuing.'

Vellin looked at her in disbelief. He had completely misread her. She was not going to co-operate. Vellin had met an immovable force in the most fragile beauty he had ever seen.

Sue Carter was staring at a computer screen covered with thin, vertical coloured lines. If forced to describe them, she would have said they most resembled a supermarket pricing code. Which reminded her. Her boys had football practice tonight and she had to stop off at Tesco on the way home or they would arrive snarling and ravenous in the kitchen to find a bare fridge. A supermarket dash was definitely on the cards. That was, if she ever got out of here.

The Sergeant standing behind her spoke for all of them. 'What is it, Ma'am?'

'Blessed if I know. Perhaps Mr Millington can enlighten us.'

Millington, who appeared paler, sweatier and even more anxious, if possible, than at their last meeting, almost wrung his hands. 'It's mass spectrometry. By passing light through any substance, the prism is broken up in a unique pattern characteristic of that substance, thereby allowing us to identify exactly what chemical compound it is comprised of.'

Tesco looming large in her mind, Uriah Heep in front of her, Sue Carter cut to the chase.

'And what substance is this?'

He would not meet her eyes. The man should be on medication, he looked so shaky.

'Er, it's too early to be sure. To be honest, it strongly resembles a number of widely available, commercial fertilisers.'

'Fertiliser, or at least manure, is not something I would have thought the Prince was short of,' she snapped. HRH was certainly ensuring plenty of it was flung around here, she thought sourly as her nemesis, Chief Inspector Briar, walked into the room.

With a sense of impending doom, Carter felt a visit to the chip shop coming on – again – for her sons' dinner. There was no chance of the old windbag cutting her any slack. Why couldn't Briar have done his usual Thursday afternoon skive off to Wentworth where his gruesome, lavishly dentured array of friends awaited him on the golf course?

'Good afternoon, Sir. Was there anything you wanted?' To her annoyance, she found herself patting her short, highlighted, mousey bob, ever the little girl anxious to please.

'Results. I should have thought that was obvious. Talk me through what we've got so far.'

Briar took up the Sergeant's position, leaning over the back of Carter's chair and staring uncomprehendingly at the coloured stripes. Her skin crawled, knowing his hand was back there. Really, her aversion to him was visceral.

'It's mass spectrometry, Sir,' said Carter, sounding more convincing than she felt, 'Every substance has its own signature on a graph with peaks and troughs and it's only a matter of time until we identify this one.' She looked around desperately for Millington's corroboration. The sweaty little slimeball had disappeared.

In the locked, disabled loo on the ground floor of the Police HQ, Millington was on the phone. 'I think we've cracked what Laffey was up to. The spectrometry results looked familiar, so I checked. I need to see you. Somewhere completely private.'

The contrast between the two men currently disrobing in the RAC Club's changing rooms could not have been more stark. The younger of the two – Vellin, looked like the predator he was. By some metamorphosis, his low friction trunks, his goggles and his black swim cap made him look more dangerous, rather than less. The same accoutrements as sported by Millington looked ridiculous. The shorts, like the belly, were baggy, the goggles had a knot tied in the side of the band and his hair was wild. He followed Vellin through the shower and footbath into the deserted pool enclosure. While he dithered on the edge and wondered about the water temperature, Vellin dived in and did two swift lengths before surfacing next to his companion. Millington watched, fascinated as the water poured off Vellin's taut six-pack. He last remembered having one of those when he was in the CCF at University some 20 years ago. Where had it gone?

'Talk to me. What was Laffey making?'

Vellin urgently wanted to know. He had known from its inception about the manufacture of a chromatothanatogen – the River Dragon – to reduce the incidence of male births in China. He had known that it went hand in glove with the fertiliser contract and that China was as concerned about redressing the imbalance created by the one child policy as it was about feeding its burgeoning population. He also knew that providing the compound was one of the reasons behind Regis' extraordinary success with the Chinese.

Amoral to the core, the idea had not particularly bothered Vellin. Indeed he had read reports which suggested that a more equitable male-female balance in China would ensure a more successful and peaceful society. But all that really mattered to him was that Lord Regis thought it was acceptable. He simply had to ensure that it was not going to be blurted out to all the wrong people by this sad sack.

'Describe it in layman's terms,' he said.

'A waterborne androtoxin. Put simply, it is a poison, which kills any male who drinks it. Irreversible.'

'Are you certain,' said Vellin. 'Actually kills them?'

'Completely sure. I have synthesized the compound and resynthesised it. While a female has two X chromosomes, a male has an X and a Y. This substance targets the Y chromosome. Therefore only males would die. Experimental projections suggest that if a woman was given it, she would survive, while a man or boy would die.'

Vellin was perplexed. This was not the point of the compound he knew about, which merely killed off male gametes before conception. It could even be argued that it was a humane way of dealing with some of China's more intractable long term problems. This, on the contrary, would be cold-blooded murder.

'But why would Laffey make such a thing?' said Vellin. 'He was asked to bioengineer a new generation of fertilisers for China.'

'He did – and they *are* brilliant. But what if the revolutionary fertilisers were really a sideshow? What if Laffey and Regis were involved in population control work for China–and the huge Chinese contract was the reward for that?'

'But why do it at all? China used to throw away girl babies. And now you say they've make something that kills off males. Why?'

As he said it, Vellin knew perfectly well why. New China, like ancient Rome, needed slave populations in the poorest and most desperate nations in order to survive. Tibet, areas of the Russian federation, vast tracts of Africa – all were being exploited by the Chinese, who needed a compliant workforce – which meant female in those countries. And they needed it fast. The chromatothanatogen took at least 18 years to come to fruition. Enter Lord Regis. Again.

Picking up on his thoughts, Millington said, 'If Regis knew about this, or was involved in it, it explains his immense sway over the Chinese.'

Vellin knew already that it was true. But to what extent? The existence of a male poison took the plot way beyond anything he had imagined.

He had to divert Millington.

'But why would Laffey put this thing in the Prince's lake? Of all targets, why HRH? He was a great supporter of International Fertilisers.'

'Often the most convoluted of crimes have the simplest of motives. Laffey was a rabid animal rights activist. The Prince hunts. Therefore he – and any male downstream of his aquifer – dies. Simple – when you're mad. '

Vellin looked down pensively as he rinsed his goggles in the pool water.

'Sounds to me as though Laffey went postal. Tonto. He was a brilliant scientist but he lost the plot. He used his access to the labs and the chemicals to do something for himself before he retired. Remember, it was only a few months off. I can't believe it has anything to do with Lord Regis and the IFL contracts. The only link is that Laffey was the Quantum scientist working on the IFL fertilisers for the past 20 years.'

'You're probably right,' said Millington. 'I thought I knew him after working with him for so long, but I suppose we never truly know anyone.'

Too right, thought Vellin. What he had imagined was a relatively innocuous tweak of a fertiliser into a subtle nudge towards nature now appeared to have a darker and more sinister aspect. Could Regis have been developing a more extreme version for a more immediate solution?

So, the source of the master's magic is revealed, he thought. Base chemicals into golden contracts. Millington's voice broke in.

'The only other thing is the name. River Dragon. The dragon, the most powerful symbol in the Chinese horoscope. Just about the only thing on the page that wasn't encrypted.'

Ah, thought Vellin. But this was a different compound. *This* dragon breathed deadly fire.

Millington clearly felt he had done his bit and now he needed his reward.

'What about my twins? What if they take them? I'm going out of my mind.'

'I will give you a number to call. Come with me.'

Vellin hauled himself out of the pool in one graceful movement and headed for the changing rooms, Millington trotting behind him.

Ping Li looked down over the garden square and listened as Vellin blurted out everything she had worked for, for the past 30 years. He was so overwrought, his usual seamless instincts for mind-melding with his audience had deserted him. Ping Li stood there, emanating hatred, disgust and distrust, and still he babbled on.

'This information is dynamite. I know you have connections. It is imperative that you inform the Chinese authorities before there is a catastrophe. I would go to Lord Regis but he is on his way back from China.'

'I do not understand.' Ping Li was exquisitely, politely blank.

'I just explained. Our supposedly harmless organic fertiliser, boon to millions of Chinese farmers, came with a pair of evil twins. The first is a compound – a chromatothanatogen – which will simply stop an entire generation of Chinese males from being born. We called it River Dragon. Population control, but for the new China.

Forget the one child policy and the discarding of female babies. Somebody high in the Chinese hierarchy has decided that women are what they need now, to correct the terrible imbalance caused by the one child policy. And they would provide a valuable workforce, particularly in China's offshore colonies. Look at Africa – the only workers there of any value are women. So make more. This is the grandest of propositions. Human farming, so China can conquer the world.'

'But China is doing well enough already in this 21st century world. Why would she need this? I think you're imagining things, Mr Vellin. Or at least, you're adding two and two and making five.'

'But that's not all. Dr Laffey tweaked that compound again, to create the second, much more dangerous one. He ratcheted it up, so that any living male who drinks it is a dead man walking. The compound targets the Y chromosome. The male chromosome. Victims die quickly of terminal cancers, leaving the women unscathed. Originally, I thought Laffey did it for his own reasons – to settle his own scores -- but now, I am not sure. Maybe the idea behind this androtoxin is that it's worth killing off a few men in advance so that we don't have to wait 18 years for the population imbalance to ease out.

Ping Li's body language was impenetrable. Vellin was not used to such a lack of reaction. He wondered whether this woman was lacking a few neuronal synapses. He decided to shock her.

'Do you understand, Laffey had gone postal, completely off the reservation, stark, staring mad. He was trying to kill Leonie's Prince, for God's sake.'

'You know I am unable to discuss my daughter's employer.'

Vellin stopped. Ping Li's glacial demeanour had finally penetrated his excitement. Suddenly he realised how much she hated him. And that nothing he was saying was in any way a surprise. Like a trapped fox, ready to gnaw his own leg off, he looked frantically around for a means of escape. This had been a mistake. He had overstepped the line. He sidled behind the white sofa but Ping Li blocked him at the door.

'And what of Lord Regis' role in all this?'

'I don't know. Certainly, he knew of River Dragon. I did, too. Laffey was working with Lord Regis on the first compound – the CMT project – to prevent male births. It hurt no one and seemed a small bonus to give our Chinese friends, although we could never admit to it. But I believe Lord Regis must have been unaware of Laffey's private project – the androtoxin. And certainly, murdering living males is going too far. But then, I think he must have known... It explains why, in exchange, Lord Regis brought home the greatest chemical contract our country has ever signed. With China.'

'China is not your concern, Mr Vellin.'

'It's everyone's concern. That male sperm killer was especially formulated for China. But what about the androtoxin? Where would China use that? Africa, the autonomous regions? Population control is one thing but genocide... if this gets out, China will be a world pariah. And I'm sure you would not want that, Miss Li?'

It was not a rhetorical question. Vellin wanted to know what she knew. Ping Li decided to bring things to an end.

'I will inform the authorities. Thank you.'

Vellin traded in information but Ping Li was not paying up. He stood there for a few, long seconds. Finally, he turned, opened the front door and slammed it behind him. She heard him walk blindly into one of the Fu dogs outside the door and curse, before the lift doors on the landing whined open.

Ping Li walked straight to the phone and dialled a number she knew by heart.

'I need to speak to you on a scrambler. Let's agree a time.'

Regis put down the phone on the desk in his hotel suite and picked up the exquisitely carved ivory Chinese puzzle ball he had bought that afternoon from his special dealer. Six hundred years old, it was one of the finest he had seen – and he had seen many. Each one took a lifetime to make, concentric globes, all wrought out of one single piece of ivory. The finer the ball, the more layers and the more beautiful the carving. Each ball represented a life sentence in that each rendered the carver blind, twisted and old before his time. Some took several generations to complete. Never mind blood diamonds, this was blood ivory.

His collection, closely alarmed and guarded in his London house, was finer than anything found in a museum. The powers that frowned upon China's imperial treasures leaving the country turned a blind eye where Regis was concerned. He rotated it in his hands, counting the layers again and marvelling at the exquisite workmanship. It was like contemplating the universe; the mind ran out of places to go. The telephone rang. He picked it up and spoke.

'Regis.'

'I hope you now find yourself unencumbered.' Vellin's silken tones.

'There is rejoicing in the streets. Nancy has gone – flown away on our company jet but it's a small price to pay. She is no more popular with our friends here than she is at home… and lunch with the Prince! I can hardly bear to ask how you swung it?'

'To be honest, I haven't, not completely. However, the Prince is known for his frequent changes of direction. None of us can be blamed if he suddenly cools off on the idea.'

'And she will be too proud to hunt for the guilty. Positively Machiavellian. You have outdone yourself.'

Warmed, Vellin expanded. 'It was the most pleasurable assignment you have given me for a long time.'

'Ah?'

'The Prince's personal assistant was *most* accommodating.'

Regis controlled himself with effort. 'You surprise me, Vellin. I never took you for a ladies' man.'

Vellin caught something untoward in his master's voice and morphed back instantly into consigliere mode. 'You know I'm not.'

'Good. I would not like us to misunderstand one another.'

Regis leaned forward and pressed the button on the phone, cutting off Vellin. Then he threw the delicate 600-year-old Chinese ivory puzzle ball against the wall, where it shattered.

As soon as he had dried off and dressed, Milllington rushed out of the swimming baths to call the number Vellin had given him.

Every time he spoke to Millington, Seb was surprised that the man on the end of the line had ever managed to hold down a job, let alone rise to the position of senior scientist at Quantum. As ever, Millington was incoherent, unable to marshall his thoughts, certainly unable to register that he had spoken to Seb several times before. A function of extreme fear, thought Seb dispassionately. The man's children were under threat, though no action had yet been taken.

No action ever would. It was time for Seb to ease up on Millington. The first few calls and photographs had kept the inside information on Laffey flowing; he no longer had any need to frighten the man.

But Vellin had been right to alert Seb. For somehow, despite Laffey's death and the erasure of his files, Millington had discovered what Laffey's plastic bottle held. Seb had known only that it was important enough to have Laffey stopped. But not how important. Now he knew. Vellin had given him the details while Millington was trying to find a private place from which to call. Which meant in turn, that Seb had been right to keep the pressure on Millington. Somewhere, there had been a loose end. He had simply given Millington a powerful incentive to find it.

'Leave it with me, Mr Millington, he said. 'I will call you back as soon as I know something.'

'But what do I do in the meantime?' said Millington.

'Go to work, behave normally. This won't take long.'

Seb put the phone down. One last, texted photograph and he could forget about Millington.

Ping Li could hear Leonie's hair drier in the distance. It was early evening and both women were preparing to go out. They rarely spent time at home together except in the mornings when they would meet in the kitchen. Leonie would be munching on granola and organic yoghurt, Ping Li eating fruit and a handful of supplements prescribed for her by the Chinese herbalist in Mayfair, whom she had come over the years to regard as a friend. Mother and daughter would exchange a few words, confirm schedules and leave for their separate worlds. But this morning had not followed the usual pattern. Leonie had not been there at all. She had come home at 6 am, long after Ping Li had woken up suddenly, staring at the ceiling, imagining nameless horrors. When Leonie came into the drawing room, fresh and lovely in blue jeans and a white ruffled shirt, her mother was waiting.

Where were you last night, Leonie?

Leonie was startled. Her mother never interfered with her adult life. In fact, total discretion in both directions was an unspoken condition of them sharing a house again after Leonie had returned from Cambridge and landed her job on the Prince's staff. Not that Leonie needed to be discreet about her mother. So far as Leonie was concerned, Ping Li had no secret life. Certainly, there was no evidence of any amours.

Leonie thought this a shame – her mother was still beautiful – but she seemed content with the arid life that she had forged in this alien land. There must have been someone, once. Leonie was evidence of that. But her mother had never hinted at a man, still less the whisper of a name. And somehow, Ping Li's conviction that this was how it would be, made it so.

Which made it all the more extraordinary that Leonie was being asked this question.

'Mum, I don't think you should be asking me that,' she said. 'I'm 27.'

'I'm your mother. I have been concerned about something. Just promise me one thing.'

'What?'

'That you will not get involved with Michael Vellin, Lord Regis' man.'

Leonie felt 12 again, caught out in some heinous crime by her all knowing, all seeing mother. The blood rushed to her head, creating a thudding sensation around her ears. She felt guilty to the tips of her toes.

'Why would you think that?'

'I saw you together at the press conference. There was something. I detest him Leonie. He's a dangerous man. Ambitious, amoral, sexually ambivalent. He will hurt you.'

'Oh Mum. You're so overprotective. I can see what kind of man he is.'

'I hope so. Just remember, it has always been you and me and no one else.

'Of course I remember that. Don't worry Mum. I can handle him.'

Hours later, after Leonie had gone out and Ping Li had returned from the Embassy, the telephone rang. The clicks told Ping Li that this was her scrambled call. Harry Regis was on the line.

'What's up?' Harry knew better than to waste time. Even the best scramblers had only a few minutes before the combined might of Chinese state security, the US echelon satellites and various other interested parties unscrambled them. Ping Li knew too.

'That man of yours, Harry. He seems to know everything, yet he understands nothing. Where did he get this information? I thought Dragon was secret, yet he knows all about it.'

'How?'

'Some scientist at Quantum. Millington?'

'I thought that avenue was closed. They were unable to decipher the encrypted disc. And we – you – wiped it off the mainframe.'

'Nonetheless, Vellin knows.'

'He works for me. He belongs to me. He is my creature, my creation. I will make sure he doesn't step out of line. And he is useful.'

'He is dangerous. He came here for more information, to trade, to strengthen his arm. He hinted at blackmail. And now he is sniffing around our daughter.'

'I will stop that, I promise. And remember, he doesn't know she's my daughter.'

'Harry, he doesn't know anything, especially how stupid he is.'

Leonie was almost hysterical. She had been ringing constantly for almost two hours and there had been no response on any of Vellin's lines. This was unheard of; his many roles demanded that he should be always in touch -- and he always was. No one worked the phones like Vellin; it was a matter of pride to him to give the impression of being ubiquitous and all knowing. Even Leonie's subterfuge of using the Prince's private line, which would certainly be flashing up as such on Vellin's Blackberry, wasn't working. He was nowhere.

Leonie was panicking. She wanted to see him, to reassure herself on so many counts: mainly that her mother was wrong and that her feelings were right. She had always been dutiful and careful not to form any inappropriate relationships. The suggestion that a liaison with Vellin was unsuitable had wounded her deeply. Her mother had ingrained a very Chinese sense of propriety and fittingness in her daughter.

There had been no significant men in her life; studying had always come first and the men – boys, really -- were merely harmless dalliances. She knew she was extraordinarily attractive and she had never felt the pain of rejection. The goodbyes had always come from her, though carefully disguised to allow her victims some dignity. She had never felt this vivid pain before. The only man in her life, her father, was gone before she knew he was there. In fact, to all intents and purposes, he had never existed. Her mother never spoke about him and had been both mother and father. And that had been enough.

This lack had spared her the pain of his loss and instead had left her free to construct an idealised man from scratch. Leonie had imbued Vellin with all the heroic attributes her ideal man possessed; whether they were real or not mattered little in the full flush of first love. But she had no frame of reference for her hero being manipulative. And now he was ignoring her.

Was it because she had refused to invite Nancy to the lunch? Leonie couldn't believe that. As the only man she'd ever met who instinctively understood the hidden power plays that swirled around men like the Prince and Lord Regis, surely Vellin understood the hierarchy her world revolved around. The Prince was at the apex; everyone else ranked lower down, including her mother, the Chinese Ambassador and Vellin. It was one of the things that had drawn them together -- Leonie was certain of it. Like doctors and actors who often married other doctors and actors, their lives required such a particular set of skills that only someone in a similar occupation could truly understand the rigours and fit in.

However, her emotional hierarchy was something quite different. And there, Vellin sat at the very top of that pyramid. She longed to speak to him.

He answered the phone.

'Vellin.'

'It's me. Leonie.'

'Yes.' Flat. In fact, it was almost completely without inflexion. Leonie was unable to tell whether he had been watching his various phones ringing for two hours or whether he had just returned from a game of squash at his club.

'I wanted to speak to you.'

'Obviously.'

'Can I see you? I need to see you.'

Vellin felt a long sedated part of himself awaken and respond to the desperation in her voice. He had enjoyed his fling with Leonie. She was exquisite to look at and surprisingly passionate in bed. It made him feel powerful. It gave him a twinge of guilt, too. But that was swiftly superseded by rage: for some reason his association with Leonie had upset Regis. Somewhere, things had broken down and Leonie was in the middle of it somehow. Regis had been utterly cold and implacable in their conversation. Perhaps the old goat fancied her himself.

He had not been interested in Vellin's hints that he had found out more about the contents of Laffey's plastic bottle – batted them away, in fact. There had to be a reason. Frantically Vellin scrolled through the past few days in his memory. Yes, he had missed Regis' departure at Denham, but that was at least half Regis' fault for changing plans and not telling him. He had met Millington to find out more about Laffey's activities. He had spilled the beans to Ping Li – rash, but not a hanging offence. After all, Regis worked very closely with her. The rest of his time had been spent with Leonie. And one of these things had badly upset his boss. He didn't know how but he would find out. He quelled the urge to be kind to Leonie. He'd been screwed over; now she could see how it felt.

'I don't think so, Leonie. I have to leave for Azerbaijan at 5 am.'

'What? How long for? Why didn't you tell me? You can't go without seeing me.'

'I found out two hours ago. It is a new venture for Lord Regis…' And what was the phrase? '..and a reassignment of priorities for me.'

It was, in fact, exile -- and he knew it. And having been specifically banned from seeing Leonie, he wasn't going to rock the boat any further. The cosy symbiosis of the Regis/Vellin axis had unexpectedly exploded, leaving Vellin surprisingly off his game. He was determined to glue the constituent parts together. He was deeply attached to his master: both the relationship and the benefits that accrued from it were precious to him. He knew that they were precious to Regis too, some in an unspoken sense, which they both understood but which would never be surfaced. Which made Regis' adamantine cruelty even harder to understand. While Leonie was pining for Vellin, Vellin was in truth, pining for Regis.

'How about a quick drink?'

'Perhaps when I get back. I'm sorry Leonie. I have to go.'

He put down the phone and returned to his packing.

An hour later the doorbell rang. Not the external doorbell, where visitors spoke into an intercom and were buzzed in, but the small bell on Vellin's front door. He opened it, expecting to see Frank the porter bearing that day's post or a last, couriered message from Regis. Perhaps a reprieve. Part of Vellin appreciated the theatricality. How like Regis to send word by messenger – like a Tudor king pardoning his errant servant on the way to the guillotine.

It wasn't Frank. It was Leonie, looking small and exotic and emotional. She slid past him and Vellin closed the door behind her.

She immediately flung herself into his arms. 'I had to see you,' she said. Fleetingly, Vellin thought about putting her away from him. But the adoration on her face and her total lack of subterfuge left him unsteady. She was so unlike anyone he knew or had ever dealt with. His head was filled with her. He lifted her off her feet and kissed her with true rage. He dropped Leonie onto his bed where she lay, looking at him with love, her arms open, intoxicating in her utter lack of guile. Vellin fell on her hungrily, as though he could take her honesty and purity and absorb it through his skin. To hell with Regis and his interdictions. She made him feel good and he wanted her, now.

There was mist on the Thames outside the glass windows and the sun was just rising as Vellin prised Leonie's reluctant arms open to release him. She murmured and turned over in his bed, abandoned in sleep like a child. Vellin leaned down and kissed her.

'Get dressed, Leonie. The car can drop you off on the way to Heathrow if you're quick.'

When he walked back into the room with two latte's, Leonie was up, sleepy eyed, rumpled haired but already putting on her coat. Without a speck of makeup, she was still beautiful. He kissed her again – she smelled delicious. But Azerbaijan Airlines waited for no man and, besides, Eric the driver had already rung the doorbell twice.

Regis was feeling strangely unencumbered that morning. The weather was beautiful, he was glad to be home and he was at the top of his game. His usual preoccupations had reduced themselves to a manageable handful in a corner of his mind. He fleetingly wondered whether it could be something to do with Foote. They would be meeting in 30 minutes and he was actually looking forward to it. The relationship had brought a new lightness to him. Having someone to talk to – however much he kept back – had given him a sense of relief. And the man certainly had a way of getting to the nub of things, of releasing pressure points which had not appeared to need releasing until discovered. But then, Regis had not risen to the very top by dwelling on his weaknesses, and he was not at all sure that those he had could even be classed as such. Without the occasional fault line, there was no way he could even begin to identify and empathise with the thousands who worked for him. He prided himself on his ability to talk with crowds and walk with kings. The common touch. Those he admired most had possessed it.

Here, by illustration, was his driver, Eric, an Essex man with whom he shared a perfect understanding. The odd drink in a pub, an occasional illicit salt beef sandwich consumed while leaning on the bonnet of the Bentley outside Blooms on the Mile End road and a reasonably successful betting syndicate at the bookies – all these cemented a relationship between master and man which was as close, probably, as Regis had ever been to anyone. He imbibed Eric's NCO wisdom, often as informed as any of the broadsheets, and Eric, in return, got to regale his mates in the boozer with the doings of the rich and famous.

The heavy front door of the Connaught Square house banged shut behind him with the rattle of brass doorknobs and letterboxes as Regis bounded down the steps and into the

Bentley. The police sentry two doors down, guarding the house of an ever absent former prime minister, had taken to removing the traffic cones in front of Regis' house just in time for his driver's arrival. And there was Eric at the wheel, newspapers folded on the passenger seat and a steaming caffe latte from Coffnascenti in the cup holder. The daily ritual was unvarying on the days Regis was in London. He sank back into his deep leather seat with an inward sigh of pleasure and buried himself in the news. Eric knew better than to interrupt him – conversation was banned until Parliament Square, after which they would exchange their usual banter for the next ten minutes or so.

As they swung right past Churchill's statue, Eric spoke for the first time. 'Got young Vellin off to Baku first thing this morning.'

'Ah, good. Who was he flying with?'

'Azerbaijan, God help him,' said Eric, who despite his global knowledge of charter airlines and their destinations, had never once flown scheduled and could not have imagined the desolation that was Azerbaijan airlines. Regis chuckled, mainly because it seemed the correct response and he was feeling good this morning, but also because he enjoyed the thought of Vellin's discomfort; so, no doubt, did Farheen, who had booked the flight.

Encouraged, Eric continued.

'Packs it in, our Vellin. Dropped off his girl on the way. What a looker. Mind you, they do say these exotic types will inherit the earth. When we were in Thailand, every single pop star and everyone on telly was Eurasian. Hotel owner told us it was all the whiteys out there marrying the locals. The results are bleeding amazing. These ugly buggers and their Thai wives have incredibly beautiful children. It's like that *Hair,* isn't it? The musical. You know, "Coffee coloured people everywhere." Though she was more golden, like, Vellin's girl.'

Regis knew. He knew exactly. He was swamped with a rage so powerful he could hardly speak. His sense of wellbeing and bonhomie had deserted him in an instant. Vellin had disobeyed him and he would pay for it.

Vellin's gratitude to Heydro knew no bounds. He had been plucked out of the endless snaking queue at Baku's Heydar Aliyev airport where so far, he had been to the passport desk, back to the immigration office where an unshaven official had made a not very discreet attempt to extort money, then back to the passport desk where he had been for 40 minutes. No one looked even remotely concerned at the possibility that this might be the all-time nadir for an airport arrivals hall.

Vellin had been braced – 'worse even than Lagos,' read an internet report he had skimmed in the car – but this was of a different order to anywhere he had ever been. A pall of

Turkish cigarette smoke hung over the terminal and everyone, so far as Vellin could see, was doing his or her best to add to it. There was an unmistakeable smell of oil adding to the miasma – a reminder that this had been the home of oil exploration and exploitation since Zoroastrian times. Women, not particularly young nor alluring but thin -- and remarkable for the amount of makeup they had caked onto their faces -- were already making friends with the numerous single men in the line. Vellin was just rummaging for dollars in an attempt to speed things up when a man in fatigues carrying a sign bearing his name came up to him.

'Mischa Villain?'

'Close enough.'

'Come.'

The man held out his hand for Vellin's passport, passport photographs and immigration form and smartly removed the $40 from his hand. Guiding Vellin smoothly past 30 or 40 mutinous passengers, he handed the paperwork over to the passport officer while seamlessly pocketing, Vellin noticed, the $40. The visa was stamped instantly and they walked through a door guarded by a man with an AK47 to the back of the carousel where the baggage handlers were just beginning to unload the luggage from AZAL Flight 34. Several of them were heaving bags from the trailer onto the rubber track; several more were removing them again, seemingly at random. Vellin watched and noticed that those tightly cling filmed in thin plastic were left untouched, those with locks were put back and those looking relatively smart were removed and put back onto an empty carriage on the trailer, which promptly disappeared out of sight. Here, clearly, was the source of Baku's reputation as the graveyard of checked baggage.

Vellin's companion turned to him.

'Your bag?'

Vellin pointed to the Mulberry Albany Duffle just coming off the trailer. He felt foolish travelling with so obvious a target. But there had been no time to buy anything else when the company jet had suddenly and mysteriously become unavailable. Farheen had been adamant.

The bodyguard took the bag and slung it over his shoulder with a grunt. He then started walking out on to the airport apron, Vellin following closely behind. A MBB BO105 helicopter, emblazoned Caspian Air, was just rotating its blades and they ran the final stretch, bent over to the door and scrambled in, helped up by a young soldier waiting in the cabin. Vellin belted himself in and put on the headset he was handed as the helicopter lifted up into the air and began to fly over the destroyed lunarscape that was Azerbaijan.

General Thalie Heydro had long since ceased to ally himself with anyone except those who served his immediate interests. He'd had a shaky start to his military career: two years as a grunt in what was then the Azerbaijani Soviet

Socialist Republic Army, fighting the endless outbreaks of independent-mindedness which afflicted all the Soviet states in the Caucasus. Then he had seen the light and joined the Azerbaijani National Oil Corporation as a humble plumber. From there he had worked his way into the upstream arm – the prospecting side -- of the Azerbaijani National Oil Corporation, and by 1986 found himself in charge of some of the roughest wells in the land. Already one of the most notorious figures on Azerbaijan's black market, he had set up his own distribution networks and cross-border trade, mainly serving the small pseudo-autonomous states (oblasts) dotted around the edges of the mighty Russian federation, when the 1990 Nagorno Karabakh war broke out. A small, predominantly Armenian region, it was fighting for independence from Azerbaijan and ultimately the USSR. Unwilling to let a good thing slip out of his hands trade-wise, and still strongly pro-Soviet, Heydro formed an armed group which, backed by the Russians, made early and significant inroads into the region. His reward was to be appointed official representative in Nagorno Karabakh and the neighbouring regions.

This was probably a mistake on the part of the newly independent Azerbaijani Government. Heydro was becoming over-mighty and certainly more important than the post he held. Strongly supported by the mighty 104th airborne division of the Soviet Airborne Troops, headquartered nearby, he was able to rely on them to the extent that when asked to disband his detachments, he refused. By 1992, aged 33, Heydro was a General; by the end of the war, in 1994, the Government made a feeble last attempt to disarm him. It ended in abysmal failure; on departure, the Soviet Airborne Division had bolstered him further by donating their arms and equipment to his forces. Subsequent attempts to indict him for treason sputtered out, especially when international bodies tasked with procuring peace in the Caucasus advised tolerance rather than toughness to the governors of the new republic. Master of all he surveyed, Heydro was left in peace to run his own, by then considerable, affairs.

He refused to return the compliment. A nationalist to the core, albeit one with Soviet sympathies, he was disgusted by the 1994 'Contract of the Century,' which allowed Western companies to extract oil from the Caspian sea. Heydro's forces marched on Baku, only halting 20 kilometres away. Almost instantly, Heydro was granted his demand to become the Azerbaijani Minister of Mineral Rights, Customs and Borders, an ideal calling for one blessed with his particular talents. He also asked for and got a seat on the board of the newly formed Azerbaijan International Oil Consortium.

It was in this role that Thalie Heydro had met and marked the man who was later to become Lord Regis of Clutton Champflower. By 1994, Harry Regis had already risen through International Fertilisers to the position of CEO; the many areas of overlap between his and Heydro's industries had necessitated many long meetings, followed as their friendship blossomed by hunting parties in the mountainous highlands of Karabakh and shooting parties on Regis' Somerset estate. Lord Regis' *ennobling* was attended by a very few select friends, Heydro among them. Negotiations over the Trans-Caspian Oil Pipeline, between Azerbaijan and Kazakhstan, had been one of their most cherished joint projects and were still in the offing. Now Regis had sent his man, this Michael Vellin, over to help lay the groundwork.

Vellin climbed out of the helicopter, its blades still rotating and walked, head lowered, over to where the General awaited him. He stuck out his hand, which Heydro ignored, instead pulling him closer in an approximation of a bear hug. 'Welcome to the wild East,' he roared over the whine of the engines winding down. Releasing Vellin, he turned, heading for a top-of-the-range Hummer parked on the edge of the helipad. Stretching out in every direction were oil rigs, drills, nodding donkeys and vast chunks of pipe in a desolate wasteland dedicated solely to denuding the earth of its wealth. Despite his disgust at his exile, Vellin felt his interest quicken at the sight. The sheer majesty of so much dedicated and monumental machinery would have appealed to the Boy's Own in any man.

In truth, Heydro was not much impressed by Vellin. Despite his blood-soaked past he held himself to a strictly macho code, and the immaculately-groomed, metrosexual Vellin gave off too many conflicting signals. Heydro had a wife and two mistresses and attended to them well, materially and physically. He wasn't sure Vellin would have the wherewithal in any department. At least Regis, despite his small stature, was a player. It was one of the things Heydro and Regis had enjoyed together. Both appreciated beautiful woman and there were many in Azerbaijan. Interestingly, he had noticed Vellin's flick of the eyes towards the young soldier who had brought him in. Was that the way he was oriented? The thought repelled Heydro but he filed it away. Knowledge was power.

Vellin walked into his suite at the Excelsior and thanked the genius who had seen fit to build a decent hotel in Baku. The all pervading scent of petrochemicals – the very essence of this oil soaked land -- was less powerful in here, thanks to the heavily-scented soaps and bath oils arranged around the palatial marble bathroom, but it had already seeped into everything he wore. He removed his clothes as he patrolled his new quarters. A bowl of caviar on ice – the very best Beluga – and a bottle of vodka awaited him on the side table, together with a note from the General, who had accompanied him back to Baku, inviting him for dinner that night. That was two hours away. Vellin decanted half a bottle of bath oil into the tub and turned on the taps.

Vellin would never be entirely clear in his mind about the events of the ensuing few hours. He had considered ignoring

363

the doorbell, then finally opened the door in his bathrobe to find the young soldier from the helicopter standing there. The young man stepped forward, his hands moving under the bathrobe with complete assurance. Fleetingly, Vellin considered that it must be a set up, equally fleetingly wondered what the point of such a set up would be, then gave himself up to what was on offer.

Dinner with Heydro had followed in a haze. The caviar consumed, the vodka drunk, Vellin had descended with his young friend to the very plush, padded dining room – like one of those Brussels dining rooms patronised by EU bureaucrats, thought Vellin. Heydro had ignored Vellin's companion and pressed yet more icy vodka on Vellin before dining. As it hit, the vodka had an extraordinary effect on him; though he was present and could still communicate, Vellin felt, with extraordinary fluency, that another part of him was also operating on a higher level. He was not at all inebriated. He felt a sense of utter clarity; that he could see all things. The food courses passed his lips without registering on his taste buds. He was beyond such earthly sensations.

The next image to imprint itself on his memory was the nightclub. He remembered the name, 'The Most', because it was illuminated in blue ultra violet on the wall behind the solid mass of dancers moving as one to the techno-trance music. His soldier lover was with him and they danced and lay on vast white leather sofas and embraced and drank yet more vodka. Slowly Vellin had become aware that the club was full only of men. The fabulous women patrolling the bar were male cross dressers; one leaned down from her vertiginous heels and said to Vellin 'You very pretty boy,' in a deep growl as she passed. 'Hostesses' wore spangles straight out of *la Cage aux Folles*. Rougher trade, looking like extras from a gangster movie, stood around in groups. Two men together seemed utterly unworthy of notice. Vellin was on a wonderful, pure high; the sensation was most akin to cocaine he thought – he had once rubbed it onto his gums in an Islington warehouse.

Very suddenly he felt sick. He knew he was going to throw up and crashed out of the double fire escape doors he found in the corridor by the bar. Leaning over a bin he heaved, then stood shivering in the underground garage he found himself in. Bed, he should go to bed. But he had left Vassily and his leather jacket in 'The Most.' He couldn't decide which he needed more. But the fire doors had locked behind him and no-one could hear him banging through the din.

He started walking unsteadily through the cars towards where he thought the front door of the club should have been. Then he hit a brick wall. A huge man in a leather donkey jacket, palm flat against Vellin's chest, pushed him backwards, up against a pillar. Vellin fought back feebly but was then surrounded by other men who punched him to the ground, kicked him and jeered. Vellin was vaguely aware of cracking sounds and blood pouring through holes where his teeth should have been. They hauled him up, ransacked his pockets, removed his watch and shoes, turned him round and pulled his trousers down. He struggled in vain as two men held him up against the wall while he was repeatedly raped. They dropped him again and then someone jumped on him. For a moment he was bleakly, horribly sober, then he lost consciousness.

Sister Edwards was crisp and brisk. Her white hat was that rare thing in a modern British hospital, a masterpiece of starched origami. On her shoulders the pips bore her rank: Queen Alexandra's nursing corps were sticklers for doing things correctly. She held the plastic cup to Vellin's lacerated lips and fitted the straw through the hole where his incisor should have been. He drank obediently, grateful for the smallest act of kindness.

The journey home in the company jet, now converted to an air ambulance, had been part of a nightmare 36 hours. Vellin, adrift in a sea of pain, had floated on morphine as images, like flashbulb memories, had intermittently imprinted themselves on his mind. Being found, more dead than alive, by the nightclub cleaners as they readied the bins for collection at dawn. Awaking in agony to find himself in his suite at the Excelsior, attended by a doctor and nurses and General Heydro. The General's face dissolving into soft focus as painful consciousness and humiliation fled with a merciful injection. Heydro's expression of complete disgust. Being loaded onto the flight in a stretcher, groaning at the bumps. The butch, expressionless, Stasi-esque female sitting by his side all the way home, changing drips and topping up his opiates. The private ambulance in London, whisking him to the comfort of the King Edward private hospital just off Harley Street. The shock of seeing his face in the mirror.

Vellin had a broken sternum, ribs, arm and leg, a fractured jaw, a ruptured spleen and a torn rectum. But none of these physical torments could compete with the horrors he anticipated at the hands of Lord Regis. He had imagined the interview with Regis in such detail and with such intensity, he was almost relieved to see his employer walk into the room behind the starched assurance that was Sister Edwards.

The relief lasted a nanosecond. Regis' face was unreadable to most but years of assiduous study enabled Vellin to see the fury holding the man's jaw taut.

After tinkering with the drips, Sister Edwards tactfully withdrew: she must have sensed the coming storm, thought Vellin. And then it broke.

'Are you utterly corrupted? Do you have any idea of the extent to which the utter squalor of your activities in Azerbaijan repels me.' Regis was quiet and articulate, at his most lethal.

'I was mugged.' Vellin's mangled jaw mashed the words.

'And buggered, yes. By a bunch of thugs set up by the pretty boy you installed in your suite almost the second you got there. Tell me, is this kind of behaviour habitual for you? Consorting with male prostitutes?'

'He was a guard. He worked for your friend. I thought he sent him.'

'I think not. Why would he have imagined that you might need such company? Heydro likes women. In fact, he loves them. Where would he have got the idea that you might prefer men?'

'He arrived at my door,' said Vellin sulkily.

'And that was enough, was it? Anyone who arrives at your door had better watch out. How about me? I've just got here. Any sudden urges you would like to own up to. The love that dares not speak its name?'

With an instinct not entirely blunted by trauma, Vellin saw clearly for the first time that there was something, or there had been something between him and Regis. Man and master had crossed a line somewhere. While Vellin had fostered an interdependence and even a symbiosis with Regis, he had never imagined that his shadowy gropings in Islington warehouses could ever cross over into real life. But here it was. His shadow side had crossed with Regis' shadow side and both were left horribly exposed. And even if Regis was not completely aware of why he was so angry, his rage was being fuelled by the sublimation of a powerful urge. Vellin hadn't just fucked Vassily; he hadn't fucked Regis.

Vellin tried to tap the remaining shreds of the bond they had once shared.

'I can't explain it. I was tired, upset. I felt I'd been exiled. I was lonely. I just needed human comfort.'

'And the Prince's assistant was not enough to provide that the night before you left? Despite my clear – very clear -- instructions? She stayed the night at your apartment. My driver dropped her home on your journey to the airport. He reported that she was all over you. Careless, Michael, very careless. And I suppose she arrived at your door too.'

'She did.'

'Am I expected to believe these people drop into your lap like ripe fruit? That for all these years I have been harbouring the Casanova of the bisexual world. I'm sure Leonie Li will be distraught to know just how catholic your tastes are.'

At he thought of Leonie, Vellin had a pang – rare for him. For some reason he didn't want her to think badly of him. He wanted to be the man she thought he was. He begged.

'Don't tell her, please.'

'What could your pleading possibly mean to me? I told you to leave her alone. You didn't. I told you it was important. You thought your physical needs were more so. Now she will be told what kind of a man you are.'

Desperate to protect Leonie – where was this coming from? – Vellin rallied. 'Why would you do that? It doesn't affect her work, our relationship with the Prince. She's utterly professional. She doesn't deserve this.'

'You're dead right. And I will make sure my daughter never has to deal with it again. I gave you a chance to redeem yourself. Instead you got sent home for bad behaviour from the very arsehole of the universe. You have failed me disobeyed me, betrayed me. You disgust me. It's over.'

For Vellin, it was over from the moment he heard the words, 'my daughter.' He might have survived the Baku incident, maybe even the thwarting of Regis's unspoken affections. But this was terminal.

Leonie was Regis's daughter, the beautiful child he had never been able to acknowledge or to enjoy. He, Vellin, had possessed her through his shallow arts, screwed her, leaving her father raging and impotent. The man who never destroyed anyone unknowingly had unknowingly destroyed himself. Vellin knew he was dead.

'If I could fire you, I would,' said Regis. 'But Human Resources would never let me get away with that while you are lying in a hospital bed, whatever you did to deserve it. Think of the law suits, the compensation. So, instead, Nancy will take control of your functions. You will report directly to her.'

The cold spite made Vellin weak. Suddenly the morphine seemed inadequate. He desperately wanted Sister Edwards. He closed his eyes.

Regis hadn't finished. He leant over Vellin for his parting shot.

'You've probably got AIDS.'

Leaving the King Edward's, Regis found himself in the side streets of Marylebone, lost in a way that he had never felt lost before. The car stayed outside the clinic, Eric unsure what to do when he saw Lord Regis stride off. Regis walked north up a mews at the back of The Orrery, making for Regent's Park. He wanted to walk and think in a way that he hadn't wanted since the time Ping Li had told him they had created a child all those years ago. He had felt then as he did now: that forces he didn't know he had released might have sent his world crashing down. He knew there was no escape, but he also knew there was no-one he could turn to but himself. It wasn't exactly panic he was experiencing, he thought, but he would have been hard-put to find a better word. Except that compared with the last time, the rage he felt now was overwhelming. He could see why men might kill.

The complete disaster of Baku was one thing. It might have been better, thought Regis, if the gang rape had simply ended in Vellin's death. At least that could have been managed. Diplomacy would have worked its magic across police boundaries, and there could have been an announcement of a tragedy from which IFL would certainly have recovered. But Vellin would now be useless at every level, damaged goods beyond any possibility of repair. And he knew too much now. He was a serious threat although a little judicious blackmail could neutralise that. Above all, Regis had to protect the Chinese interests, come what may.

But much worse than that, Vellin had possessed his daughter and he, Regis, was the unwitting cause of the misery that Leonie would now endure. He would be forced to endure the scorn that Ping Li would heap upon him. She had, after all, warned him. He had utterly failed Leonie at every conceivable level of what a father might be to a daughter. And there was no thinkable way of repairing that.

It was then that he realised how deeply he had yearned over many years that one day Ping Li would agree to Leonie knowing who he really was. He had seen Leonie in recent weeks operating as the young and independent woman she had become under Ping Li's influence, and had felt the great emptiness of his life with Marcia. There was nothing in it he would ever want to hang on to, and now this realisation flooded through him, creating a level of despair he had never known before.

And then he found himself taking out his telephone to call Foote.

'It's Regis,' he said as Foote's picked up the phone on the first ring. Regis was so bound up with his own pain he was unable to recognise the strain in the other man.

'Can I see you? There's something you might help me with.'

Foote was trying – and failing – to write. His mind was full of terrible imaginings of what could have happened to Hester and Freya, and as he always had in times of stress, he resorted to the certainties of his work. But no words would come. His mind betrayed him. He was blank. Blank and scared. In a distant way, as though he was prodding a poisonous snake, he sampled the realities of the amygdala hijack, where the emotional part of the brain suspended all

377

rational thought, replacing it with raw fear. He had taught countless clinical psychology students how to recognise it; now here it was, up close and personal. He was stunned at how paralysing it was, despite his wealth of knowledge and understanding. He could do nothing useful at the greatest crisis of his life, except wait impotently. Regis, at least, would provide some valuable displacement activity.

'Of course. Come now,' he said.

Regis handed the phone to Eric so that he might hear the directions, then remembered with a pang that Foote was facing his own demons. When Eric handed the phone back again, he dialled Seb, his man. No answer. He would try again later.

Within 15 minutes, Lord Regis was banging upon the door of a tall, thin house that he recognized as one of London's gems. By a church, in one of the quieter and greener Kensington squares, it was a perfect – though surprisingly expensive – bolt hole for two unworldly academics.

The door, particularly finely made and painted a dark forest green, opened to reveal Foote, looking unshaven and unkempt. His eyes were red ringed and he looked profoundly worn.

The unaccustomed words came pouring out of Regis,

'I am so sorry. My man is doing all he can.'

Foote said nothing, simply gestured to a narrow hallway and a door leading off it. Regis found himself sitting opposite the psychologist, each of them in a winged armchair with the roughness of uncut moquette beneath the palms that lay on the chair arms. A small fire flickered in the grate.

Foote sat in silence, partly because he found it hard to generate any rational speech. He consoled himself that he was leaving Regis time to think. More importantly, he was leaving him time to feel. There was a danger, of course, that Lord Regis would simply use the time to re-assemble his feeling system into its usual impenetrability. But Foote would take a risk on that because, for Regis to have phoned him in the way he did and have come to see him was unusual enough for there to be other ways in, if necessary.

'If I knew exactly why I called you when I did,' said Lord Regis, 'I would tell you. But the fact is that a number of things have happened that... I feel less sure of things than I normally am. And I thought you might help me settle my thoughts.'

Foote kept his silence. Having real time to think was such an extraordinary luxury for a man in Regis's position that it worked a magic of its own. Foote kept a gentle, steadfast gaze upon Regis whose own gaze wandered until it came back to rest on Foote's from time to time, almost as if to check that Foote was still there before another peregrination took place.

Ten minutes or more elapsed like this. Neither man registered time passing, only the sense of an immediate presence. Foote watched Regis closely, although without appearing in any way inquisitive. He knew that to look as if he was about to raise a question would immediately take Regis away from exploring his own inner workings. Foote had no idea why Regis was there and could have hypothesised endlessly, trying a series of more-or-less clever questions. But his own miseries kept him mute and observant, which seemed to be as effective as anything he could conjure up. The safest thing was to wait, however long it took.

'I can't see my way out of this one at all,' said Regis eventually, more by way of a reflective comment to himself than a deliberate communication to Foote. And then he lapsed back into silence, looking only at the toe-caps of his highly polished shoes. Foote had thought, about four minutes previously, when Regis had stretched his legs and crossed his ankles, that something might be said soon: as if stretching the legs signalled an easing of some process that had let Regis unwind a little. Now he saw the legs gradually being withdrawn again and Regis losing the slightly more relaxed posture he had been slipping into, as if a decision had been made that would require his feet for action.

'Thank you, Dr Foote,' said Lord Regis. 'You have given me time gather my thoughts. Forgive me if I do not tell you what is troubling me. I need to give it more time. But I feel calmer than I did. We are to meet the day after tomorrow, I think, and I shall look forward to seeing you then.'

Foote stayed sitting while Lord Regis left the study with no more social interaction than if he were quitting his own house.

Foote let the whole episode settle into his system. Lord Regis had been through something so profound that he had actually asked for something by ringing him. Foote considered the extraordinary possibility that he had developed some deeply-felt level of trust with Regis. Only a future session would make it clear exactly where and how deeply the levels of trust lay. He felt unusually exhausted by what had passed. He closed his eyes, his head turned against the wing of the old armchair and slept.

Nancy was not a frequenter of hospital bedsides. With a start, she realised she had never been into a private hospital in London before and found, as she did with so many things that she derogated as 'British', that somehow the systems were designed to disquiet her.

King Edward's Hospital for Officers, located in quietly efficient opulence in a small side street off the Marylebone High Street, had managed not to let itself be sucked into the rapacious maw of the National Health Service at its founding in 1948, when the British Government had done the deals it had to grab the real estate, as well as keep the doctors quiet. But none of that history was known to Nancy. What she experienced was an institution still run with a humming order which she found disquieting. There was nothing here that was not properly placed or not entirely understood and therefore, not a world that Nancy knew or trusted. She only felt safe when she knew where the enemy was.

The fifth floor nursing station made sure they knew who she was before letting her knock on Vellin's door. Even that seemed to her like a violation of her rights. It was as if clinical care outdid security considerations, and that was an entirely unfamiliar possibility to Nancy's machinating mind.

Vellin would come to wish the system had been quite impenetrable to Nancy. Physical pain was one thing. At least endorphins could do their bit to suppress it, and help from opiates was at hand. But the emotional pain Nancy could inflict was something else.

Nancy had not primarily come to see Vellin because of corporate matters. Lord Regis had assigned all Vellin's functions to her. There were doubtless useful pieces of information that were to be had from Vellin that could be extracted in due course. But Nancy had a score to settle and she was not one to bear humiliation lightly.

Nancy's arrival back in the UK for the Prince's lunch at the Palace was something that would forever rankle in her soul. After the corporate jet had touched down in the early morning, Nancy had rung the Prince's office as soon as she decently could. She had thought she could engage with Leonie in woman's talk. With only four hours before presenting herself for the luncheon, Nancy had had some serious preening to do. And the chance to chat on a more intimate basis to Leonie was not one to miss.

However, she had had difficulty getting through to Leonie. That irritated. If her own name didn't ring bells with the functionary who had answered the phone, she was surprised that her title and company didn't seem to speed things up. It was only when Nancy had impressed the functionary with the urgency of her need to talk to Leonie about that day's luncheon that she had been put through.

Nancy had launched straight into her girly chat. She had been told she did it very well and she rarely used it, but on this occasion it had come out full force and brilliantly polished. But far from getting the reception she had expected she heard Leonie say: 'But Miss Hammer, I think there must be some confusion. I very much regret that you are not on the Prince's luncheon invitation list today. If there's anything I can do to help on dress codes for some future occasion, I should be delighted, but today's luncheon is entirely to do with His Royal Highness's interests in architecture and International Fertilisers has not been an active participant in these discussions.'

Nancy had not felt a lurch in her stomach like this since she was chosen last for the baseball team at the age of 10.

Even prepared, Leonie felt the full, unrelenting quality of Nancy's ire. She remained implacable however, and Nancy realized it was a lost cause. All Nancy knew was that she had been led into making the most profound social gaffe by

Vellin. As her rage and humiliating despair gradually shifted into cold, long-term revenge, she understood that Regis must have been complicit in too.

Clearly he had not wanted her in China. Vellin had pressed exactly the right buttons to bring her back to London: he had read her vanity like a book. He had it coming.

A heavily bandaged and surprisingly pathetic Vellin did not put Nancy off her stroke one bit. That he was awake was a slight disappointment. She had imagined him waking to find her standing over him. As it was, she had to appear more as a visitor than the avenging angel that she intended.

'So,' she said, asking nothing of his state of health, 'are you going to tell me now, quickly, or will I have to drag it out of you?'

Vellin lay there, eyes staring to the ceiling after the first flicker of contact to see who had arrived. 'Fuck off' was what he most wanted to say, but he wasn't sure he could get it out with enough conviction in his jaw-locked state. But it was worth a try. Ventriloquists could do it without having to move their jaws.

But ventriloquists practice a great deal to use the muscles of their tongues very adroitly, and his weren't in the best of shape. 'Suck off' was what it sounded like, and not very forcefully at that.

A more generous woman than Nancy, even one seeking revenge, would have known in that instant that Vellin was finished and that he knew it. A more astute woman would have turned on her heel and left, leaving Vellin only to dread the coming storm. But Nancy had scores to settle and she was neither generous nor astute.

'Let's start with your job description, then, shall we?' she said.

Vellin knew she couldn't know the particular horrors of the injuries from which he suffered. There were stories he had heard of European mercenaries being locked in African jails where they were used at will by African prisoner gangs for the wildest forms of buggery. 'Slow puncture' it was called, a reference to the HiV they invariably contracted. Vellin's only relief was that he was at least in the care of those trained by Queen Alexander's Nursing Corps to turn crisp sheets down precisely. But he knew that Nancy was going to do her best to do a slow puncture on his ego. Little did she know that Lord Regis has done the deflation job already. There wasn't any air left. 'Go away,' said Vellin, mustering what reserves he could. 'Thith ith harassment.' Again the sibilants let him down.

'I don't think so, said Nancy. 'In any event this conversation never happened. So let's get back to your job description.'

Vellin went deep inside himself, to a place that he had only been once before. Somewhere around the age of eight, in the orphanage that had been the only home he had known, he had been surprised to be told that an aunt and uncle were going to come and take him out for the weekend. He wasn't quite sure what was involved but it seemed to excite the interest of the other kids, who said he was lucky to go on a Saturday and not come back until teatime on Sunday.

What happened he could never quite describe, even to himself, for he could not place it at all. As soon as he had been put into the back of a car -- the first one he could ever remember being in -- a lady had said there was a game they were going to play and everything was a great secret and they were going to go to magic place and have lots of fun but it was so magic he had to put a hood over his head so it stayed really, really secret. And she had slipped a hood over his head and had tied it quite loosely at the back, but enough so that he couldn't ease it off, not even in the night by himself, and it had stayed there until he came back to the orphanage the next day and the lady wasn't there any more.

No, that wasn't quite true, about it staying there all the time. He was given something to eat and drink two or three times, but for that he had to sit at a table in a completely dark room and the hood was taken off and someone stood behind him and guided his hands to food that came in crunchy bar shapes and a beaker of orange juice. And his face was washed with a flannel after he had eaten and before the hood went back on. And he must have slept at some stage but he couldn't remember that.

But he remembered quiet grown up voices and hands all over his body and things being pushed into him. He couldn't understand it, any of it.

For days after he came back to the orphanage little Vellin had not spoken. He didn't answer the other kid's questions. When he wouldn't speak they teased him. He just stayed silent. He didn't now know how long it was before he spoke willingly again. He half remembered seeing the doctor who paid a weekly visit to the orphanage. He asked him why he wasn't speaking; but he wouldn't tell them. He never saw the aunt and uncle again.

Now, unable to escape physically, Vellin found that same place of utter silence within himself again. It did not require that anything be explained or understood. Indeed, that was its beauty. It was a place completely without explanation or understanding. In there, he just was: completely and utterly uncomprehendingly self-sufficient. It wasn't even frightening. In there, he could survive. And, curiously, it was Nancy who had triggered the opening of the door through which he could pass. The pain of Azerbaijan had kept him too much in his present. Nancy had required that he retreat. And lo and behold, there was a place to which to go, and this time it felt good. He would stay here, he thought.

Nancy had been waiting for some kind of a response. She needed him to be in play. This complete withdrawal was not something she had expected at all. It stoked her fury.

'It's no good playing catatonic with me,'said Nancy. 'We get down to business or I fire you. Which way is it going to be?'

Vellin hardly heard her, but deep inside himself he knew she wouldn't fire him. At least not yet. He understood that Nancy would need some public displays of her triumph back in IFL.

And then he remembered suddenly that there was a way out. He stretched out a hand and pressed the button for the nurse who appeared almost before the bell ring had died away.

'I'm hurting, Nurse,' he lisped, and the nurse needed no further suggestion.

'I shall have to attend to Mr Vellin,' she said, indicating the door, 'and Mr Vellin will have a sedative.'

'Good for you, nursey' thought Vellin in mild triumph, and he closed his eyes as he heard Nancy rise from her chair. He took no further part in the proceedings, but as he floated off on a cloud of morphine, he heard her say to the nurse: 'Tell Mr Vellin that I shall keep in contact to see how his recovery is progressing: and I shall come to see him as soon as we are able to sustain a conversation.' And with that she left.

Vellin knew he had only won a skirmish in what would be a long war of attrition; but at least he had won for now.

Vellin swam up to alertness with difficulty after hearing his name, spoken again and again, in a sweet, low voice, which he associated with good things. He knew he had to get past the tendrils clinging to his consciousness, pulling him back down into drowning torpor. With a last, fierce kick of his mind, he emerged into a hospital room with Leonie sitting looking down at him.

She looked anxious, tearful and relieved. 'Michael, thank God.' She leaned forward and kissed him. He flinched. Leonie noticed, misinterpreted, and put her hand out to stroke his ruined face.

'It's OK, don't worry. I'm here. I'll look after you. We'll get you better. Your face will be fine.'

Nothing would ever be fine between him and Leonie again, but her sweetness and beauty lulled him into a reverie of what life could have been. Time stretched out while he contemplated the imminent and terminal demise of his finer self. He thought about his interview with Regis, about the utter hopelessness of his position now. The scene with Nancy had been the final nail in the coffin. Leonie and he settled into a pieta of injured hero and sorrowful lover: all false, thought Vellin bitterly. She was leaning her head on his bandaged ribs now, her arms spread across him, and he used the sudden agonising twinge to sharpen him into action.

'No.' He pushed her away. Leonie sat up, confused. 'Never again. We're finithed.' He could hear the hiss, like a drunk's lisp, coming from his tattered lips and through the gap in his teeth. He tried harder. 'I never want to theee you or your father again.'

'My father?' Leonie was bewildered now.

'Regis'

'What are you talking about?'

He summoned up every ounce of his strength and tried to enunciate clearly. 'Regis ith your father. He taught your mother at Cambridge. He has ruined my life. Tho I am ruining yours. Now get out.'

Leonie stared at him madly for a few seconds, then picked up her bag and ran.

Out on the terrace, a cigarette smouldering unattended in her fingers, Ping Li gazed out over the Square and wondered, for the millionth time, whether she had made a terrible mistake. Her daughter, always the very essence of collectedness, had flung the front door open and walked straight to her room, where she still lay, sobbing on her bed. Ping Li could only gather that she knew at last who her father was and that Vellin had told her. But how did he know? She and Harry had always kept their secret and neither had ever told. She was sure of that. She had to talk to Harry. She stubbed the cigarette out in a planter, flicked it over the edge into the garden below and went inside to find the phone.

Regis was just attending his ivory collection, removing motes of dust with a camera lens puffer – as a general indicator of his mental state, the more minute the activity, the higher his stress level – as his private line lit up. He picked up immediately.

'Harry, Leonie knows everything.'

'How?'

'Your man Vellin.'

Regis felt the blood drain away into his feet, a sensation he had not felt since he was carpeted at 15 by the head man for smoking. He did not bother to deny he had revealed the truth to Vellin.

'How is she?'

'Distraught. Of course. '

He let that hang there while he thought in his new, detached way. Ping Li attacked again.

'Why did you let this happen?'

There were so many answers to that. Ping Li would understand none of them. Indeed, several might enrage and disgust her.

'I must see her.'

'She doesn't want to see you. She says she hates you.'

Regis felt a clutch of anxiety. He had driven the raptor Vellin away from Leonie but he had damaged her in the process. Now, she was even less attainable than before. He struck out in frustration.

'Why didn't you let me tell her before now?'

Ping Li couldn't resist twisting the knife a little. Twenty five years earlier she had felt a similar agony as Regis married for his head, not his heart, leaving her with a one year old infant. It was only luck that she had left his name off the original birth certificate – luck and a desire to make sure that her family, who had long eyes, as they said in China, would not know his identity.

'You were married to Marcia. It was not suitable. Better an imaginary father than the reality.'

'I haven't done so badly in the world.' He was proud of what he had achieved, this prodigiously clever boy from nowhere, who rose through grammar school via Cambridge to become a master of the universe.

'You have succeeded at everything that matters, except this.'

She put down the phone.

Harry Regis didn't really know how to take such damning criticism. Since their rapprochement, Ping Li had always had an unerring eye for his welfare and had guided him away from many diplomatic minefields, especially with the Chinese. He had been dimly aware that this suited the direction in which they all wanted to go and had been happy to allow it to carry him along. But somewhere he had imagined she still loved him. His vanity, and his enduring love for Ping Li, prevented him from looking more deeply.

If he had failed at being Leonie's father, it was because Ping Li had ensured that he failed. She had left him in the wilderness for almost eight years, when she was so angry about Marcia. He still had no real idea why she had contacted him again after the big chill – except that by then, he was clearly on his way to the very top. Her excellent brain and level of education, combined with total intransigence about returning to China, had finally resulted in her being made the Chinese Scientific Attaché, with the assurance that she would remain in London for the foreseeable future. Nothing if not pragmatic, the Chinese. And Ping Li's friends in high places were unequalled in their altitude.

By the time she contacted him again, their child was nine and Harry Regis was lonely. His wife had been exposed for the grasping, shallow, snob that she was. All he had to do was keep Marcia in the style to which she was accustomed and she would tolerate him. With his meteoric rise, Marcia obviously felt that she had done all that was required of her and could now reap the rewards.

The heroic sex had worn off with the honeymoon. The lack of children and the ensuing basic and intrusive medical investigations had separated them further. Inwardly, the knowledge that he had fathered a healthy child gave him a small, psychological advantage over his stick-thin wife. He was sure that she was sleeping with the Prince and he found he didn't care much. He was mildly impressed by the Princely assumption that another man could fund his pleasures – polo teams, yachts, planes, gifts, women. Marcia was just another freebie for this Prince, and some would have felt honoured to become a gilded cuckold. Regis did not, particularly.

As a result, after eight long years, when the call came from the lover he should have married, Regis leapt at it. He was grateful, where perhaps he should have been more questioning. After all, Ping Li had managed total silence without a single waiver. But Regis had missed her, and even when she made it clear that there would be no physical relationship, he was glad just to have her friendship. It was lonely at the top: not only was the air thinner, there were very few, true friends.

Ping Li had carefully kept him away from Leonie, too. She was always at school or boarding or overnighting with friends when he came to Cadogan Square. Photographs around the apartment showed the exquisite child, teenager, graduate, he was missing. Leonie had never had an ugly day in her life, and she was obviously clever and industrious — a perfect mix of her parents' finer attributes.

Yet he had missed her entire childhood. He couldn't think too hard about it or he might howl with anguish. Regis had discovered a well of sentiment within him that he had never suspected. These days, on occasions, it threatened to overwhelm him. He blamed – and needed – Dr Andrew Foote. But he had his own misery to deal with.

Ping Li sat on the edge of Leonie's bed with a cup of tea and a marmite and cheddar sandwich. It was an unlikely favourite of her sylph-like daughter, but a favourite nonetheless. Leonie was lying motionless on her front, her face protected by an arm flung up, but her mother could tell she was awake and alert.

'Leonie, listen for a minute. Don't say anything, just listen. I didn't tell you about Harry Regis to protect you. He was my tutor. It would have ended his career if it were known that he had seduced a student and fathered a baby. I didn't want that. I owed him a great deal.

'Anyway, I didn't need to. I was secure enough. You know enough about our family in China to know I had no life there. Luckily, because of your father, I had finished my PhD in inorganic chemistry and was valuable here. Eventually I persuaded the family in China that I was of more use to them here, too. Which meant I could bring my daughter up in Britain, free and unencumbered. I could educate you as I wished -- and I did. Your father hardly mattered, in a way. We became friends again later, for different reasons. We were useful to each other then.'

Leonie spoke from under her arm. 'Did you love each other?'

The question asked by every child of every separated parent. 'Yes, of course. Completely. But then he hurt me.'

Leonie was too immersed in her own pain to hear her mother's – still acute after 26 years. 'You could still have told me.'

'I could. Maybe that was a mistake. But you seemed so complete. I didn't want you wishing for something impossible.'

'I always wondered. And you always let me think he had died.'

He did die, in a way, thought Ping Li. That was how she had managed to get over the greatest misery of her life. At the time, she could not believe that Harry would marry someone else: she had loved him so much. So she had killed him off in her mind. Eight years of rigorously expunging all lingering traces of affection had done the trick and then she could sublimate what was left into a perfectly affable friendship.

'That was how I managed it. I'm sorry if it left you with nothing to hold on to.'

Leonie thought about the elegant but grey man whom she had rarely seen but who had always been one of her mother's friends: a dull grown up, who always asked her about school, university or her new job if they met en passant.

'Who *is* he really, Mum?'

'He is probably the most successful businessman of his generation. He has forged links with China, unimaginable to others. He has turned a chemical company into a supranational entity. Governments defer to him, he is always in the loop on any decision affecting this country's trading posture, he can change national policy. Prime Ministers and Presidents will always answer the phone to him.

'When I met him, he was the youngest Professor of Inorganic Chemistry at Cambridge. When he joined International Fertilisers, he was the youngest MD in their history. Over the past 20 years he took them East, when everyone else was looking West. You already know he speaks Mandarin and collects Chinese ivories with an expert eye. He is also a lateral thinker, an absolute innovator.'

'Is that why you liked him, Mum?'

'No. He was brilliant and funny. He changed my life. He gave me you. He understood the Chinese mind well enough to protect me from my family. And for a long time, we were really in love.'

'So what happened?'

'He married someone else.'

Leonie turned over onto her back and stared at her mother. Ping Li looked back.

'That must have been hard.'

'It was.'

There was a silence as Leonie thought about her mother's loss and the magnitude of her own welled up inside her. She sobbed.

'Michael hates me now.'

Ping Li looked at her daughter and marvelled at self absorption of the young.

'That may be just as well,' she said more calmly than she felt.

Leonie was crying openly now. 'He told me he hates my father and therefore me. Why? What has Lord Regis done to him? We had something special.'

Ping Li reacted now. 'You never had, nor will you ever have anything special with Michael Vellin. He is not fit. He is not your equal in any way.'

Leonie was raging now. 'You don't know him. I love him.'

'You don't. And he certainly doesn't love you.'

Leonie was hysterical now.

'How would you know anything? You're cold, controlling and you hate men. You've never liked any boy I met. Even that man you say is my father ran away from you. I hate you both -- you've ruined my life.'

In her head she could hear Vellin's words echoing, almost the same. She didn't wonder why.

'Have you been told why Vellin is in hospital?'

'Of course. He was mugged in Baku.'

'He was not mugged. He was beaten up in a gay nightclub by the cronies of his male lover. Who had been living with him in his hotel room since his arrival in Baku.'

'I don't believe you.'

'I'm sorry. But Michael Vellin has… appetites that you will never be able to satisfy. He is perverse. He has a history of random homosexual activity. Long before your friendship with him, the Embassy kept watch on him for other reasons. I have pictures, names, dates and times. He risks everything -- by cruising, cottaging, whatever you call it. Three years ago he was picked up by the Police but was let off with a caution. Twice, he was roughed up by men he took home with him. This time, he was on their home territory and he was not so lucky.'

Leonie turned over again onto her face as she imagined other hands, other mouths, on the man she thought she loved. She thought of passion in a vast white bed in a docklands warehouse. She wanted to be sick.

Foote shivered in the bitterly cold air. He wore an ancient ski jacket as proof against the biting wind, which blew across the airfield. He looked up at the clear, night sky and watched the thousands of twinkling stars and thought about the millions more he couldn't detect by eye. He remembered his father, one of the first generation of jet pilots, telling him that when flying in the troposphere you could see that every single degree in the arc of the sky subtended hundreds of thousands of stars. The infinite possibilities up there defied the mind. As it was meant to, he thought.

He had always thought of God as a useful hypothetical construct. But there was something about the grand design, the majesty of space, which made him consider that there might be more. Certainly, he would be more inclined to believe if his wife and daughter were restored to him. As it was, he had never prayed so much to a hypothetical construct.

He looked up, huddling further into the down jacket, straining for warmth. He had been summoned by the telephone ringing in the dead of night. It was Seb, who had sounded a million miles away.

'Denham Airfield, West London,' he said. 'Zero three hundred hours.'

He looked at his watch. Two am. But he was disinclined to go back to the car and wait. Keeping his own, cold and lonely vigil out here on the grass by the runway, he felt more able to will his family back to him.

A shooting star sailed across the sky. He closed his eyes and wished, like a child. Another one came a few seconds later. It must be a meteor shower, he thought. But then the star began blinking and turning and gradually coalesced into aircraft lights. Still far up and high, but coming closer.

He couldn't allow himself to hope. It was probably bound for Heathrow, to the southwest. But he kept watching. He could hear jet engines now. And the lights were lower and faster and the G5 executive jet was visible and definitely on finals for the runway in front of him.

Foote thought his heart would burst. In a miracle of self-control, he stayed still and watched as the sleek jet touched down and decelerated fast in order to stop before the end of the runway. Engines screaming, it turned through 180 degrees on the piano keys at the end of the tarmac surface and came back, turning off towards the tiny club building where he stood.

The engines wound down and the main door just behind the cockpit opened, the stairs unfolding out and down. Foote could see a shape in the doorway, male. Then another, both casually dressed. They jogged down the stairs, round to the back of the plane and opened the baggage compartment. There was a pause, then a familiar figure with leonine hair stood in the doorway. Foote croaked and ran forward. Hester ran down the stairs and into his embrace. As he hugged her, he felt Freya's arms wrap around them both.

Two nights later, Foote was sitting sleepless in his snug, enjoying the warmth of the little fire Mrs H had thoughtfully banked up for the night. He felt again as he had felt that first night after Freya's birth – as though there was a wonderful present lying in a cot upstairs. Except this time, there were two presents; presents he had thought he would never see again. The sensation reminded him of being a boy, a sense of anticipation and excitement, like Christmas Eve. It was, he realised, unalloyed joy.

He didn't see Freya's head appear through the doorway then withdraw. But minutes later, she and her mother, both with bed hair and smudged eyes, appeared in the snug bearing frozen crumpets, plates and butter.

'We can't sleep,' said Freya. Foote picked the toasting forks out of the coal scuttle and handed them to his girls in an old family ritual repeated many times before. They sat around the little fire, toasting the crumpets and revelling in the sense of shared security.

'Butter tastes weird now,' said Freya wrinking her nose. 'After all those *arrepas*, I'm not sure I can ever eat normally again.'

'You will,' said her mother, stroking Freya's hair as she sat on the floor, leaning back against her mother's knee.

'*Arrepas* and chocolate. Every morning.'

'Except the last,' said Hester.

'Except the last,' agreed Freya. 'The shooting started just before dawn. We thought it was more guerillas. They were always shooting at each other, fighting over the drugs. Then this man with a gun came into our hut. He was English. He said he was Seb and that you sent him, Dad. We had to follow him out of the back of the hut. We ran with him and some others across some maize fields to an open area. And then this helicopter came down. All these men in green spread out around us and were shooting back at the huts. Then they jumped in and we flew away.'

Foote leaned back and closed his eyes. He knew the story from there on. Regis' Gulfstream V, complete with medical staff, was waiting at Bogota airport and the girls were flown home. He would never be able to thank Regis enough. Ever.

And the girls had their own hero. As far as Hester and Freya were concerned, Seb Johnson, Regis' 'man in black', could do no wrong.

Despite his domestic bliss, in his professional life Foote was feeling hemmed in. Not exactly trapped, but harassed in a way that was unfamiliar to him. To his surprise, both Nancy and Vellin were each a source of his discomfort. In combination they felt like a really sore point of pressure.

Foote was beginning to feel uneasy within himself too and couldn't quite resolve the conflicting signals. This was unfamiliar territory. He prided himself on knowing where he stood on most of the complex ethical questions that might arise in the course of a practice where he heard many secrets. Total discretion had always been his rule and it had served him very well.

But the way in which Lord Regis had mobilised his formidable resources to secure Hester and Freya's release had left him with an unexpected weak spot.

It was not Foote's custom to feel gratitude to his clients. His relationship with them was always rigorously well-defined by the professional boundaries that total privacy required. Invitations to the weddings of clients' children about whom, over a number of years, he learned a good deal, were always politely turned down. 'I should only be a spectre at a feast,' he would say, and if pressed would add 'Well, people always ask how one knows the family. And without telling a lie I couldn't say I knew you professionally because that creates all kinds of untoward questions.' If pressed even harder he would say firmly that it was his practice always to say no to even the kindest and best-meant of invitations, and that had always ended such matters there.

But when Foote discovered that his wife and beloved only child had been abducted in a South American jungle, he had not given second thought to accepting Lord Regis's offer to do whatever was necessary to secure their release. Only later did he find himself thinking that it had taken him over a boundary that he had never before transgressed.

Foote could never work out why lawyers, especially lawyers, spent so much time being commercially friendly with their clients. He took it as a given of professionalism that it did not spill over into anything other than a professional encounter. There were no obligations allowed to intrude upon such a relationship, other than those of using one's best endeavours.

Yet here he was, deeply indebted to Lord Regis, who had utterly refused Foote's offer to bear the cost of the rescue.

'Put it down to stress testing our systems,' Lord Regis had said. 'We will have garnered much that is of value to us.'

Being utterly honest with himself, Foote was very relieved that something near a quarter of a million pounds worth of costs would not be billed to his account. It would have been near impossible to find.

But it left him feeling compromised. And the fact that both Nancy and Vellin knew of the arrangements seemed to him to bear some relationship to the sudden increase in their demands.

What Nancy wanted from Foote was anything she could get hold of. What Vellin wanted was much the same. Neither knew exactly the questions they wanted to frame. But both knew that if they could get Foote talking, they might steer the conversation in a way that, if it did not yield immediate results, would give them the basis for another, more stiletto-like attempt later on.

Nancy had tried it on with Foote whenever they met. But now he had a telephone call from her.

'Andrew,' she said, though they had never agreed on a first-name basis.

'I am starting a review of the senior executive coaching programme, of which you are a part. I am inviting all the coaches involved to meet me privately so that I can get an overall view of how it is going, and whether we are getting a proper return on our investment. I should like to get our diaries together.'

That approach had floored Foote. He hadn't known that his work with Lord Regis was being seen in such a corporate process context. He could immediately acknowledge that it was a legitimate concern that Nancy should be able to justify her budget, though he hadn't given any thought as to whose budget he was in: so far as he knew, Lord Regis authorised his monthly invoices, and they went through Farheen. But he couldn't legitimately talk to Nancy. Stalling, he had said: 'Well, you know I deal with all matters in the utmost confidence. I am sure some of the other coaches you have will be seeing more than one client and so can make composite observations for you that are unattributable. But that is not the case with my work with Lord Regis. So I don't think I can be of much help to you.'

Nancy was entirely unwilling to take no for an answer after the Beijing disaster had so unsettled her. 'I completely respect your privacy; but in order to do my own job properly I do have to have had some regular contact with the senior coaches we have invited in, which I am sure you will understand. So perhaps if we could find some time, I would value your cooperation.'

Foote had no other card to play. He fixed an hour with Nancy for three days hence, but was troubled by the fact that he had. He wondered if an appeal to Regis might get him off this particular hook. Or would it put him even more on Lord Regis's debt? Shouldn't he fight this minor corporate battle by himself? He wasn't used to such indecision.

Then there was Vellin, whose re-allocated relationship to Nancy had been explained by Lord Regis. But the explanation Foote had been given didn't entirely seem to him to merit Vellin being cast aside in such a brutal manner. There hadn't yet been a chance to explore it in a session with Lord Regis, but this was high on Foote's agenda. Meanwhile Vellin had rung him more than once from his hospital bed.

'Dr Foote,' Vellin had said on the last occasion, 'it would help me a great deal if I might speak to you in confidence. Could you possibly visit me in hospital?'

Foote had been fascinated by such an open request, which he assumed was done without any corporate approval, and which he knew was well outside the brief of his relationship with Lord Regis. Yet Vellin's request had a sinister and yet slightly pleading and helpless element about it that went deep into Foote's own psyche. Perhaps, he thought, it was an occasion when he ought to break his own rules.

What was really rattling Foote was that he had somehow lost contact with Lord Regis. Since the South American rescue, he had felt their sessions no longer held the same sense of trust in them. It was as if the whole episode had redefined for Lord Regis the person who Foote was: an employee of some kind, rather than the only person in the corporate world – maybe the *entire* world -- before whom he had ever let his guard down.

But that was not Foote's only concern. On the two occasions when he had probed into the China visit, Regis had stonewalled him. Had Regis said to Foote that there were matters which were so confidential that he was not free to talk about them, even within the confines of his relationship with Foote, Foote would have accepted it. But that was not what had happened.

Foote knew, in consequence, that there was something that was so secret that Regis had blocked the real knowledge of it from himself too. That was the difference between privacy and secrecy. And considering how much secrecy Foote had been able to shift into privacy within Lord Regis during the course of their conversations, finding an area of secrecy so completely off limits left Foote troubled.

Foote realized that he had begun to trust the relationship with Lord Regis, rather than continuously question it as was his normal procedure. That was not good. And now here were Nancy and Vellin, for whom he felt no trust of any kind, pressing upon him for their own ends.

Nancy's office was unlike any other in IFL. She had feminised one half of it but without much taste. Foote found himself sitting on a small deep purple leather sofa facing Nancy, who sat across a coffee table on a similar piece of burnt orange interior designer expense. He couldn't work out whether it was an uncomfortably large chair or a small sofa. There seemed no good way of sitting on it except upright, the seat being too deep with no cushions of any kind in evidence. Foote smiled a little internal smile. Of course, that was exactly how Nancy would have had her office arranged. Anyone present had to sit up and feel uncomfortable and face her. Foote felt momentarily better for that flash of perception, as if he had acquired a useful piece of enemy intelligence.

'Let me put some cards on the table, Andrew,' said Nancy by way of opening gambit. Foote was much more interested, as was his habit, by the cards she wasn't putting on the table. But he could only start where she began.

'I think there is something very untoward happening in China. You know I went there recently with Lord Regis and had to return unexpectedly early. The India problem needs my close involvement. But far from being welcome in Beijing, it was obvious that Lord Regis wished me off the scene completely. I know that he finds compliance a pain the ass. But that's my job and he understands that very well. I have no complaint about his professionalism on the subject. But this seemed different, and I thought you might have some insights that would be helpful.'

Foote had to admire the subtlety of her appeal to his superior knowledge. If he had had any insights, he might even have been tempted. But he knew nothing of the circumstances of Nancy's return from China, nor indeed, that she had gone there at the same time as Lord Regis. There was no reason why he should. In Lord Regis's absence, he had no cause to be at IFL. Also, Nancy was not on his professional radar except as someone within Regis's purview.

India had been all over the press. A serious toxic blow-out in a southern factory there had created a mini-Bhopal problem that needed managing in all kinds of ways. Nancy's story was entirely plausible and not one to give him pause for thought. But the drift of what she was saying chimed with his own anxieties. She had him surprisingly hooked, and he was curious as to how he could get anything from Nancy during this encounter.

'Tell me a little more,' he said, allowing himself time to find his own position.

'What worries me is this,'said Nancy. 'The China contract was a great triumph –indeed a reward -- for Lord Regis's skilled relations with that country over many years. I would have imagined a visit there could be nothing more than a follow-up, almost a celebration, you might say. But I saw nothing of that and heard of no plans for it. It seemed to me that something else was going on. It's just a hunch but it's one that doesn't go away.'

Now Foote found himself with a tiny and unexpected glimmering of professional regard for her. He had never imagined anything other than a relentless drive for a top job as the key to understanding Nancy. But here she was with antennae functioning in a way that he recognized as a fellow expert in human attunement.

He needed to get some control of the situation and make Nancy believe she was going to get more than she really was.

'Can I presume we are speaking under Chatham House rules?'

'Too true on both sides,' said Nancy, immediately conveying she had no idea of the convention that a Chatham House agreement in conversation meant absolute discretion, with nothing ever to be revealed of it. But for now, Foote had hooked Nancy into a secrecy agreement, even if she was only half aware of it.

'Then what I can say,' said Foote, spinning it out for effect, 'is that you mirror some anxieties of my own. I ought to make it clear though, that I know nothing that would resolve your hunch one way or the other. I only know about China through what I have seen in the press and the fact that I knew Lord Regis was going there last week. The purpose of his visit does not feature in our conversations, and I have seen him once since his return, when it was not discussed. So I am not sure I can be of any real help to you.

'What I can say, is that I have sensed an increased stress in Lord Regis recently, to which I have not been able to assign any particular cause. That's all. It is not in any way specifically related to China nor, indeed, to anything else I can pinpoint.'

'You have been more helpful than you might imagine,' said Nancy. 'I won't take up more of your invaluable time. Thank you for coming to see me. Perhaps we should be in touch more often.'

'Perhaps,' said Foote, in a tone that conveyed the negative side of Nancy's intention. 'In any event, I hope the meetings you're having with the coaches who are looking after the senior people are proving productive.'

'Too early to say,' said Nancy. 'You are the first.'

Foote left with a slightly sinking feeling. How had he had allowed Nancy to hook him into this meeting? It surprised him that he had walked straight into it without checking whether any other coaches had been invited. It left him feeling slightly foolish. Was he losing his touch? The only thing he knew for sure was that Regis was moving out of his orbit. But to where?

He decided to see Michael Vellin.

King Edward's was a hospital that Foote knew and admired. In his own work with the military, he had lectured over the years to a senior strategy course on the neuro-psychological aspects of leadership. Through this, he had gained a profound respect for the excellence of the senior people he met. It was true that that a great deal of their time was spent in training for a variety of situations that might never arise. But when they did, how extraordinarily well they moved into action. Then, when they brought back the stories of their experiences to examine, their practical experience became embedded as the wisdom from which all could learn.

It was so different from the commercial world, Foote always thought: there the trick was to hide one's mistakes or attribute them as fast as possible to someone else. In the military, there were no hiding places -- but nor was there any shame in not having succeeded *if* one had done one's absolute best. Better to have come out on top, of course. The default position was that soldiers knew they were responsible for each other's lives, whereas in commerce, others were expendable.

Michael Vellin sat in bed with the litter of a convalescent around him. Books and magazines on every surface made it clear that clinical concerns were no longer the major part of his recovery, and he was working at a laptop on the bed table in front of him as Foote knocked and eased his way around the door in response to a peremptory shout of 'Come!' It was the custom that doctors and nurses did not knock.

Patients were, after all, there to be treated, and not as guests. Clinical staff time was infinitely more precious than the patient's. But all other visitors knocked. Hence Vellin's curt invitation to enter that he had enjoyed perfecting once he had learnt the system. Actually he had expected a tea tray, and felt ever so slightly embarrassed when it was Dr Foote who appeared.

'Thank you for coming,'he said, making immediate amends by pushing the bed-table away. 'Clear that chair and come and sit down.'

Foote did as he was bid, preferring as always to get a sense of the occasion by being more an observer than a participant until active participation could no longer be avoided. So he sat, in silence, not wishing to convey any sense that he was there in any guise other than a professional one, and at Vellin's request.

'Tea's due in a moment,' said Vellin. 'I shall ring them and make sure they bring one extra.' As Vellin picked up the phone, Foote observed with surprise that he went straight through to the nursing station for such a request. He thought how forbearing the nursing staff must be when there must have been a method of contacting housekeeping directly. But he said nothing. It was a ploy to raise Vellin's anxiety a little and get him off his guard. Foote was not entirely sure he should be there, and wanted to treat the situation as coolly as he could. He certainly knew how to lift Vellin's situational anxiety.

'I'm not sure where to start,' said Vellin when the tea had been delivered and dispensed. 'But it goes back to the Lord's visit to China.'

Still using his old coy reference to Regis, thought Foote. Not quite down and out yet.

'After the China deal,' went on Vellin, 'Regis went out there to start a new phase of work. I don't exactly know what it was. Nancy went with him. She thought it was a chance to see the China operation. He didn't know she would be there.

When he found she was, he wanted her out of the way as quickly as possible. I got her back to London fast, though not entirely fairly.'

Vellin paused. Foote kept his silence. He knew from long experience that a question would only betray the limitations of his knowledge. What he wanted to know was what was in Vellin's head. Only Vellin could let him in. Over-directing him with a question was not the way to open up anything.

The silence hovered between them. Vellin gazed at the foot of the bed. 'The wrong foot to be looking at,' thought Foote, who kept his gaze on Vellin and betrayed nothing of his silly inner pun.

'The problem is,' said Vellin after an indeterminate pause, 'I have been reassigned by Regis to Nancy in all my functions. It can't possibly work. He knows that. Everything tells me there is something very strange going on that is unlike anything I've come across ever before. And I thought you would be the one person who might have a clue.' Only then did he shift his gaze directly to Foote's face. Foote saw a crumpled, pleading, haunted look in the eyes that had never been apparent before.

This was one of many occasions in Foote's professional career when people had attributed to him more knowledge and insight than he possessed. But with his recent meeting with Nancy reverberating in his head, this was not the time to be self-effacing.

He kept an engaged and attentive silence. Vellin needed time to think, and Foote would facilitate that by creating the conditions between two people where the brain becomes most flexible and creative and manages its networks at their most flowing. The anxiety that had flooded Vellin needed quietening down if Foote was to hear as much as might possibly be said. And so Foote remained very alert and very relaxed, and deliberately tried to make Vellin aware that he was utterly tuned into him and ready for the next downloading.

Slowly, but entirely predictably, Vellin started to calm down. His inner world responded to Foote's capacity to regulate it from outside him. Suddenly, he gave a slightly wry smile, and said 'Do you know, I think the Lord is up to no good in China. I'm not sure what it is but something's very odd.'

Another pause. Vellin wanted to see if Foote would start some questions, but it was becoming clear that he would not. And so Vellin started again.

'I've been puzzling a lot, lying here... I'll tell you what I think .'

Foote was now exactly where he had hoped to be. Although Vellin had initiated the visit, Foote had quietly turned the encounter through one hundred and eighty degrees, so that Vellin was now going to find the answers that he wanted for himself. And Vellin was doing that, not through any interrogative process on Foote's part, but through exploring what he deeply knew and had not yet entirely connected. Foote was simply creating and maintaining the conditions for that to happen. Like any fine skill, it looked simple when very well done.

This time, it was very well done indeed.

'It's like this,' said Vellin. 'As you know, I have been an aide to Lord Regis for a long time. Frankly, there's nothing I thought I did not know about him. It's been a delicate balance at times, staying as a trustie, while sometime having to help him see that what he was doing was not in his best interests. But by and large we have worked it out pretty well.

'I realised a long time ago that power appears in two guises. You can either fight your way up to be leader or you can make the leader the best that he can be. I have chosen the second way, that of the consigliere -- you know everything but are very discreet at all times and manage anything that needs managing. In that way you become indispensable.

'Nancy wants power *over* the leader while I only want power *through* the leader. It's an important difference. It makes Nancy very ruthless. The only way I know of combating that kind of ruthlessness is to make it clear to such a person that you can make them fall flat on their face. In fact, I made that happen, though it wasn't premeditated and, in retrospect, wasn't wise...'

His voice faded out. He was still exhausted.

'Could you put a little flesh on the skeleton of your story?' said Foote, not even addressing Vellin by name as he said it. He wanted nothing to intrude that might in any way take Vellin off the neural networks he was on.

'Regis rang me from China,' said Vellin, 'He sounded cross and even a bit panicked, now I think about it, that Nancy had turned up. He wanted her out of the way fast. And so I intimated to Nancy that HRH had especially asked for her to be at a luncheon after meeting her at the China bash we had at the Royal Academy. She has that American fantasy thing about the Royals. She swallowed it, hook, line and sinker. She took the company jet straight back to London, only to find HRH's office very frosty. There was no luncheon invitation of any kind. She'll never forgive me, but at least she was out of the way in Beijing. That's my job. But I can't help wondering why he needed to get her out like that.'

Foote gave no sign of any knowledge. It still didn't explain Regis' desire to crush his former aide out of all existence. Something was being held back.

'I started putting two and two together,' said Vellin. 'And there's much more which you must hear if you are going to advise me.'

Foote wondered whether he should query the assumption about advising. His only responsibility was to Lord Regis. Yet he found himself being too absorbed by the prospect of what might come next to deflect Vellin's assumptions. He let it pass. As he did so, he knew he was committing the worst professional sin of collusion in his very clear canon of correctness. Yet he could not leave.

'You may have come across Leonie Li, the assistant to HRH. Anglo Chinese, very pretty, ferociously clever. Her mother is Ping Li, scientific attaché to the Chinese Embassy and an old crony of Regis'. There has always been a connection there, which I have never completely understood, but it has served us well at IFL. My path has crossed with Leonie's many times over the years and more frequently over this collaboration between the Prince and IFL.

'We became lovers not long after the Academy bash. It may surprise you. Most people think I am gay. I have, I suppose you would say, a foot in both camps. Lord Regis warned me off, several times, but I thought I could manage it, so long as we all remained professional. I even thought he might be jealous. Of me, at first. Then, of her. I saw him speaking to her intently at the Academy. I even wondered whether he wanted her. Then he came here, cold with rage and told me she is his daughter. '

'Ah,' said Foote, stalling for time on every front. His tone was consulting room sympathetic, not social sharing. He was struggling hard to work out where to start.

Had Vellin been a properly defined patient or coaching client, there would have been no problem. But in the present context, he was talking with Vellin about matters deeply involving his actual client, Lord Regis, without any permission to be doing so. He couldn't properly advise Vellin without drawing on his knowledge of Lord Regis, when that knowledge was professionally privileged and protected.

If Foote had been able at that moment to switch his thinking towards theology, he would have known what the mediaeval mind really understood about temptation. 'The evil in me that I would not, that I do,' as the Prayer Book so succinctly puts it. Deep inside, Foote knew that he had made the wrong choices.

Yet having got in so far, it seemed easier to go on than pull back. The justification had been that he might find out something that would help his understanding of Lord Regis. But deep down he knew that was only a rationalisation. Here he was, justifying the actions in himself that he spent every day of his working life unravelling in others.

He wanted to know whether Vellin had any understanding of the gift of herself that Leonie had made to him and what it meant for her. He expected not. Clinically, he wondered whether Vellin saw Leonie androgynously, as a vent for his unresolved sexuality. And somewhere in the back of his mind he trembled for his own daughter as she went out into the world, so dependent for her fundamental well-being on the worthiness of the man who might tell her he loved her.

So Leonie was Lord Regis's daughter. He mentally kicked himself for not pushing harder. He had known there was a lover, and now he knew who it was. How had he missed it? There was a time when he had always been very systematic and very thorough. As he got older and, he had hoped, wiser, he had allowed himself all sorts of corner-cutting. The price of that was that he knew nothing about huge and relevant chunks of Lord Regis's life and the way life experience had shaped him. Had he been getting lazy or just arrogant?

Yet he could neither articulate nor pursue any of this. A professional mask came down upon Dr Foote. Vellin would not have noticed the slight clouding of his gaze, for his posture and apparent concern remained intact. But Foote was storing stuff inside himself in a private place that would later require deep and painful exploration with the psychoanalyst that he himself consulted when he needed support. He realised with a shock that it had been too long since the last occasion.

'Michael,' he said, wanting to get out of the situation he had allowed himself into, 'you have told me some extraordinary things. What I think would be best is if I were to go away and mull them over quietly to myself, to see what sense I can make of them. Then, perhaps, we can have a more meaningful conversation than I feel prepared for at the moment.'

Vellin looked quizzical. It was not the reaction he desired. 'It's pretty urgent for me, though,' he said. 'I need you to help me see what I'm going to do about it all. It's a disaster and I can't see my way through it. In fact, I feel quite desperate. And I feel angry – very angry - at the way I've been treated. After so long and after all I've done for him.'

As though a curtain had been drawn back, Foote suddenly had a glimpse of Vellin's pain at his rejection and the fury that now consumed him. He wondered whether Vellin would be able to control a desire for revenge. He doubted it.

He was desperate to get away.

'I promise you I will come back at 2 p.m. tomorrow and I shall be free until 6 pm. We can use as much or as little of the time as we need.'

The headline, TIBETAN MYSTERY DEATHS was emblazoned across the whole of the front of the Evening Standard.

Dr Foote picked the freebie up as he slipped into Bond Street tube station. The Central line would get him back to Holland Park and the seclusion of his private thinking space, even if the girls were now home and scattering their paraphernalia over every surface. The thought filled him with a joy he had not felt for a long time. His wife and his daughter home and safe under his roof! Despite the importunings of Vellin and Nancy and the feeling that somehow, he had bartered away his carefully constructed professional distance, it had been a price worth paying.

How precious Hester and Freya were to him. He could understand Lord Regis' desire to protect his Leonie – now revealed as his lost and most desired child – from the rapacious Vellin. And he could see how Vellin's betrayal of his master had become terminal when Regis realised that his own, subconscious seduction had been accomplished in reality with his daughter.

Idly, Foote spread the paper across his knees as he sat down in the airless, half-empty compartment.

Joanna Lumley, he saw, had been asked for her comments about the 'mystery deaths.' The editor knew very well that the Great British Public totally understood that she had something to do with the well-being of people in the Himalayas, even if they didn't distinguish too readily between Tibet and that equally mountainous home of the Gurkhas, Nepal. Indeed her photograph and comments took up most of the front page. What a good chance to link something very foreign and potentially disturbing to something very familiar and deeply attractive through a picture. Clever editor, he thought – and not least because the story details seemed sparse.

Among the many hundreds of valleys in Tibet, where high snow waters flowed down through infinitely networked river system and where, along the valley floors, little villages managed their subsistence existences as they had done for hundreds of years, there was apparently one valley where a surprising number of male deaths had occurred in the past four weeks. China was not allowing any of the international agencies access to find out what was happening. A Chinese government spokesman had given a bland and totally uninformative comment about the situation which, it seemed, had been reported to the outside world by a Chinese railway construction surveyor, who had been mapping that territory recently and who had lost two colleagues in whatever the epidemic was. He had posted his story on a website when he returned home. An international press agency scanning the worldwide traffic for titbits from such sources had seen the posting and put it on the international press wires.

The source of the story had not been contactable. His phone number rang dead, so the story could not be confirmed. But its essence was that along the river system, many men and boys had died in many villages. But no women had died, and no female children, it seemed. That was the extent of what was known. There was speculation that a leak from a remote cadmium mine could have caused the poisonings but the location was not clear, as the original website posting gave the name of a village that was not on world maps, and lacked any other identification. The source had been on a unspecific surveying trip with his two colleagues in difficult terrain, and there were no earthworks of the kind that there would eventually be if any railway lines were forced through the valley. Therefore, there was nothing that satellite surveys might pick up by way of fixing the locale.

The story occupied Foote from Bond Street to Notting Hill Gate. More of the story was inside the paper than the photograph of Joanna Lumley would allow on the front page. He got ready to get off at the next stop, cross the Bayswater Road, and take the short sharp hill up to Campden Square.

China was in his semi-conscious awareness when he got to his study, a mug of tea in hand, and as he sat down in his most comfortable armchair and let his mind go into free play. His mind spun the finest of threads to Nancy and to Vellin. Was it chance or real synchronicity? Was that distinction real anyway?

China was connecting Nancy, Vellin, Regis, Ping Li and now Vellin's sexual conquest, who was Regis's half Chinese daughter. How had Regis ever made that connection, more than a quarter century ago, with Ping Li? How had he, Foote, missed it? Regis had told him there was a woman, a child. Foote knew enough about the byzantine twists of fate to know that they would not have been consigned to dusty oblivion; of course they were part of the story unfolding in front of him.

And what did Vellin's and Nancy's anxieties about Regis and China mean? He didn't know; he didn't understand either.

More free play was needed here if there were connections to be found. So Foote sat back, closed his eyes, and found he couldn't settle. Needing some help to shift into a contemplative mood, he opened his eyes and went over to the CDs lying next to the Bang and Olufsen in which he had indulged last year. Schubert's *Trout* quintet was on the top of the pile and he slipped it into the machine, turned the volume down quite low and went back to his chair.

'Water,' his mind said to him, and it then shifted to that newspaper report. 'Water.' And China again thereby. He would stay with 'water' and see where that went.

Regis is the central character, he thought. Everything revolves around him. Stay with Regis for the moment and with water.

An image of the first time he had gone to IFL came into his mind, the very beginning of the story that was occupying so much of his inner time these days. He saw the headlines of the newspaper that had been lying on the back seat of the car sent to collect him: they had announced the IFL China deal. And then there had been that extraordinary business, just as he had getting involved with the company, about something happening on the Prince's estate. That had involved water. Were China and water connected in some way and that incident, with Lord Regis the lynch pin?

That thought produced an odd little feeling of elation: not quite a tingling of the spine, but a sense that some kind of new connection had just been forged – as if he were a child suddenly spotting the piece that would lock the jigsaw together.

Foote picked up the sounds of the music again that he had not been tracking for several minutes, opened his eyes, and knew he had something to test. The question was, how? And did he have enough to go on?

Better trust his intuition. Thinking wouldn't get him anywhere nearer the truth that he sought. It might direct him to where it was, though.

And then he paused. Only Regis was connected to every bit of the conundrum. Whatever truth there was to be found must lie with Regis. So the practical question was: how to conduct the encounter that could not be avoided? And how did that play with the promised meeting with Vellin tomorrow?

Foote heard the peremptory 'Come' as he knocked on Vellin's room door one minute before 2pm the next day. No embarrassment shaded Vellin's face on this occasion. He was as determined as a man in pyjamas in bed can be to assert his position. Foote was not in the least surprised. He had, after all, on his own terms, abandoned Vellin the previous day.

'I think we ought to start by being clear about what our relationship is,' said Foote, as he sat down. 'I do not have a professional relationship with you; I am employed by IFL to act as an executive coach to your employer, Lord Regis. As such, anything he says to me is completely privileged and I am unable to disclose it for any reason whatsoever.'

Vellin was surprised. But he recovered quickly.

'I'm sure you're right,' said Vellin, in his most emollient tone. 'I understand perfectly. What I *was* hoping was that you could help me see my own situation a bit more clearly. I don't have anyone I can really trust to talk to about it. Could you do that with me?'

Foote had not expected such an elegant response. Vellin had touched upon Foote's innermost motivations. Could he do what Vellin wanted and keep the boundaries that he must with regard to Regis? The way he *ought* to have managed the situation was entirely clear to him. He ought not to have visited Vellin in the first place without first having agreed it with Lord Regis, with whom he was in a very clear professional relationship.

'Let's see where we get to then,' said Foote. Both knew then that the question of the precise definition of a professional relationship was being shelved, although while Foote made a mental note to return to it, Vellin made a note that he shouldn't.

'So what have you thought since yesterday?' said Vellin, wanting to keep the initiative.

'Let's start from where your thoughts are,' said Foote, trying to keep Vellin responding to the therapist, not the other way round.

'I still can't make much sense of what happened and why,' said Vellin. I can't see whether my getting attacked was just chance or something that was planned. Why me? And why then?'

'Tell me your darkest thoughts about it all,' said Foote. 'Let's see what hangs together in there.'

'Let's start with the facts, then,' said Vellin. I was sent to Azerbaijan by his Lordship to start a discussion with General Thali Heydro, someone he knew very well and whom I had met twice. Heydro was a General by 33 and the Azerbaijani Minister of Mineral Rights, Customs and Borders by 35 – a position he still holds and an ideal calling for one blessed with his particular talents. Essentially, it is a fast track to wealth and insider knowledge on everything.'

'The deal I was asked to go and facilitate seemed nebulous in the extreme. Deals are always a long-shot, but this was even more amorphous than usual. In retrospect, I wonder whether it was real at all. I arrived in the late afternoon and we agreed that we would leave business discussions until the following day. Needless to say, they never took place.

'The entertainment that was arranged the first evening was entirely set up. The guard in the helicopter was a beautiful young man, but there was absolutely nothing ambivalent about his behaviour. He walked straight into my suite and seduced me. He accompanied me to dinner with the General Heydro. We drank vodka and ate caviar. Later, we went down to the nightclub, The Most. I remember the blue neon sign. And well named. Full of exquisite men..'

'What exactly happened?' said Foote.

'About one o'clock I had to throw up. I can't drink vodka and my head was spinning.

I got out of the fire doors then tried to get back in again. They had shut, so I walked through the garage back towards the front door of the club. Vassily was still in there. And my jacket.

'These men in leather coats came up to me, pushed me around, knocked me against a pillar, then beat me. They held me there while they took turns to rape me. Then someone jumped on me. The cleaners found me at 6 am.'

'Then I was in my hotel room again. There was a doctor, nurses, Regis' fixer and ... the General. He looked angry, sickened, but I was too tired to speak.'

'A doctor said they were flying me back to England as soon as possible to the best medical care. And after some time I arrived here, though I don't remember much of the detail of the journey. I was out of it. And that's it.'

There was silence for a while. Vellin stared at the ceiling. Foote kept his gaze on Vellin. He knew that the next statement he made would be critical.

'Is there another fact somewhere?' he said. 'Has this happened to you before?'

Vellin lay back, too exhausted in mind and body to move. After what seemed like an age, he reached out for his bedside telephone, dialled 0 and spoke to the hospital operator.

'Put me through to Scotland Yard, please,' he said.

He waited a few minutes as the number rang in the Police headquarters off Whitehall. When the call was answered, he gave the name of the photogenic policeman he had read about with increasing frequency in the newspapers. A man with a top flight degree from a top flight university, the new face of the Police, a meritocrat, who showed neither fear nor favour in his pursuit of malefactors. So far, he had landed some plum victims; from those who had bought their peerages to those who abused their public office.

And now, he would be the architect of Michael Vellin's revenge.

'Inspector Ware, please,' he said.

Sue Carter knocked off at seven 7 pm, half an hour late. The boys would be tearing the kitchen apart by now in their endless search for food. It didn't matter how much she stuffed the fridge, it was always empty. Her attempts at healthy eating -- yoghurts and the like -- were met with derision. The boys wanted vast amounts of carbohydrate three times a day, accompanied by equally vast amounts of protein at least twice. She knew she sounded like her mother, but it was impossible to imagine where they put it. Too easy to see where her salary went, especially as her ex had sodded off to Australia and given up on alimony. They had both inherited his lanky frame and insatiable appetite.

'Hollow legs' had always been the old family joke about her ever-hungry brothers. Too right.

She drew up outside her house, which was ominously dark -- where the hell were those children? -- and climbed out of the car. She was reaching into the boot for her case when a movement in the corner of her eye startled her. She jumped, then turned around to face it, fully expecting it to be one of her starving sons.

It was Millington -- the sweaty toe-rag from the lab. In her garden, standing on her unweeded flowerbed.

A jumble of thoughts flowed through her head, the last of which was mild alarm. Sue Carter did not scare easily, especially when the threat was shorter and lighter than she was and, by the look of him, about to succumb to a stroke.

'What are you doing here?' she said.

He thrust a damp, mangled piece of card into her hand. Her immediate inclination was to recoil and she dropped it. He picked it up again and held it out. A photograph.

'My children,' he gasped.

The adrenaline was pumping now, finally, making her sound more aggressive than she felt.

'Why are you showing me this?'

'They've threatened to take them.'

'Who?'

'The people who want the formula. The Quantum formula that Dr Laffey was working n. The stuff in his bottle. I know what it is. It's not a fertiliser. Not at all. It's a... a de-fertiliser -- except it stops people, not plants, from growing. In fact, it stops them dead, if you get my meaning. They say they'll take my kids if I tell the Police. But I've got to. It's gone too far.'

He was so anguished he could barely stand up.

Sue Carter locked her car door, picked up her briefcase and motioned Millington towards her front door. She made a mental note to text the absent boys. They could have pizza on the way to football. The only person who would feel bad about it was their mother. Extra vegetables tomorrow.

'Come this way, Mr Millington.'

Half an hour later, Sue Carter had something she could work with. Although terrified, Millington had all his ducks in line. Some nerd called Patrick, working freelance for Millington and Quantum, had copied the original formula and unravelled its makeup. So far as she could understand, there were three strands that Laffey had been working on. The first was what it purported to be. A new fertiliser to be mixed in water, designed to help an exploding population support itself agriculturally by boosting production. The kind of product IFL was famous for and for which it had made its reputation over the years.

The second was more sinister. The same fertiliser, tweaked. This time, when added to the water supply, it ensured the death of male gametes in the human reproductive system. They called it a chromatothanatogen, a CMT in lab speak. The name they had given it was River Dragon. By using the River Dragon in the supply, China's bias in favour of male children would be historically reversed. Only girls would be born. Girls, who would grow up to be women untormented by testosterone or troublesome ideas of freedom.

The third was Laffey's dark secret, his androtoxin: a compound, named Dragon's Breath, which would kill males of any age, the only critical qualification being the possession of the crucial Y gene. This was what he was pouring into the aquifer at the Prince's estate, his intended victims being the entire male side of the royal family.

Carter thought back to that disastrous day at Surrey Castle. The Police had known that an animal rights extremist had the Royal Family in his sights. There had been enough 'chatter' on the usual websites and communications to alert them that something was up. Therefore, they had been prepared for an attempt upon the Prince, whose insistence upon continuing to hunt made everyone's lives much harder. Yet it was his uncontroversial passion for early morning mushrooming that had almost been his undoing.

She realized that they had had no idea of the gravity of the attempt. Laffey had looked like a foolish, elderly cyclist, almost doddering. His Heath Robinson equipment, the plastic bottle with the tin foil seal, none of it suggested the utter lethality of the substance, which leaked harmlessly away into the grass. No one could ever have imagined the havoc it could have unleashed on the rulers of England's green and pleasant land.

And although the Police had been prepared, they were not expecting to have their target shot from under them by forces unknown. Unknown still, thought Carter ruefully.

She had to think through this carefully. Why assassinate Laffey? The only reason she could imagine was that the perps knew what was in the bottle. Which meant that someone other than Laffey knew he had designed it to do what he was attempting to road test it for. She thought hard. Where had she seen something like this tonight? There. Her eye went to the headline of the Evening Standard she had brought home. All those men and boys dying in Tibet. Laffey worked at Quantum for International fertilisers, and IFL was deeply involved in China? Didn't China keep Tibet in servitude, as an 'autonomous region'? She had heard the Dalai Lama talking about it only recently. And Lord Regis had just won a world beating contract from the Chinese.

So, the huge numbers of male deaths it in Tibet might not be accidental. What Carter found chilling was that the only reason it was ever discovered was that Laffey had kept some back in order to pursue his own agenda. Lord Regis had some questions to answer.

She decided to speak to Scotland Yard. They had a man who specialised in taking down the rich and the powerful and she suspected she would need his input.

At the same time, she must deal with Millington, who was in a bad way. She had started the ball rolling by sending his wife and children in a Panda car to a safe house in

Gloucestershire. Their father would disappear into a safe suite at Paddington Green Police Station.

The quiet of Lord Regis' office had become familiar to Foote. But he could not entirely quell perturbations within himself as he sat down and Regis assumed his familiar place. He had arrived five minutes early, and chatting with Farheen about the next evening's China Ball had allayed some of his unaccustomed nervousness. For Foote knew he stood upon the swampiest ground professionally of his entire lifetime. Now that he needed to be on the firmest of footings, there was nothing that supported him.

'Thank you for the invitation to the Ball,' he said, and knew immediately what Lord Regis would say in reply.

'I am delighted you can both come,' said Lord Regis. 'What a pity we could not find room for your daughter to come too. But I hope this will make a homecoming for Professor Foote that she will remember.'

They both knew that Lord Regis had complete control of the agenda. The little formalities ('Professor Foote'), the reminders that he was in charge ('I am delighted' and 'What a pity'), the reminder that the homecoming was entirely to do with him, the generosity that was completely unsaid but could never be ignored. He had the most difficult task in which to engage Lord Regis, and no grounds from which to engage. He realised, with wrenching dismay, that his professional independence had been completely suborned.

'Lord Regis,' he started, feeling feeble, 'I wanted, rather unusually, to start this session by checking my thoughts out with you, so that I know we share the same frames of reference. If my thoughts are wrong, I need to know if I am to be of the detached and dispassionate adviser that is my role with you. If my thoughts are right, or close, then I also need to know, as we shall be much involved with those matters of secrecy and privacy which so occupied us when we first started these meetings.'

'Of course,' said Lord Regis. 'Trust is of the essence of the way we have agreed to work together.'

Foote could not immediately tell why he so distrusted that statement as he heard it. It brought none of the relief it ought to have done, but he couldn't be sure whether the false notes were his own or emanating from Lord Regis. It was as if every third key on a piano was missing. Something didn't sound quite right, though there was nothing wrong with the notes that were being struck. It was a quite different encounter from anything he had experienced before with Lord Regis.

'I have been putting a number of disparate thoughts together,' said Foote, speaking slowly as he monitored his own thoughts carefully in the half-second before they became words. 'I am curious about China and Tibet. They are not topics we have touched upon very much, but I know

the first engages a huge amount of your time and energy –
and that is without mentioning the success it has brought you
– and I wonder about the second.'

'It's not a topic upon which the Chinese like to discourse,'
said Regis. Foote could also hear the slight caution on
Regis's speech as if he were mirroring Foote.

'But there are no Chinese present in our conversation,
Lord Regis,' said Foote, trying a little probing thrust.

'In the back of my mind the Chinese are always present,'
said Regis.

That touched the target then, thought Foote. No denial
about Tibet, but a very clear statement about the fact that he
has to safeguard what he says about it.

'Nevertheless, Lord Regis, would you like to tell me about
Tibet?'

'I wonder what is making you curious?' said Regis. 'Is it
something specific which brings you to me on this?"

'Not at all, Lord Regis. I would not in any circumstances talk about IFL in any setting at all, let alone that one. My involvement with you is entirely between us.'

As he said it, Foote knew he was lying. What about his meetings with Vellin and Nancy? This, then, was the consequence of the lack of integrity he had known he was displaying then with regard to his working relationship with Regis. Perhaps Regis already knew about those meetings. That thought would have to wait.

'All I can tell you about Tibet,' he heard Lord Regis saying, 'is that if there are specific questions you wish to ask me, then I shall consider whether I can answer them. That's as far as I can go.'

What a curious position this was, thought Foote. Here I am invited to play a guessing game in which he holds all the cards, and anything I say lets him know about me, not me about him. It's a one-shot game.

'Let me ask you just one question then, if I may,' said Foote. 'Are you involved in any capacity in the deaths in Tibet that have recently been reported?'

'That's such a preposterous question, Dr Foote, that it makes me doubt whether we have the basis of any kind of working relationship.'

So it was true. Foote knew it immediately. Nothing would have induced Lord Regis to make such a statement in the light of what had gone before -- unless he had hit a bulls-eye. Now what? He thought a little silence might go a long way.

And it did. Much further than he would have thought. For ten minutes neither said anything, neither knowing who could cause most damage by what was said next. Lord Regis broke first.

'I think that brings this session to an end, Dr Foote. Neither of us is clear what we wish to say to the other, I think. Let us both go away and reflect upon this meeting. Perhaps I do not need to remind you, but I should be failing

470

in my duty to the company if I didn't: anything you have learnt about me, or the company, through your involvement with me is bound by complete confidentiality in the contract you signed -- and, I imagine, by your own rules of professional conduct.'

'I understand your need to make that statement, Lord Regis,' said Foote. 'And what you say is quite correct. But I have not, as it happens, yet signed a contract with the company at all. Nancy was so keen to get this started, it turned out that procurement did not have an appropriate contract in place for my kind of professional services. They are, I am told, conducting a best practice survey to determine what the detail of the contract should be. Meanwhile, I am here under some programme for innovation that Nancy established to get round procurement's systemic delays. That's how matters stand at present. My answer to your implied question -- as to whether you can trust me -- is that you will have to rely entirely upon my professional integrity.'

Lord Regis rose from his chair, saying nothing. Foote followed. Keeping control in his own office as they both moved towards the door, Lord Regis said:

'I will see you at the Ball. After that, I am not sure whether or when either of us will have the need to contact the other again. In any event, please make sure your account is up-to-date, when you have time.' He opened the door letting Foote into the outer world again. Foote said nothing, his mind spinning as he wondered about the long shadow that lay over them both.

Once home, Foote went to his study, stopping only to let Hester know he would be thinking about something and didn't want to be disturbed under any circumstances. So he sat into the small hours, sipping whisky intermittently, and reflecting on the failure of which he had just been a part. His relationship with Regis was over. Nothing could re-create what had begun tentatively to flower as Regis had explored aspects of himself he hardly knew. Of course, Hester and Freya had been restored to him with the kind of despatch that he doubted the Foreign Office could or ever would have organised. But he had committed sins of which only he was aware, and had compromised himself thoroughly in the process. Was it even possible to redeem himself?

The biggest question, and around which all else revolved, was what should he do about his knowledge regarding Tibet? He had no facts that would stand in a court of law, but his strong suspicion was that Regis and the deaths in Tibet were somehow inextricably linked. Who would take action on that if they knew? He had utterly no idea.

At first, Foote resolved that he could only do what he was best at, which was to wait. For what, he was not sure. A knock on the door? Answering questions somewhere? Himself arraigned before some court or enquiry?

And then he decided, at about three in the morning, that action would be better than waiting. Of course there were agencies of the State that knew how to manage difficult situations quietly. He thought that somehow he could make a clean breast of matters and resolve his own doubts about his actions by doing what he had never done before: break his own code of conduct. And then he remembered that he had done that already, when he visited Vellin, and that his last meeting with Regis was somehow the outcome of that lapse. Nevertheless, MI6 seemed right. That's what he would do.

So he switched out the lights and made his way to the bathroom. And as he did, something that H.L. Mencken had once said came into his mind. 'For every complex problem there is a single solution that is clear, simple and wrong.' 'Damn,' he said, as he went to find whatever sleep he could.

Meanwhile there was this accursed Ball to get through. And they would.

The golden dragons on the long, Chinese banners outside the Royal Academy spat flame in the spotlights as cars drew up by the archway. They deposited the guests at the beginning of the red carpet, which crossed the open courtyard and continued up the steps beyond.

Locals and tourists on the pavement goggled at the dresses and the jewels and the glamour of the women. The cars, uniformly dark, quiet and expensive, glided up to the entrance point and away, like manta rays swooping.

The China Ball, attended by HRH Prince Edward, Duke of Cumberland, had only just begun and was already the party of the year. Designed to showcase the Imperial Chinese treasures and lavishly sponsored by IFL, it was a spectacular demonstration of power, goodwill and glamour.

Expensively wrapped in her glittering Badgly Mischka – some events just screamed for the real thing -- Nancy stood just inside the doorway of the Academy, barely able to contain her excitement. She felt like a young girl at her first prom.

The floor to ceiling mirrors lining the doorway reflected her silhouette, and she was satisfied. She would have to make sure one of the Press photographers caught her looking hot tonight. They already had her email details as IFL's organiser-in-chief of anything remotely Royal. She would email the shots home to Chicago first thing in the morning – her Mom could wake up to views of her daughter looking like a princess.

She stretched out a leg in front of her to admire the Manolos – only Manolos would do on a night like this. She sipped on a rare glass of champagne – she deserved a treat -- and waited for her date to show.

As protocol required, the Prince would arrive at the last minute. He would be led into dinner with his party first and only then could the assembled company sit too.

Nancy would not be at the Prince's table. That privilege was reserved for the Chinese Ambassador and Ping Li, Lord and Lady Regis, and the President of the RA and his wife. Finally, for some inexplicable reason known only to Lord Regis, the psychologist Dr Andrew Foote and his wife made up the ten.

His invitation annoyed Nancy beyond all reason. The man was immune to her attempts to get him to spill the beans on Lord Regis's state of mind. Her increasingly leaden hints that, as IFL was paying for Foote's services as an executive coach to Regis, IFL should be allowed some insight into Regis' thought processes, had met with the blankest of walls. Foote had kept her neatly at arm's length.

The only other minor shadow was that Michel Vellin was her date for the evening. And in truth, that wasn't so bad. Since Lord Regis had handed over his management on to Nancy, he was now securely under her thumb. And as a date, he was seamless. Beautifully dressed, charming, a good dancer and she could enjoy his masculine beauty. No wonder she had thought he was gay.

Vellin had changed since his 'accident' in Azerbaijan. And not just physically. He had a scar on his face – positively Phantom of the Opera -- and a limp to his right leg, but there was more to it. He was much less assured, less cocky. He had submitted to the treatment handed out by Nancy without overt protest. He had sat in on her interminable briefings with colleagues and contributed more than she had expected. He had actually seemed to be listening as she dry-ran the new, corporate governance booklet of rules on him. His suggestions were intelligent and reasoned. Which, she had to admit, had sucked much of the joy out of it.

She began to realize that he was more able than she had imagined and not just the scheming consigliere, forever in his master's shadow. Lord Regis had been clever to spot such ability. She was beginning to cherish high hopes for the Hammer-Vellin axis herself.

She turned back towards the staircase and walked into the man in question. He bowed slightly, looking, Nancy thought, like the devilish hero in a bodice ripper. Even she was not entirely immune to Vellin's considerable charms.

'Ms Hammer, you look magnificent, if I may say so,' he said.

'You may,' said Nancy, thrilled, despite herself. If she had known the degree to which she repulsed him, she would have been shocked.

'I see you have a drink. However, I think we can improve upon it.'

Vellin turned to the waiter and deposited Nancy's lukewarm glass, taking two chilled ones instead from the tray.

'Confusion to our enemies,' he said, raising his glass to her. Nancy wondered whether it was a dig at her, then decided not. She most certainly had been Vellin's sworn enemy, but now that he was no longer in thrall to the Dark Lord, she could forget, if not forgive. Anyway, she now understood his value to Regis.

They were co-hosting the second most important table in the room, the one devoted to the senior diplomats, the curator of the Chinese collections, Leonie Li and a floridly gay royal equerry. They would shortly be required to gather them up and play the hosts, but until then, Nancy was enjoying celebrity-spotting. There was an eminent judge with his famous actress wife, a pop singer with her Brit Art boyfriend and a grizzled, Booker prize-winning author with his unfeasibly young, oriental wifelet.

There also was that annoying man, Doctor Foote, accompanied by his Professorial spouse who, in Nancy's opinion, should have done something to her hair. Hester Foote's figure was neat enough and her dress quite elegant, though not by any designer known to Nancy. But her hair was unadorned grey and badly cut. It didn't matter how many degrees the women had – and Nancy had heard she had many – she should learn how to present herself. Particularly as she was sitting on the Prince's table. Being rescued from drug lords, or whatever they were, in the jungle was no excuse. Freelance hairdressers existed. Nancy had their numbers on speed dial on her Blackberry for emergencies.

Over in the corner of the first room, Lord Regis and the Lady Marcia – groomed, Nancy saw with approval, to a T -- were holding court. Until the Prince arrived, this was the only game in the room and the ambitious, the worldly and the terminally bored flocked around them. She could hear Marcia's shrieking laugh and Regis' low boom. Waiters stood around them, bottles at the ready, like moths drawn to a flame.

There was a disturbance near the front door and Nancy moved forward. It was the first limousine, conveying the Chinese contingent. The Ambassador and his wife stepped from the first car, together with Ping Li. Although the Scientific Attaché had little to do with China's cultural treasures, she was virtually one in her own right, being high-born and closely related to the Ambassador.

She dazzled tonight, in lacquer red, with her hair done up on top of her head. It was easy to forget what a very beautiful woman Ping Li was: her daytime personality was so dead pan that searching for any glimmer of personality felt doomed to failure. Her professionalism was beyond doubt but she managed to make Nancy, who admired that characteristic above all, feel inadequate.

Nancy watched as Lord and Lady Regis crossed the room to greet the Ambassadorial party. And kept watching as Regis smoothly manoeuvred himself to the edge of the group next to Ping Li, though it must have seemed completely natural to those around him. The two began talking without preamble. What was going on there? Nancy had wondered for years. The couple were connected – she prided herself on being able to spot these things; it was almost as though they were invisibly linked. She would have dismissed them as contented old marrieds, but for two things. Firstly, Marcia Regis was standing there too. And secondly, what could the English Lord and the Chinese ice queen possibly have in common?

The Royal party had arrived. Nancy fell into the receiving line next to Vellin, some way down from Regis and waited. She had practiced her curtsey at home in front of the bathroom mirror, mentally thanking Miss Chloe, her ballet teacher at elementary school who had told her that, though too tall and gangly to dance, she could still be graceful.

The Prince appeared to be in a jovial mood. With his equerry hovering behind him, supplying tiny biographical details when required, he wrung hands warmly, kissed Lady Regis excessively warmly and moved down the line without undue haste. When he reached Nancy, she was overwhelmed to be addressed by name as she rose from her curtsey.

483

'Miss Hammer, I am grateful for all that I know you have done to make this occasion a success.'

'It was an honour, Sir,' said Nancy, meaning it with every fibre. Her mother would be ecstatic.

Out of the corner of her eye, she could see Leonie hovering and looking unusually awkward. She had noted the complete lack of interaction between Leonie and Vellin. Leonie wasn't looking at him; nor he at her. That was it. Whatever had been going on there had blown itself out and it was still hurting. Nancy felt the warm, vicious glow of schadenfreude.

She was still rankling over the way they had made a fool of her at the polo match. Secure and oblivious in their bubble of mutual absorption, they had made her feel ridiculous and shrill. And then, there had definitely been a note of triumph in Leonie's voice over the Prince's luncheon that never was. If Nancy was honest – and prided herself on being brutally so – that had been the killer blow. Now, to have so completely emasculated Vellin was a small consolation; to see Leonie looking marginally less self-assured than usual was another.

Still, the Prince's charm and interest in her personally this evening had gone a long way to healing old wounds. He was a most charming man. Nancy had heard it said that, when he focused his attention on you, it was like being the only woman in the world. Well, it was true. And of course, he had never known about the lunch invitation at all. That had been cooked up by Regis and Vellin. So the Prince could remain at the very pinnacle of her firmament without being tarnished by their machinations.

Farheen was beginning to find the attentions of the special branch troublesome. The man in charge – she knew his name from several high profile investigations by the squad – was persistent, that was certain. He had been badgering her for days about Regis' connections with China and something that was happening in Tibet. She was aware that there was a huge natural disaster in Tibet. The waterways feeding the country's many lakes and reservoirs had somehow become polluted. There was a rising death toll, males only, being reported breathlessly on every news bulletin.

She assumed that like the Yellow River, which the Chinese had poisoned so many times that it flowed stiff with the corpses of rotting fish, the Tibetan waterways had been corrupted by their mighty neighbour. But she could not see how Regis was involved. And she suspected that the Police interest might just be troublemaking: after all, Regis was at the absolute pinnacle of his career and such success made other men mad.

Inspector Ware had just arrived in her office, determined not to be fobbed off any longer. He had been on the case since DCI Sue Carter had spoken to him and it was taking much longer to see the man at the centre of it than it should. It was late on a Friday night. Farheen had remained at her desk in order to solve any last minute glitches in preparations for the China Ball, and she could tell he was not to be diverted.

He was that new brand of policeman – neither fish nor fowl – a First from Oxford with a slight estuary accent. A man of the people, with the mind of a QC. Why did he not just go off and make money like his University chums, she wondered. What drove him to be a superior policeman instead? Destined, no doubt, for the very top, so long as he kept bringing in his high profile felons.

She was faintly amused by how very PC he was – this elite PC. As soon as he saw she was Indian – not obvious from their many conversations on the telephone -- his tone changed. He had obviously undertaken one too many cultural awareness seminars. Farheen, who was also supremely well educated and gifted at sussing people out, could smell it on him.

Nicholas Ware was nonplussed by the beauty before him. She had held him off for several days – Lord Regis had been unavailable or on meetings or out on private business – but now she had allowed him into the eyrie Regis used as his office. A bored security guard buzzed up to the 36th floor, spoke briefly, then pointed to the express lift in the left-hand corner of the foyer.

Ware had stepped out of the lift into another world, like the panelled interior of a private club. And there was Farheen, graceful and beautiful and utterly unhelpful, as she had been on the phone.

He had been expecting a dragon, someone old enough to wield her boss's power with the assurance she had shown on the phone. But Farheen could not have been more than 35, albeit with the bearing and diction of a princess. And Ware, veteran of investigations into cash for peerages, the affairs of real princesses and corrupt potentates, found himself at a loss.

Without his sidekick, he might have remained at a loss for longer. But anxious not to lose face in front of young Ben, he pressed his case.

'It is urgent that we see Lord Regis,' he said, 'the situation has become critical and it appears than he is in possession of information that we need.'

'Well, as you see, he is not here,' said Farheen. 'He is at the China Ball, having dinner at this very moment with the Prince and his Excellency, the Chinese Ambassador.'

Ware sighed audibly. This was never going to be easy. But DCI Carter had backed up Michael Vellin's story from another source. He knew Regis was his man. But there was no way he was going to march into the China Ball and haul out a peer by the scruff of his neck, no matter what had happened. And Farheen knew it.

Harry Regis felt unusually out of sorts. Normally, this was the kind of occasion at which he shone: one of the reasons for his stratospheric ascent, once he left academia. He wondered why he felt uncomfortable. He was seated with the man who would one day be king, and the social muscle that alone would give him among his peers was unimaginable.

Perhaps it was the conversation with Foote. Damn the man. He had always doubted the wisdom of allowing anyone to look into his mind, and here was proof.

Then he realized that, for the first time in his life, his shadow side was on overt display for all who were able to read it. He was sitting across the room from Leonie, his precious daughter. To one side was Hester, the wife of the man he could now honestly say knew him better than any other. To the other was Ping Li, mother of his child. He had never seen Ping Li so forbidding. He assumed it was the presence of her uncle, the Ambassador, which required her complete transformation. She was still beautiful to him. But she was utterly unreadable tonight.

Marcia, his wife, was, as always, giving the Prince her undivided attention. Watching her dispassionately, Regis was finally aware of what everyone else must have known for years. He was being cuckolded by the future King. His wife was passionately in love with the man and that passion seemed to be returned.

It was not really surprising, Regis thought. He, Regis, had been the interloper. Marcia and the Prince had played together as infants, climbed trees and skied together as children, experimented together as teenagers. The Prince's doomed marriage to a bovine foreign princess had left Marcia temporarily high and dry.

She had found Regis and he had been delighted to be found. With Marcia's contacts and his ability, they had been the consummate power couple. Marcia's faith in him had been confirmed when he had been ennobled. By then, he didn't care.

There were only two people at the table not intimately connected with Regis and his fortunes. One was the director of the RA, a well-known specialist in Chinese antiquities, and the other was the Prince's equerry, an ex-army officer with reputed links to the SAS and beyond.

As he looked at his companions he felt a sense of detachment, a loosening of ties. The world outside, the chemical plant explosion in India, the mounting death toll in Tibet, the myriad annoyances, which had begun piling up seemed to fall away.

He knew it was a turning point in his life, *the* turning point. Everything so far had led him here and now, finally, he knew what he wanted. The company, his creation, would be fine. He had headed it up for as long as he could and now it was someone else's turn. He was now more aware of who he was and what drove him than he had ever been. Funny, that.

The arrangement with Foote, though foisted upon him by the company rules, had brought him great gifts. It was time to explore them. He raised his eyes to search for those of Ping Li.

Andrew Foote fumbled several times as he tried to put the keys into the lock of the front door of house. The taxi, which had deposited him and Hester had promptly disappeared and the light was bad. They could usually rely on the light over the church porch, but the bulb had not been replaced since it a vandal had smashed it a week ago.

He got the door open and Hester swayed past him into the hall. They were both fractionally the worse for wear, but he liked seeing Hester slightly out of control. It suited her and reminded him of a time when they had both been struggling students, not pillars of the community.

'Tea?' she said, not waiting for an answer, as she headed towards the kitchen.

Orlando shot between his legs and out of the door. Foote turned and followed him out into the night. He would have to wait now or the cat would be locked out all night. Perhaps he should install a cat flap. The thought of gouging a hole in his beautiful front door, even for Orlando, was too much. He preferred to hover in the dark outside his house for a few minutes every night.

He sat on the bench by the church, enjoying the 3am silence, so rare in central London. The low clouds reflected the orange glare of the city and blanketed the metropolis in warmth. He could see the cat, digging up the bulbs in the urn next door but he didn't have the energy to stop him. He would be back soon enough. A hand passed him a cup of tea and Hester said, 'See you upstairs.'

He leaned back, closing his eyes and enjoying the gentle spin brought on by a vestibular apparatus under siege from champagne, Chablis, claret and port. Then a voice spoke.

'Dr Foote.'

Andrew Foote was wide awake now.

'Yes?'

He looked and for a first, panicked second, saw a stranger. Then the man's features composed themselves out of the shadows and he became known. It was Regis's man, Hester's hero, the man in black who had brought Foote's wife and child back from Colombia alive and safe. It was Seb.

'Don't worry. I want to talk to you. I followed you home from the Ball.'

Foote moved up the bench and motioned to the seat beside him.

'Of course.'

Seb Johnson sat down, leaning his weight forward on the balls of his feet, as though ready to leap into action. It stirred a strong sense of recognition in Foote but the memory wouldn't come. What did that remind him of?

'I want to tell you. The Police know what Lord Regis has done. They're coming for him tonight. Inspector Ware has full details of the Tibet project and he will be able to build a prosecution case out of it. Regis is finished. His fall from grace will be biblical.'

Foote braced himself for the next bit. He knew better than to ask what it had to do with him. He had strongly suspected what Regis had done, he had spotted the clues but had not gone to the Police. He felt like a criminal, an accessory to the crime. Hiding behind his professional code, he had compromised himself personally and professionally. He had failed his own, self imposed standards. He had stood knowingly by while Regis wrought great evil in the world. He had allowed himself to be bought off by the rescue and restitution of his family. Like Regis, he had sold his soul.

Johnson came to the point.

'Regis's man Vellin has turned Queen's evidence in exchange for immunity from prosecution. He's singing like a canary. And, in exchange for my for allowing his story to go unchallenged, I have been airbrushed from the entire history. Which suits me fine.

'As for you, Professor Foote, I reckon you seem like a good bloke who got in with some bad people.'

Even in his bleary state, Foote wondered how Johnson could have divined such a thing. Like a mind reader, Johnson answered him.

'You helped my mate. Ricky Boyd. We were in the Squids together. Then he lost it. Froze in the battlefield. He thought he let his mates down. It crushed him. We thought he would top himself. But he didn't. You were the reason why. His wife, Sandy, told us.'

Ah, that was what had been tweaking at the edge of his memory. This young, fit man, poised for action like a coiled spring. It took his mind back to the dreary street in

Hamworthy by Poole Harbour. He remembered the pale, strained wife and the angry young man, fatally blocked by his stepfather's brutality and his own terror as a child, hiding from the beating his mother was taking.

He could see Corporal Boyd, sobbing as he relived the horror of being paralysed by fear while those he loved were in mortal danger. And he realised that it was not all one way. Just as he had helped Boyd, Boyd was now helping him.

'Thank you,' he said fervently.

'Nah, mate. Thank *you*,' said Seb. 'And stop that ginger cat crapping in your neighbour's garden.'

'It's over,' said Marcia. She was standing by the marital four poster, her face a slimy mask, her hair drawn back in a wide, stretchy hair band.

Regis, who had not been attracted to her for longer than he could remember, was now actively repelled by the unguents she applied so lavishly. He turned so that he could not see her out of the corner of his eye and resumed packing.

'Indeed it is,' he said, 'and I would venture to suggest, has been so for some time. You clearly have other priorities.'

'I do. And I shall be moving into Cumberland House immediately.'

Regis fleetingly pitied the Prince who was stealing his wife. Would he really enjoy paying for the delights he had until now appropriated free of charge? As with his polo, he was content for other rich men to underwrite his pleasures. Well, not any more.

'We will, of course, need to share out the proceeds of this house.'

She took his silence for acquiescence and continued, 'And the flat in New York is still in my name.'

Yes, she would get away with that. But Regis would get away with more. He wished he could be able to see the look on her face when she found out.

Ping Li waited in the Chinese Embassy meeting room on Portland Place. She had instructed the hovering functionaries to show in her guest and then not to disturb her on any account.

She sat in the long, thin room and wondered at the imposition of Chinese restaurant décor on the priceless Robert Adam masterpiece that the house had once been. Now decked out in vast red leather chairs, the walls a miasma of watery silk paintings and the carpet a pale symphony of beiges, the proportions, the height and the decoration of the room were completely wrong. The Embassy had been demolished and rebuilt in 1973, the year that Ping Li had been starting her PhD under the attentive eye of her fascinating tutor. The British Government of the day had insisted only that the front of the building be perfectly restored. After that, the Chinese could run riot. And they had, spectacularly so.

Ping Li realized that her shock at the room's decor signalled, if any sign were necessary, that she was now completely assimilated into her adopted country. She was now, for better or worse, British. This was her home now. Her daughter was half British, and though she carried a proud Chinese ancestry, it was one still not spoken of in the People's Republic.

Her daughter's father walked into the room. Harry Regis looked surprisingly fresh for a man who had attended a Ball until the early hours. In fact, he looked positively rejuvenated and greeted her with enthusiasm.

'My dear,' he said, taking her hand. 'Marcia and I have parted. I should have done it years ago. I should have seen the kind of woman she was.'

'Harry, don't deceive yourself. You always knew the kind of woman she was. Which is why you chose her.'

Unused to people disagreeing with him, Regis assumed that she had not, and carried on.

'I have a little local difficulty,' he said. 'Farheen was kind enough to warn me last night. There is a warrant out for my arrest over the Tibet matter. I have sought advice from the Ambassador and he was kind enough to offer me a future as an honoured guest in your country.'

'My country?'

'China.'

'You mean you have sought asylum in China.'

'You could call it that. I would prefer to say that I have switched my allegiances to the country my true wife and daughter call home.'

'We do not.'

' You do not what?'

'We do not call China home, Harry. Leonie has been there twice in her life. I go there now only when duty calls. We live here, in London, and we have no desire to move.'

'But we can be together now.'

'Now that your wife has thrown you over for a bigger prize? Remember, Harry, you left me for her. You didn't think twice. You knew I would survive. And I did.'

Regis opened his mouth. But Ping Li was not to be silenced.

'You were so hungry for the contacts, the social prominence, the networking opportunities she could give you. And, my God, have you used them! No one could say you have left any potential unfulfilled – except, perhaps, your chance to be a good man.'

'But you always gave me to understand that you still held me in affection.'

'I do, Harry. Despite everything. Despite being deserted with my infant to survive alone in a foreign land. Despite you not thinking me presentable enough for your future. Despite the terrible human beings you surrounded yourself with. Your man, Vellin – he is contemptible. Yet you allowed him to ooze around you like a toxic scum. And I watched as you metamorphosed into someone unrecognisable.'

Not any more, thought Regis.

'But I do not love you enough to go back to China after 30 years. What would I do? What would my daughter do? I have made my life here. Yours, I'm afraid, must be lived there.'

It was the most shocking moment of Regis' life. All pretence was stripped away. He could no longer hide behind what he imagined she thought he was. He knew she saw his rapacity and ruthlessness clearly.

Harry Regis was like an ancient oak chest banded with iron and riddled with secrecy, like wormholes. One touch and the whole disintegrated into a handful of dust. And, as he saw all avenues close inexorably before him, the Pilates, the facials, the careful diet all fell away and he aged a hundred years.

Kathryn Balfour, partner of Carter Burke, specialized in the dissolution of high profile marriages. She was herself a veteran of one, but a recent, late flowering romance with an old friend, with whom she had done her pupillage decades earlier, had made her a believer again. Newly married and installed in a Mayfair house with her equally successful husband, she was happier than she had ever been. As a result, she tried to dredge up a smidgeon of sympathy for the woman in front of her.

However, Marcia Regis was making it difficult. Although their paths had frequently crossed in the higher echelons of London society – Kathryn's first husband had been given a peerage after considerable donations to a grateful party – Lady Regis was refusing to acknowledge any common experience.

She was, instead, standing on ceremony. Even though her husband had been disgraced and was even now boarding a

Chinese state jet, bound for a life in exile, she was insisting upon being addressed as Lady Regis.

Accompanying her was the sharkiest shark of them all, Michael Mason, divorce lawyer to the stars. Kathryn could almost see the shards of flesh streaming from his sharp, white teeth.

To cap it all, she had earlier spotted a liveried Royal driver dropping her clients on Southampton Row far below her window. The rumours, which had been circulating London for years, were clearly true. Lady Regis now saw herself as far elevated in status above the lawyer she was here to consult.

Well, this would be interesting. Kathryn opened the Regis files and looked up.

'I have received a letter faxed from Lord Regis' office, laying out the situation. Some you already know and some, I am afraid, will shock you.

'We will start with the certainties. The house in New York, which has been in your name since it was purchased, will of course remain so. The house in London, is in trust for a Miss Leonie Li – a daughter of whom I believe you have no knowledge.'

She caught a look between Lady Regis and the shark and instantly understood that Marcia had known, or at least suspected, there was a child.

'I think that will need to be proven,' said Lady Regis.

'It may or may not complicate matters for you to know that Miss Li works in the private office of Prince Edward, Duke of Cumberland where she is, I believe, a valued member of staff.'

A palpable hit. The Prince was a legendary defender of his staff. Years ago, he had stood up to the Queen over a particularly avaricious aide who had been exposed in the tabloids for selling various unwanted baubles donated by Arab princelings. Despite the scandal and his subsequent separation from the Prince's household, the aide had gone on to make millions by arranging parties for his patron's rich friends.

Marcia Regis would know of her lover's reputation and would not want to rock the boat, guessed Kathryn. Certainly, Lady Regis visibly subsided. And Kathyrn continued.

'As the settlor of the Trust, which he established 10 years ago, but also as the beneficiary in living there, Lord Regis has for 10 years paid a market rent to the Trust for the house in which you have both been living. That rent has accumulated to a sum not far short of £1m of which the Trustees have the disposition. I can inform you that Miss Li is the sole beneficiary and I am the single trustee.

'So far as the other assets are concerned, Lord Regis has, over the years, made arrangements for the accumulation of capital to be available to him well outside the jurisdiction of Her Majesty's Revenue and Customs. Certainly, my understanding is that we have no extradition agreement with the People's Republic of China.'

There seemed little else to say. Michael Mason QC was too expert an operator to niggle now; he would go away, examine the documents and pick holes in them later.

Well, he would find it difficult, thought Kathryn. Lord Regis had spared no expense on making his arrangements watertight. And anyway, he was now out of the country with the cash. So what could anyone do?

'Thank you, Miss Balfour,' said Marcia grandly. 'We will be in touch.'

Was that the royal we, or was she referring to her expensive bagman, who was even now collecting up her papers?

The letter to the Chinese Foreign Minister from the Foreign Secretary to Her Majesty's Government was succinct.

'From the office of Richard Cavendish, Secretary of State for Foreign and Commonwealth Affairs, Foreign and Commonwealth Office, King Charles Street, London SW1A 2AH

Her Majesty's Government understands that the People's Republic of China has seen fit to offer political asylum to the Baron Harold Regis of Clutton Champflower.

As you are no doubt aware, Lord Regis is being sought by the authorities in this country for a number of transgressions relating to the manufacture and export of prohibited chemicals. Furthermore, the International Criminal Court at the Hague is seeking the extradition of Lord Regis on charges of genocide after the alleged use of those chemicals in Tibet.

While the people's Republic of China is not a signatory to any extradition arrangements with the United Kingdom, we would hope that countries wishing to maintain an Embassy in this country would abide by the same high standards as the UK government in maintaining the rule of law, respect for human rights and integrity in public life.

We would like to indicate, in the strongest possible terms, the displeasure of Her Majesty's Government over this matter. We shall continue to pursue the extradition of Lord Regis.

We will be seeking an interview at the earliest opportunity with your country's representative to the United Kingdom.

Yours faithfully

The Rt Hon Richard Cavendish MP'

Ping Li put the letter down on the table. The Ambassador had included it in his most recent bundle of communications, no doubt aware that it held a special poignance for her. In truth she did, briefly, feel a pang of nostalgia for what might have been. But what might have been was more than a quarter of a century ago; not three months ago, when Harry Regis had begged her to go with him into exile in China. She did not regret her decision. Nor would she. It was over now.

Leonie had decided to walk home from Cumberland House. The Prince was in town this week; his duties did not always allow him respite at his country home. She needed the air and time to think, although she was not certain how much oxygen she was actually getting as she walked along the railings by Number One London, the glorious Apsley House, given by a grateful nation to the triumphant Duke of Wellington.

Leonie was finding the certainties of life a great deal less certain at the moment.

Her father – she found it hard to use that word of Harry Regis – had been the subject of every headline for a week now. His crimes, his defection, his marital breakdown provided a feast for the tabloids and glutted that least pleasant and most pleasurable hunger in the British character: the tall poppy syndrome – the irresistible desire to see those who had once lorded it over their compatriots brought low.

Lord Regis could not have been brought lower. He was the arch villain in a world-beating scandal. He had sold his soul to the devil. Peace loving Tibet, oppressed and beloved of every right-thinking liberal and movie star, was, quite literally, poisoned by his works on behalf of the evil giant next door. Regis was the deranged scientist, involved like a Bond villain in nefarious plots to rule the world. And he had escaped, unscathed, to life as an honoured friend of China. Or was he so unscathed, really? Recent events had shown

513

that China was not so forgiving to those who had embarrassed them upon the world stage. Bo Xilai came to mind. Leonie wondered what fate held in store for the man who had given her her life.

Meanwhile, Marcia Regis had escaped to Leonie's boss, the Prince. Perhaps this explained why the Prince was in unnecessarily querulous mood, demanding ridiculous and nitpicking changes to letters, arrangements and staff. It happened periodically, when his smooth running world wobbled temporarily on its axis. It had happened when he divorced his foreign princess. The Prince had not enjoyed the comment, much of it critical, which had accompanied his divorce. Nor had he enjoyed the gossip about his lengthy relationship with Lady Regis, although he would not give her up. 'Non negotiable' was the phrase used by inner members of the household. Certainly, he relied upon her to an extraordinary extent.

It would really be better if they ended the pretence and married, thought Leonie. The Prince had three beautiful and talented daughters who would soak up the press attention increasingly from now on anyway. He and his mistress, newly installed as a couple in Cumberland House, were finally free to live as they wished.

Then there was Ping Li. Leonie was amazed by her mother. Ping Li had shown a ruthlessness in protecting herself and Leonie which her daughter finally understood. It had been bred of necessity by years of dealing with some of the most powerful and single-minded men on the planet. She had evaded the clutches of the Chinese, while making herself invaluable to them; finally, she had exacted a cold revenge on her lover for his desertion.

Next was Leonie's love affair with Vellin. She allowed herself to approach the thought gingerly, like a tongue seeking out a sore tooth, to see if a touch would set off a cascade of pain or whether it had dulled a little.

She realized how she had been duped, but she knew that somewhere inside the construct Vellin had created, there was someone who had, if only fleetingly, been capable of giving her the love she gave him. With the unending optimism of the young, she resolved to look for that again. Meanwhile, she would pick up the strands she had neglected and start over. She was thinking vaguely about learning to play polo and the friends she would call and the bridge she would take up.

As she opened the door to the Cadogan Square flat, her eye alighted upon a large, legal envelope bearing her name.

Leonie stood in the hallway of her house and looked around. The furniture was mostly gone, stripped out by Lady Regis before she would relinquish the keys, but the light poured in through full-height sash windows onto the bare, oak boards in the ground floor salon and illuminated the graceful airiness of the building. For the first time in her life, Leonie felt grateful to her father. This was her own home, long overdue, and she felt thrilled by the prospect.

She had been barely able to believe it when Kathryn Balfour had explained the situation to her. Harry Regis, now of Beijing, had left her a house of her own, with the funds to run it. It was overwhelming. While Leonie had never been poor, working for the Prince was never going to make her fortune. The thought of moving out of her mother's home had just begun nibbling at the edges of her consciousness, and this was an elegant solution.

She would divide the house, which was too big for one, or even one small family, into two apartments and rent one out to provide an income. She would have a cat. Her mother would be within walking distance. She would find love again. And all would be well.

Nancy wasn't quite sure who had lost the plot. The corporate environment in which she had been trained was one that took no hostages. It espoused a continuous creed of personal responsibility whilst at the same time making sure that whatever bad happened was someone else's fault. No-one had ever prepared her for the possibility of meltdown when there was no-one left to blame.

But the fates had been kind to her. On a trip to Washington two months ago she had been dined by a couple of heavy hitters with high level government connections. She hadn't been sure whether they were inside or outside government. Perhaps, she had reasoned after the meeting, somewhere in-between. Scouts, perhaps, for the White House Chief of Staff. She liked that thought.

The upshot of the dinner had been an invitation to think about a government job nailing Chief Executives through working with the kinds of people that she had herself been in IFL.

'It's like this, Nancy,' one of the scouts had said, 'the corporate world is always sucking up to government, and always trying to get everything it can out of it, but blaming it at the same time. It's wearing. Government wants a bit more bite-back capacity. So a new high-level job has been created that would get us focused on whether corporate responsibility targets really are being met. Guys who look like the big beasts of the corporate world come whining to the President about all sorts of things. His office needs to be able to give him the dirt, if there is any, before he meets these guys. If there isn't any dirt, it allows him to choose the people he speaks about in public wisely. We need someone who hasn't been in corporate America recently, so they're not tainted, but who really knows how this whole compliance industry works, and knows their way around big organisations. You have been suggested as ideal for this position.'

Nancy had been as flattered, as it had been intended she would be. Vellin had called in a whole bank of favours. The

519

job on offer had been created without there being any real meat in it; in practice it could lead nowhere and had no teeth. Whoever took the job, and Nancy was the only candidate, was going to find themselves totally rejected by the corporate systems and powerless within government for an inability to create any added value. The salary had been pitched a bit on the high side to make it look more senior than it was.

That was going to be rather embarrassing in due course for someone who was supposed to be a compliance hot shot who would bring the corporate world to task for their compliance failures. But it would have needed a less self-interested set of feelings than Nancy was capable of deploying to see *that* flaw before being in the job. For Nancy, it looked like a career move that took her back to the Stars and Stripes covered with battle honours achieved abroad. Before the dinner was over, she knew she wanted the job. Going away to think about the offer was only to make sure she didn't seem too eager. IFL was no place to be and hard to market oneself from, since the disaster. At every level Nancy felt good about the prospect before her.

But now was no time for self-congratulation. It was time to accept her colleagues' congratulations and good wishes. Her leaving drinks were in two minutes' time, being held in the great corner office that Lord Regis had so recently inhabited. Nancy had announced her impending departure only three days before Lord Regis had put himself outside the long arm of British law. That had just been a lucky chance. But it signalled absolutely that she was not involved in his scandalous demise.

Arriving one minute early seemed about right, just in time to be the centre of attention for busy people looking in to say farewell. The two waiters holding trays of drinks and canapés were in place exactly as they should have been: the in-house catering manager was there to see that Nancy approved.

Nancy had declined a drink as she arrived. Best to have both hands free for greeting people. Difficult to manage the variety of social gestures that were required these days with a drink in one hand, and entirely impossible if a canapé was in the other. They could come later. So Nancy took herself about a third of the way into the room and waited expectantly, gazing out of the corner windows and down over the river towards the Palace of Westminster, where that great building looked like a Victorian child's cut-out. The view had hugely impressed Nancy the first time she had met Lord Regis there. She watched a tug pulling a string of barges up through Westminster Bridge, the Eye in the distance and Lambeth Palace trying to hide its Tudor charms on the opposite side of the river. The mix of the old and new in England was something that never ceased to fascinate Nancy and here it was laid out before her, just as she was going off to something new.

Nancy was in one of her rare reflective moments. Spending so much time as she did investigating others, she rarely had time to wander around her own musings. This thirty seconds waiting for colleagues to join her was a rare occasion and a pause for thought.

To her surprise, she could see that Big Ben's minute hand had slipped past the five-minute mark. Had she been standing there so long? Where was everyone? She half-turned towards the door with an unformed anxiety beginning to cloud her brow when Vellin strode in, lifting a glass of champagne from the hovering tray.

'Here's to change, Nancy,' he said, not missing a beat. 'Heavens, you don't have a glass at your own party. That won't do. Let me get you one and we'll make a toast to total uncertainty.'

The flunkey who had appeared immediately by his elbow, relieved to have been able to move from the stiff posture by the door, had the tray exactly positioned for Vellin to be able to ease a glass into Nancy's hand before she had a chance to make any comment at all. Secretly she was rather relieved that Vellin had slipped effortlessly into his social control mode.

'It's a funny old world, Nancy,' said Vellin. He wondered whether Nancy recognized the phrase from Mrs Thatcher's departure from Downing Street, when she made that remark. Old certainties, turned over by events that no-one had foreseen.

'Too true,' said Nancy, not being quite sure how to play a farewell party that seemed to be just a tête-à-tête between them. 'I guess we'll have to toast that. Here's to a funny old world, Michael.'

'Funny old world it is,' said Vellin as they did the ritual raising of glasses before drinking to their separate conceptions of how funny their old worlds were.

Nancy had an immediate sense that her new world was bright with promise. She would have real power, she thought, and it appealed to her very much indeed, as if it was a just reward for the battles she had fought.

Vellin knew there was only disappointment ahead for her, a vacuum existence where she would be slowly starved of the oxygen of corporate effect that had fuelled her for so many hard-fought years. As for himself, he did not know. The future would emerge. His skills were well-known, and in many places admired as well as despised, and there would undoubtedly be a place for his dark arts.

He could manage the uncertainty for a while. Regis' fall from grace had necessitated Vellin's staying on as a safe pair of hands while a new, corporate star was sought to head up IFL. But there was no future for him there. While his cooperation with the Police remained secret, he was forever tainted by his close association with Regis, poisoner of the innocent masses.

There were bruises of all kinds that still needed time to diffuse, as with a boxer who has suffered an unexpected knock-out instead of the world title he thought was within reach. Boxers were known to come back and Vellin would do the same. Machiavelli had written his great work on the practicalities of statesmanship whilst out of office and without favour from the Prince he sought to impress. That had left quite a mark on the world.

Mrs Thatcher's favourite bag-carrier, Alastair McAlpine, had produced a not-dissimilar codification of his views as to the way a person could keep in the shadows but appear to shine a light for greater others. It had been Vellin's bible at one time. Lord McAlpine had retired abroad, and though Vellin was not contemplating such a move, he knew that he still had options. Somehow his mind could piece all this together in the instant of silence as he and Nancy lowered their glasses.

Big Ben had moved its great minute hand almost to the quarter-past position. When it reached that place the sounds of striking did not penetrate the former office of Lord Regis. Thick glass had always kept out the interruptions of the world.

Vellin's gaze shifted towards the ivory balls still resting in their Chippendale cabinets and he suddenly wondered, whose were they now? Lord Regis was not going to be in a position to demand their return.

'I had better clear out the Lord's office for him,' said Vellin, looking around.

'I guess someone's going to have to do it,' said Nancy.

'I'll take that as an order,' said Vellin.

His earlier doubts as to whether he would bother to attend Nancy's farewell party were entirely dispelled. The world was offering him one of those serendipitous chances that he had never even envisaged. He had always admired, even envied, Lord Regis' collecting eye and capability. Now, if he played it well, he could be a beneficiary.

'I'll catalogue it and let you have a list,' said Vellin, putting his forthcoming act of larceny on what seemed to be an official footing.

'Do that,' said Nancy, knowing that the way things were, it had no special meaning for her one way or the other. If pressed, she would have presumed Vellin would arrange for everything to go into store.

Nancy could not ever have imagined Vellin appropriating what was displayed in Lord Regis's office. She had no knowledge of how the great museums of London housed storerooms full of objects liberated from the conquests of Empire; and that Englishmen had few scruples about plunder. Elizabeth the First had encouraged Drake to become the master of it at sea, and prize money for the taking of ships had sustained the Royal Navy at all levels for three hundred years. The army had practised the same on land. The alternative to death was financial glory.

Time had passed in a curiously inconsequential way.

'Let's finish our drinks and go, Nancy,' said Vellin.

It was not until many months later that Nancy, in the misery of her own powerlessness in Washington, ruminated on the ending of her involvement with IFL and wondered

why no-one had turned up to her departure drinks. Somehow,

in her memory, Vellin seemed to have been totally in charge.

She had not realised that he was almost not there at all.

CPSIA information can be obtained at www.ICGtesting.com
Printed in the USA
BVOW02s1754081213

338527BV00001B/25/P